ALL THESE THINGS

ALL THESE THINGS

by
Dana Pride

Everlasting Publishing
Yakima, Washington
USA

ALL THESE THINGS
was written by Dana Pride
entirely during NaNoWriMo,
National Novel Writing Month 2004.

Cover art by Jahla Brown

This book is a work of fiction.
Any resemblance to any person,
living or dead, is purely coincidental.

"Go For It," "Rock You By the Fireside,"
and "Are We Each Other's Angels"
copyright Dale Fram, used by permission.

All other songs copyright Dana Pride.

ISBN13: 978-0-9983858-7-7

2nd Edition
Everlasting Publishing
PO Box 1061
Yakima, WA 98907
USA

This book is dedicated to my family:
my husband, Pastor W.F. Pride, Jr.;
my children, Jahla and Nathan;
my parents, Joe and Dixie,
and my brother, Dale.

Special thanks to my Nano coworkers,
Ginger and Piper, who encouraged me
every step of the way.

ALL THESE THINGS

I

"And now, the band you've been waiting for, all the way from 48th and Englewood, let's give a big welcome to The Others!"

As the announcer scooted off the stage, the lights flashed on as the first note of the music blasted through the enormous speakers. The huge crowd cheered loudly, greeting the valley's most popular band to the stage of the state fair.

Dash kicked one leg high up in the air while striking his guitar strings on that first note, the energetic entertainer in his natural forum, with a huge smile on his face as he played one of his favorite original songs. He stepped up to the microphone amid the screams of the hundreds of fans and began to sing.

> *"So you think, you think you want to be a star,*
> *Go for it!*
> *If you think, you think you can go far,*
> *Go for it!"*

The music accented the words and the audience screamed more loudly. Dash's fingers flew across the guitar strings almost faster than anyone could see.

> *"Well, we've all got a dream,*
> *Sometimes they rip at the seams, (seems to me)*
> *You better do somethin' 'bout it, don't ever doubt it,*
> *Go for it!"*

Dash leaped up in a scissors kick, synchronized with the music as the cameras flashed on the band. His smile and enthusiasm during the performance made the audience feel as if they were participants in the performance, not just spectators, interacting with Dash and the band.

"If you see someone sweet walking down the street, what do you do?" Dash asked in his song.

"Go for it!" the audience shouted.

"If you see a dude you want to meet," Dash sang.

"Go for it!" the audience replied.

> *"Well, we've all got a dream, (all got a dream)*
> *Sometimes they rip at the seams, (seems to me)*
> *You better do somethin' 'bout it, don't ever doubt it,*
> *Go for it!"*

The music got louder through the musical interlude. The people at the front of the crowd were either waving their arms to the beat or just screaming. Dash kept smiling at them.

Dash glanced at the other band members as he played his guitar lead. He jumped up and kicked his long leg over guitarist Paulie Barrett's head. Dash began to sing the final verse.

> *"If you've got something that's got to be done,*
> *Go for it!*
> *If you can make money doing something fun,*
> *Go for it!*
> *Well, we've all got our dreams, (all got our dreams)*
> *Sometimes they rip at the seams, (seems to me)*
> *You better do somethin' 'bout it, don't ever doubt it,*
> *Go for it!"*

As they finished the song, they made the transition into the next song, a lively love song written by Ham. Ham and Dash harmonized beautifully, and again, Dash played an intricate lead. At the end of the song, Dash addressed the crowd.

"How ya all doin' tonight?" he asked.

He was answered by more than twenty thousand people, shouting and screaming their approval.

"We are The Others, and we are glad to be here with you tonight. I'd like to introduce the members of the band. Joe Sellers on the keyboards and backing vocals..." Dash paused while Joe took a bow to the screams of approval.

"... Ham Hockinson on bass and vocals..." Ham smiled and hit a chord and raised his hands.

"...Paulie Barrett on rhythm guitar..." Paulie waved. He looked like a smaller version of Dash: he dressed like Dash on stage and imitated his movements during the performance, though Paulie did not go to such extremes as Dash did.

"...and always on time, never missing a beat, more reliable than a drum machine: Lenny Hand on the drums!" Lenny hit the symbols.

"And I'm Dash, on lead guitar, and sometimes vocals," he told the shrieking fans, as he struck the chord to signal the beginning of the next song.

The performance went well, without a technical error or artistic mistake. The crowd was screaming and singing along to most of the songs, as Dash took every opportunity to play with them, not to them. He was so touched when he saw tears in the eyes of most of the girls when he sang the love songs, he began to get a lump in his throat. He was connected to his audience, not as a performer on a pedestal, but just another one of them - the one who happened to be singing and playing his guitar.

After three encores, the band left the stage as the cheers and chants grew louder and louder.

"Others! Others! Others! Others!" they shouted.

Dash led the band out for one last bow and the crowd went wild, throwing phone numbers, flowers, socks and various undergarments on stage as the cameras flashed again and again.

Backstage, reporters and photographers from the local newspaper and TV stations were crowding around with pens, paper and cameras, each desiring an interview with Dash and the other members of The Others. Lindsey Station from one of the TV stations cornered Dash and began to question him as the cameraman wiggled to get in place for the interview. The other reporters turned to hear Dash speak. Dash, in his outgoing way, extended his hand over his guitar as the rest of The Others gathered behind him.

"Hi, I'm Dash," he said with a genuine smile.

Lindsey, caught off balance, yet already comfortable with the young star, shook his hand and shuffled her notes, regaining her composure.

"I'm Lindsey Station from Channel 23, and it's nice to meet you. Dash. How does it feel to be the leader of the hottest band in the Northwest?"

"I'm not the leader of the band. I'm the lead singer and lead guitarist, but not the leader. I'm just twenty percent of the band, the same as the other four members. We all write songs and we make all of our decisions together," Dash explained. "But to answer your question, I feel great."

"But you are the leader, each of the 20,000 fans tonight could clearly see that," Lindsey protested.

"No, we are all equal members. I sing some songs and Joe sings some, and Paul sings some, and even Ham sings a few."

"So, in what direction are you going to take the band from here?"

"I'm not taking the band in a direction, because I'm not

4

the leader. We make all of our decisions together."

Not flustered, Lindsey referred to her notes. "Our viewing audience would like to know how you got started in the music business."

"I've been playing guitar since I was about 6 years old. My older sister had a guitar and I picked it up when she was at school. I watched her learn how to play, and she taught me to read music. We went to Disneyland when I was 7 and I saw a band performing on a stage. From that moment, I knew I wanted to play music. My sister stopped playing after a couple years or so, and she gave her guitar to me."

"So you have been playing guitar for 15 years?" Lindsey asked, astonished.

"Yeah, a little more than that."

"But you weren't born with a guitar in your hand?"

"Well, it feels so natural, I guess God gave me the gift of music at a young age, as well as the desire and ability to play."

"What are your plans for The Others?" Lindsey asked.

"I don't have plans for The Others, because I'm not the leader. I just plan to stay with them and keep playing. Things have been happening fast for us, ever since we toured with Clear Blue Castle. We plan to record some of our songs and play as much as we can."

"On stage tonight, you interacted with the audience throughout the show. Do you always do that?"

"I can tell this is the first time you've seen us in action," Dash teased. "We get energy from the people there with us. We don't see them as an audience, they are part of the show too. The more they participate, the better we can play with them."

"One last question, what goals do you have set for your band?" Lindsey read from her notes.

"Okay, this time I am the leader," Dash said, flashing a smile at the camera, "and I would like to see the band playing on a regular basis. We also have enough material to record at least two albums, and as soon as we do that, I hope you and all of the viewing audience will buy copies of each." The rest of The Others patted his shoulders and shouted in agreement.

"Thank you, Dash, leader of The Others," Lindsey said, turning to the camera. "This is Lindsey Station reporting for News 23."

Other reporters began to shout questions at Dash, and he stayed another forty-five minutes answering them while the rest of the band changed their clothes. Security guards were holding the fans back, out of the dressing rooms and hallways. When the reporters were finished and hurrying to edit their stories, an older man approached Dash with a smile.

"Hi, my name is Benny, and I own Brubrack Moons down on Second Avenue. I heard you playing tonight and you are excellent! You are just the kind of act we've been looking for. I was wondering if you and your band would be willing to play as our house band?"

"I'm sure we would love to, but I need to discuss it with the other members of the band. We make all of our decisions together," Dash repeated for the third time this evening.

"Oh, I was under the impression that you are the leader," Benny said.

2

O.K. was waiting for Dash in the dressing room. Oliver Khalif Knott had been a close friend to Dash since junior high school, when Dash had nicknamed him O.K., since O.K. could not stand either of his names: 'Oliver,' so named because his mother's favorite movie was "Love Story," and 'Khalif' after the cab driver who had delivered him on the way to the hospital. Teachers had always called him Ollie, but that named didn't fit. Dash loved to call him "O.K." or "O.K. - Knott!" or "Okay-K." Besides being a close friend, O.K. loved to act as Dash's personal assistant, his promised position when Dash would become famous.

"You were in rare form tonight, my friend," O.K. told him, slapping his hand and then staying out of his way. Dash was all over the dressing room, getting out of his damp clothes, still energized from the show.

"The people were great! Have you ever seen such a group?" Dash asked.

"Yeah, but they're nothing compared to the group waiting at Pike's. That's where the party is tonight," O.K. said, handing Dash a bottle of water. "Did you invite Lindsey Station to join us?"

"No, she had to rush back to her station and put the story together before the eleven o'clock news."

"How are you feeling?" O.K. asked.

"Mt. Hood head," Dash replied.

"Ah, sharp as a tack, huh?"

"Yeah, or pointy head," Dash said. "What about you?"

"The concert blew me away," O.K. said, "so definitely Mt. St. Helens head."

The rest of the band flooded into the dressing room, buzzing with excitement.

"Come on, Dash, let's get going so we can see ourselves on the news!" Joe shouted above the noise.

"Go ahead, O.K. and I will meet you at Pike's," Dash said.

"Okay," said Joe.

"What?" asked O.K.

"Okay, we'll meet you." Joe said.

"Yes, and Dash too," O.K. said.

"Dash to it!" Joe said.

Pike lived in a huge house on the hill, and by the time Dash and O.K. arrived, the driveway and lawn were covered with vehicles. O.K. parked across the street and Dash grabbed his acoustic guitar.

"I hope Kandi isn't here," O.K. said.

"I thought you liked her," Dash replied.

"Yeah, until she smiled and I saw her teeth. I can't believe it's not butter," O.K. said, disgusted.

"Oh, man! Really?"

"Yeah, man, and the breath to go with it."

"Oh, Mansville, Arizona!"

"Man, oh, man alive."

"What about Donna?"

"Donna Quintana?"

"Yeah, wasn't she going to come with you tonight?"

"Man, she never combs the back of her hair."

"Seriously?"

"Yeah, she combs the sides and front, but not the back.

She got really mad when I asked her about it."

"Hey, what ever happened with Anna?" Dash asked.

"You mean Rexie?"

"Rexie?"

"Yeah, Anna-Rexia. Did you notice how thin she is?"

"That's rather obvious, I mean, her bones stick out all over the place."

"She's obsessed with food, or, really, with not eating food. Every thing I ate, she was, like, 'Chocolate chips have twenty-five calories each, and that cookie has at least seven of them,' or 'Do you know that taco has more than four hundred calories?' or 'that mocha latte has more calories than you should consume in an entire day.' I told her I was trying to gain some weight, but she didn't take me seriously."

"Doin' a gainer! Seriously?"

"No, seriously. I need to do a gainer."

"Me too! Seriously!"

Dash laughed. O.K. was good looking with his tall stature and light brown curly hair, but it seemed as if only the strange girls were attracted to him.

They made their way to the door and joined the party. Dash was glad that none of his friends smoked, so the house was filled with the scent of nachos and beer, and it wasn't cloudy or smokey inside. Someone tried to hand them a beer as soon as they entered, but both Dash and O.K. declined as they squeezed through the crowd to the dining room. Dash was still full of music and he had to let it flow out of him. He sat down and began to pick and strum, more gently than during the show, but still with skill and precision. Several girls he knew sat around him, but he didn't feel like conversing. He smiled at them in a friendly way as they each looked longingly at him.

"Look out, here comes Sweaty Betty," O.K. warned.

Dash chuckled to himself as he closed his eyes to listen to his music. Sweaty Betty veered in another direction.

Dash was not ready for another relationship right now. He had lived with Amanda (or as O.K. had called her, 'Demanda') for nearly two years and her young son, Matthew, had called him Daddy. The three of them had gone all over town as the little family until she decided that getting high was more important than buying food for Matthew. When Dash had mentioned the fact that Matthew was hungry, Demanda began to scream and shout and slap and hit Dash. Later, he had tried to talk to her about her outburst; but when she said Dash deserved to be hit because he wasn't sensitive to her needs, Dash told her he didn't deserve to be in her company any more. He moved out that day and although he missed Matthew, he had never seen him or Amanda again.

The Beauhahnaphish twins, Beaudry and Jabry, greeted Dash with identical smiles.

"Bo-Bo, Jab-Bo, how's it going, dudes?" Dash asked.

"You and The Others were excellent tonight!" Beaudry said.

"Massively," Jabry agreed, as they blended into the rest of the crowd.

"Hey, Dash," a girl with spiky hair called. He thought she looked about 14, too young to be at this party. "I'm Jenny, and, like, I've been hoping we could meet and, like, we finally are! This is, like, so cool! Like, I can't believe it! I'm, like, right here with Dash, like, in the flesh!"

Dash didn't know how to respond, so he smiled, shrugged and said, "How's it going?" as he continued to play his guitar a little more quietly.

"Oh, this is, like, the best night of my life!" Jenny squealed. "It's like, oh, I mean, I don't know, it's like, you know? I mean, like, we all saw you live in concert and, like, now we are seeing you live here! Like, I mean, it's like, SO cool!"

"Isn't it?" Dash asked, not wanting to be in this conversation but too polite to tell her to get lost.

"I was, like, at the concert with Kari, she's like, my best friend, oh, there she is over there -- Kari! Come over here!" Jenny shouted. A slightly older girl, who looked as if she were about 16, with long pink braids stepped around people to get near her friend.

"Omigosh, I can't believe it! It's like, we were talking about what we would do if we ever met you, and Jenny is like, 'we won't ever meet him,' and I'm like, 'you never know,' and she's like, 'but he's so popular,' and I'm like, 'you never know' and she's like, 'where would we ever meet Dash?' and I'm like, 'maybe we can, like, go to a party or something with him,' and, like, here you are!"

Dash smiled as he increased the volume of his guitar to try to cover up the irritating quality of her voice.

"Can you believe it, like, here we are, like, sitting with Dash, like, the leader of The Others!" Kari squeaked.

"Like, I can't believe it, can you?" Jenny agreed.

"I'm not the leader of The Others," Dash protested.

"You're not?" Kari asked, visibly disappointed.

"Are you, like, just being modest, er su'm'?" Jenny asked.

"Er su'm'," Dash agreed.

"Hey, everyone!" Pike shouted. He had been a big boy ever since seventh grade, and now he was a very large man whose voice carried throughout the house. "The Others are on TV!"

The entire group turned toward the large screen TV in the living room. Dash stood up to see it from where he was.

Lindsey Station's voice came across at top volume as Pike turned up the TV.

"Famous local band, The Others, played tonight at the state fair in front of tens of thousands of fans. Afterwards, I had the opportunity to speak with their leader, simply known as Dash, who is said to be one of this generation's greatest guitar players. He has been compared to Jimi Hendrix, Eddie Van Halen, Carlos Santana, Randy Rhoades and even Brian May; and we got a taste of Dash's expertise tonight. During his guitar solos, his fingers flew across the strings, as he was creating beautiful and unique musical sounds that made the audience wonder what instrument he was playing.

"Dash, as the leader of The Others, how does it feel to be a part of the hottest band in the state?"

"I'm the lead singer and lead guitarist, I feel great. This time, I am the leader," the edited version of the story stated.

"I didn't say that!" Dash announced. "You were there, you heard me, guys!"

"Yeah, yeah," they teased.

"SHHH! She's not finished!" Pike shouted.

"What goals do you have set for your band?" Lindsey asked.

"I would like to see the band playing on a regular basis. We also have enough material to record at least two albums, and as soon as we do that, I hope you and all of the viewing audience will buy copies."

"Thank you, Dash Farrah, leader of The Others," Lindsey said, turning to the camera. "This is Lindsey Station reporting for News 23."

"Doesn't she know her station in life?" O.K. asked no one in particular.

"So, like, are you the leader, or aren't you?" Kari demanded.

"No!" the entire band answered together. Dash smiled, amused, as Kari and Jenny moved away from him. They spotted the Beauhahnaphish brothers and Dash heard them ask in unison, "Like, are you twins?" Dash kept softly playing his guitar late into the night, a new song that had come into his head, as couples paired up and left. Finally O.K. came to give Dash a ride home.

"Dash, ready to dash?"

"All right, O.K."

"Yes, it is all right," O.K. stated. "Hey, what's up with those chicks?"

"Oh, man."

"What, man?"

"Man, they must be in middle school or something. Like, you know, I don't know, and he's like, I don't know, and she's like, you know, and I'm like, not wanting to be in this conversation," he said, mocking them.

"Great conversationalists, are they? Well, talking isn't everything," O.K. said.

"With them, it was nothing," Dash said. "Even Oprah couldn't have an intelligible conversation them."

"Ooo, that is bad, man," O.K. agreed.

"I go, 'Man!'" Dash said.

"I go, 'Boy,'" O.K. replied.

"I go, 'Man!'" Dash continued.

"I go, 'Boy,'" O.K. completed as he pulled his car into the driveway.

"Thanks, man," Dash said as he climbed out of the car, grabbing his guitar.

"No prob, Bob," O.K. replied, winding up another typical night in their lives.

3

Dash opened the door quietly so he wouldn't awaken his parents. A glance at the clock on the microwave told him it was nearly three in the morning. He realized he hadn't eaten all day, a habit of his. He was never hungry when he woke up or at noon, and sometimes he didn't get hungry until about eleven o'clock at night, when he would have leftovers or a bowl of cereal. His mom was a fantastic cook, but Dash wasn't usually home at dinner time to enjoy a meal with his parents.

He looked in the refrigerator and considered the fresh tamales and enchiladas. He decided that the microwave would beep too loudly, so he settled on a bowl of cereal. As he poured the milk, Hpsyloughehe (pronounced Silo, most of the letters were silent, or hpsy-lent, as Dash often said), his big gray and black striped tom cat, wandered sleepily into the kitchen.

"Meeeooow," he squeaked. He had a tiny meow, like a kitten, which did not look like it could come from that huge body.

"Shhh," Dash said quietly.

"Meeeeeeooooooow," he said, even more loudly.

"Shhhh!" Dash said again.

"Meeeeeeoooooow," Hpsyloughehe repeated.

"No, 'shhh' means to be quiet, not get louder," Dash whispered. Hpsyloughehe stood on his hind legs on the floor and tried to stick his face in the bowl on the table.

"No, boy," Dash whispered, petting him on the head and around the ears. Hpsyloughehe's purr machine turned on, and Dash continued to pet him, holding him back from the cereal.

"You can have some when I'm finished. Don't worry, I'll save you some," he promised. Hpsyloughehe cuddled up to him, waiting patiently for his cereal milk and wanting more attention. He nipped at Dash's elbow.

"Ow! Hipsee!" Dash finished the cereal and put the bowl on the floor for Hpsyloughehe to drink the milk. Dash looked in the refrigerator again and didn't see anything appetizing so he decided to make a sandwich. After getting out the bread and some cheese and lunch meat, he changed his mind and put everything away, as Hpsyloughehe chased an invisible pest across the floor. Dash went down the steps to his room and scribbled a few lyrics in his notebook before going to bed.

That evening when the band met at Lenny's house to practice, O.K. arrived at the same time as Dash, and grabbed one of the guitar cases Dash was carrying. They approached the front door.

"This is a door," O.K. said, in his Inspector Clouseau voice.

"Yes, that is a door," Dash said, immediately in character with an English accent. "Would you like me to open it?"

"Stand back," O.K. warned, "I prefer to handle this alone." Dash just smiled, having gone through this routine many times before. O.K. knocked on the door and Lenny let them in.

The whole gang was there along with the band: Joe, Ham, Paulie, Gary, or Goliath, as they called him, since he was gigantic, at six foot eight and two hundred fifty pounds, Pike, Kevin (Hevi-Kevi), Frank Lee, whom they called Frankly, and Walter Nellen, affectionately known among the group as Watermelon, and the Beauhahnaphish twins. They all had been friends since grade school and they all knew each other well. They had had thousands of shared experiences, millions of conversations together. They had a dialect of their own, snippets gleaned from movies, songs,

TV programs and their own intertwined lives, each with a history and usually a funny story to go with it.

"Last night Benny, the owner of Brubrack Moons, asked if The Others would consider becoming their house band," Dash announced, as soon as everyone arrived.

"So what did ya say?" Ham asked. Ham's real and forgotten name was Aristar. Everyone called him Ham, a remnant of his grade school nickname of Hamhocks, so given because of his stocky legs and last name of Hockinson. He liked Hamhocks better than Treetrunk, which the girls in first grade had called him.

"I said I'd have to talk about it with you guys," Dash said.

"I thought you were the leader," Lenny teased, his long hair falling onto his drums as he made some adjustments.

"So what's to discuss?" Paulie asked.

"Well, what else do we have going on?" Joe asked.

"Do we want to stick with playing in a bar three or four nights a week, or are we going to record and then go on tour?" Dash asked them.

"Since we have no prospects for a tour and we don't have the money to record right now, let's do the bar thing. What's he paying?"

"We'd each get about eight hundred a week," Dash told them.

"I could live on that," Joe said.

"Me too," agreed O.K.

"Hey, you're not in this, man!" said Lenny.

"I'm not saying I am, I'm just saying I could," O.K. said.

"I'm not saying, I'm just saying," Goliath explained.

"So let's go for it!" Paulie suggested.

"Okay, O.K.? Let's vote. All who think we should take

the run at the bar, raise your hand," Dash proposed. Dash saw all hands go up except Lenny's.

"All who think we should wait and record and then go on tour?"

No hands were raised.

"Lenny, what do you think? You didn't vote."

"You know I never vote. It's against my principles," Lenny explained.

"But you have a say in this," Dash told him.

"I figure if it's the thing to do, we'll do it and my vote won't matter one way or the other. If it's not the thing to do, we won't do it. What about you, Dash? Did you vote?"

"I didn't need to vote. I'll do whatever you guys want to do. I'm NOT the leader. I'm just twenty percent of the band, you know."

"Let's go for it!" Lenny shouted.

"All right!" Joe agreed.

"Right on," Dash said, glad to have the support of his friends and band members.

"Hey, guys, this song just came to me this morning," Joe said, and began to play on the keyboards. The guys listened for a few minutes, enjoying the oddly familiar tune.

"That sounds kind of like it's from 'Dark Side of the Moon,'" Dash said before Joe finished playing.

"Yeah, like part of 'Us and Them,'" Lenny said.

"Wow, no wonder it seemed so familiar," Joe said.

"Hmm, must have been a Floydian slip," O.K. said.

"Man, that's lame," Paulie said.

"I believe the politically correct term is 'physically challenged,' not 'lame,'" Lenny said.

"What do you know about being politically correct?" O.K. asked. "You don't even vote!"

"Hey, O.K., I saw a friend of yours at Fred Meyer this morning," Lenny teased.

"What were you doing up in the morning?" O.K. asked, trying to change the subject.

"No, really, she said she knew you, took a business class with you in college?"

"Who?"

"Um, let's see, she's kind of hefty..." Lenny began, grinning, trying to recall her name. "She had a weird name."

"Is she the Hefty man?" Frankly asked.

"Maybe she's a Hefty bag," Watermelon suggested.

"Or a bag lady," Pike added.

"Is she burly?" O.K. asked.

"No, not burly, she had on lots of make up, and her hair looked like it was plastered down," Lenny replied.

"It wasn't Franchesca, was it?" O.K. asked.

"Yeah, that was it! She likes you!" Lenny remembered.

"Oh, man!" O.K. exclaimed.

"What's wrong with her? I thought she was really nice," Lenny said.

"Yeah, if you like that type!" O.K. said, disgusted.

"What type?" asked Dash.

"Can I be frank?" O.K. asked.

"No, I'm Frank," Frankly said.

"Well, frankly, Frank Lee, she has back boobs!" O.K. explained.

"Back boobs?" Joe asked.

"Yeah, I was sitting behind her and it looked like her head was on backwards," O.K. explained.

"Oh, Mansville," Dash said sympathetically.

"Oh man, oh man," Goliath added.

"M and M head!" said Pike.

"Just another chick in the fall," Ham said.

"Not a duck in a shawl, not a heck in my squall," Joe quoted.

"She's not a store in the mall, she's not livin' in St. Paul!" Dash added.

"After all, after all, AFTER ALL, Dude," they said, all quoting one of their songs, "She's just an Other Chick in the Fall."

"Back boobs can be cool," Lenny said.

"Lenny," O.K. said, "I can understand why you are the drummer. You really are in a world of your own."

"Traveling to the beat of a different drum," Lenny agreed.

"Hey, listen to this song I wrote last night," Dash said. "It came to me, just like that," he snapped his fingers, "but I don't have it all together yet. Oh, does anyone have a Susan B. Anthony dollar?"

"What for?" Ham asked.

"It makes a cool effect when I use it as a pick for this one part in the song," Dash explained.

"Here ya go - catch!" Lenny said as he tossed the coin to Dash.

Dash began with a beautiful lead on the guitar, then he changed the sound by using the coin. He hummed a portion, explaining that it would be played on the keyboards, then he made the sound of a drum solo with his mouth. The Others and their friends were impressed and excited.

"Do you have any lyrics yet?" O.K. asked.

"Just this one part," he said, as he repeated a portion of the song on the guitar, singing with it.

"Does your heart skip a beat
Just to hear the sound of her name?
Is she all you'll ever need, all you want to know?
Do you think about her when you are apart?
Do you long for the moment
When you will be with her again?"

Dash went into the intricate guitar lead, then repeated the entire song. The Others practiced that night like they never had before, while their friends played video games and discussed the fate, fame and future of The Others and how they each would fit into the picture.

4

After playing three nights a week for nearly seven months at Brubrack Moons, Dash considered his life. Things were going quite well for him. He worked with Goliath in his business, Get Wired, wiring homes, businesses and schools for cable and Internet. Goliath worked full time and the business was profitable, and Dash only worked with him two days per week. His schedule was booked for the next month and he enjoyed working with Goliath. O.K. did the scheduling and book work, and occasionally joined them on a big job. The Others played on the weekends Benny paid them well, and the crowds were always large. Dash was financially stable. He had actually saved some money, for the first time in his life, and The Others were planning to go to the studio to record a few songs. They hoped to be able to tour as soon as they had recorded enough for a full album. Dash was considering moving into an apartment with O.K.

Dash examined himself in the mirror as he got ready to go to Brubrack Moons. At 24, he was tall and thin, nearly 6'2" and only 135 pounds, yet his shoulders, arms, chest and legs were bulging with muscles. He could still wear the same jeans he had worn in high school. His long, curly brown hair naturally fell into place, with the curls so precise it looked as if each one had been wrapped around a pencil. Women were always asking him who styled his hair, and they expressed jealousy when he said he just shakes his head when he gets out of the shower, and the curls fall that way. His brown eyes were kind and friendly, and his easy smile revealed perfectly straight, white teeth. Hpsyloughehe jumped up on the counter and examined Dash's arm. He rubbed his head against Dash's elbow and started to purr loudly.

"Good boy," Dash said, petting him. Hpsyloughehe stood on his hind legs and put his paws on Dash's shoulders, rubbing his face against Dash's cheeks. Dash continued grooming himself by reaching around Hpsyloughehe's big body.

After shaving, brushing his teeth and putting on his stage clothes, Dash went upstairs with Hpsyloughehe at his heels. Dash's parents, Daniel and Victoria Farrah, were just coming in the house after their evening walk. His dad was tall, lean and handsome. His Lebanese features, the black, curly hair and deep brown eyes made him look very distinguished. When he wasn't smiling he looked almost formidable, but his constantly smiling eyes comforted those who were in his presence.

"So are you about ready to go?" Victoria asked with a smile. Dash was thankful that his mother was so beautiful. Her stylish blond hair accented her sparkling green eyes. She looked neat and trim in her bright pink and white walking outfit.

"Yeah. Are you going to be coming tonight?" Dash asked, as Hpsyloughehe wove in and out of his legs, around his feet. His parents came to watch him play at least once a week. Dash scooped the cat's huge body into his arms and Hpsyloughehe cuddled against his face, still purring loudly.

"We're meeting Della and Bill, and then we'll all come over," his mom said. Bill and Della Lewis were good friends of Dash's parents. Bill was a local TV newscaster who was very charming and handsome, and his wife, Della, was a beautiful, petite literary critic who had recently had three nonfiction books published.

"Don't forget, Dari and her family will be here tomorrow," his dad reminded him.

"Oh, that's right!" Dash remembered, smiling with anticipation, picturing his sister, his brother-in-law and his niece. "I wonder how much Kwee has grown since they were here?"

"Dari says Zaqui is walking and talking now, not just standing and babbling," his mom said.

"I wonder if we'll be able to understand her now?" his dad asked.

"Dad! Too mean! It's baby talk! You have to make that leap, and know what she's talking about, or at least pretend," Dash said.

"She is a little rascal lady," his dad said.

Dash watched his parents go out to the patio. They joked and laughed together and, even after all these years, they were still happy together. He loved his life but knew something was missing. He wanted a special lady to share his life. Ever since Dash had met Tammy, his first girl friend in high school, he had been very romantic. She was so petite, so pretty, with her long brown hair and big, round, brown eyes, and she adored him. He loved to prepare simple dinners to share with her by candle light, then he would take out his twelve-string guitar and serenade her with love songs that he had written just for her. The first time he kissed her, he pledged his love to her. They stayed together for nearly three years, until she decided it was time for them to get married. At 18, he wasn't ready. Tammy gave him an ultimatum: either marry her or break up with her. Although his heart was breaking, he just wasn't prepared to get married. He had to follow his dreams, so he told Tammy goodbye. She had found another guy who was ready to marry her. A couple years after they got married, they already had two children. Now Dash longed for a loving relationship like the one he had had with Tammy. He still had so much love inside to share.

He wondered if God had someone for him who would work together with him, so they could be a team, like Dari and her husband were. Dari had been married for nearly four years to Pastor Wright, and together they accomplished many things. Dari's weaknesses were her husband's strengths, and she was strong where he was weak. He was good at seeing the big picture and getting them to focus on their joint goals, and she filled in the details so the two of them could work together toward those goals. Pastor Wright was a people person, and Dare was an organized-number-and-word person; so they could keep the different aspects of their ministry in order. Dash was impressed by this excellent pairing of talents. Pastor Wright explained it simply as God's plan, which has always been better than man's plan.

On the other hand, Dash had his goal to really make it in the music business; it had been his dream ever since he had been a child. He knew having a girlfriend could cause problems with someone who wanted to be famous. He had already seen the jealousy in his recent girlfriends, and he wasn't even famous yet. He figured that when the time was right, God would send the perfect lady into his life and they would work together. Dash didn't need to try to set up anything for himself.

O.K. came by the house and they went together to Brubrack Moons. The place was packed tonight, much more crowded than it usually was on a Friday night. Dash and O.K. made their way to the stage and got things ready for their sound check. The crowd was ready for the music and began to cheer when the band stepped on stage, before they even started to play. Dash noticed a pretty young lady he hadn't seen there before, gracefully carrying two drinks across the dance floor. She had flowing blond hair and she seemed to glide across the room. He couldn't take his eyes from her.

"Do you know who she is?" O.K. asked, noticing Dash notice her.

"No, who?"

"Know who?"

"No, who?"

"I don't know, I thought you might know."

"I don't know, I thought YOU might know."

"Know? No."

"No? Oh."

"I'll find out, and then I'll introduce you."

"Who said I want to be introduced?"

"I saw that look in your eyes when you looked at her."

"What look?"

"THAT look."

"What look?"

"You know what I'm talking about, man."

"No, man, I don't know. I don't want to meet her."

"Are you saying you don't want to meet her?"

"I'm not saying, I'm just saying," Dash said. He wasn't ready to meet anyone that beautiful. He still had to keep his goals in mind, as his top priority.

"Okay, then," O.K. said.

"Okay, O.K."

"Kay."

"Kay."

"Mansville! You want to meet her and you know it."

"Man!"

"Boy."

"Man..."

"Boy!"

They both looked over to the table where she sat down with an older lady. From the matching upturned noses, Dash guessed that they were related.

"Who goes to a bar with their grandmother?" O.K. asked.

"Maybe they came to hear the music," Dash suggested.

"Her grandmother came to hear The Others?" O.K. said.

"Ya never know, man," Dash answered. "Maybe she has good taste in music."

"Or maybe she's like most of the other chicks here, and came to meet someone."

"Yeah, whenever I meet a new girl I always ask her if she has a friend for my grandfather," Dash said sarcastically.

"Well, ya never know," O.K. said.

"Never 'no,' you know."

"Never say 'never.'"

"Always say 'always.'"

"Always say something."

"Dude, you know I never pick up anyone in bars," Dash reminded him.

"Hey, Dash!" Hamhocks called. "You ready to get started?"

"Let's go for it, man," Dash replied, and the band went into the first set, starting with Dash's song "Go For It."

When the band took a break, Dash noticed that another young lady had joined the girl who had earlier caught his eye. The second lady was very tall and thin, and they were laughing and laughing with the older lady. Dash walked slowly to the rest room and took a closer look at the trio on his way.

The blond girl was smiling sweetly, and her lips moved. Dash strained to hear the sound of her voice, but there was too much noise in the place to hear her at all. The tall one, with her back to Dash, took a drink and guffawed loudly. All three of them began laughing. Dash could hear a gravely, wheezy laugh and guessed that it was coming from the older lady. From this distance, he could see that her teeth were various shapes, gray and decaying, each outlined in black. Her hair was stringy and laced with white, and her face was a road map of wrinkles. She pulled another cigarette out of her purse even though she still had one at the corner of her mouth. One eye squinted against the smoke, and as she spoke, the cigarette bobbed up and down on her lips, the ashes falling on the table. The upturned nose perfectly matched the young lady's nose. Fortunately for the younger lady, that's where the resemblance stopped.

He didn't want to act like he was staring (but he was) so he continued to the men's room. Another man followed Dash into the rest room. Lenny was there, leaning down to look in the mirror, brushing his hair. Lenny was even taller than Dash.

"Hey, man, I like your hair," the other man said.

"Thanks," Lenny said.

"No, I mean the one with the curls," he corrected.

"Yeah, I like it too, that's why I wear it this way," Dash said.

"How did you get it like that?"

"It's natural. I inherited it from my dad," Dash said.

"What is your dad, a hair dresser?"

"No, he's Lebanese."

"How can he be, if he's a man?" the man asked. "Wouldn't he be gay? Well, a lot of hairdressers are, anyway."

"No, he's not a hairdresser. Lebanese means his family is from Lebanon. Since my dad is full-blooded Lebanese, I'm half Lebanese," Dash said.

"I thought so! I knew you couldn't be straight! Not with hair like that!"

"No, seriously--" Dash began again.

"They look so perfect, each curl is so -- curly. You were shaking your head all over when you were on stage and not even one curl is out of place," he said, astonished.

"Amazing, isn't it?" asked Lenny.

"Do you have a perm? Because I was thinking of getting one. I wonder if my hair would look like that." He moved around Dash, examining his hair from every angle.

"Yeah, I was born with a perm. If you weren't born with one, you can't get a perm. You'd have to get a temp."

The man stopped moving.

"A what?" he asked, confused.

"A temp. It wouldn't last forever, it would just be temporary. Mine is like this all the time. It's permanent, a perm," Dash explained. "Get it? Temporary means it doesn't last forever, but permanent does last forever. Temp? Perm?"

"Wow, man, you are heavy. But, you know, I bet I could stick a pencil up one of those curls and not even touch your hair," he said, reaching for a curl.

Dash leaned out of the way. "Uh, no, man."

"Dude, don't try sticking Dash with anything, he's with me," Lenny said.

"Oh, sorry, man, I didn't know you were taken," he apologized, stepping back and holding his hands up as if he were being arrested.

"No problem," Dash said. "Come on Lenny, we have a show to do."

"I like your show!" the man called after them.

Dash and Lenny stopped at a table in front to visit with

Dash's parents and their friends for a few minutes. Dash resisted the urge to look toward the beautiful blond. He chortled as Lenny told them what had just happened in the men's room.

"You should have seen it," Lenny said, unable to contain his smile.

Dash and Lenny laughed as they returned to the stage. As Dash put his guitar strap over his head, he glanced out at the crowd and saw the man from the rest room wink at him. Dash quickly turned his attention to the music, called out, "1, 2, 3, 4!" and they started the second set.

When the show was over, O.K. came on stage to help Dash pack up his equipment.

"So, did you say anything to her?" O.K. teased.

"Who?" Dash asked innocently.

"You know who," O.K. replied.

"She has a friend, you could go introduce yourself," Dash suggested.

"No, thanks, I'm trying to cut down on dating giraffes," O.K. said.

"Man! She's not that tall."

"Did you see her neck? And she looks like a giraffe, with those stubby, spread apart teeth, like little agates. Even her hair is giraffey. You go talk to the blond, and I'll stand behind you. But I'm not saying anything. Don't even introduce me. As a matter of fact, I'll stay over here while you go over there," O.K. said, considering the possibilities.

Dash contemplated going over to thank the three ladies for staying for the whole show, but just as he was about to decide, three Hispanic guys approached the table and began to talk to the three ladies. O.K., always aware of Dash's situation, stepped in and tried to change the subject.

"Hey, man, want to go to the Donut Hole and get a French dip?" he asked.

"No, I think I'll just go home and share something with Hpsyloughehe." Dash glanced at the table and saw that the men had seated themselves. The blond girl noticed Dash looking at her and she smiled at him. Dash looked away from her as he followed O.K. out the door. Something seemed familiar about her, but he couldn't quite place it. He was sure they hadn't met before... yet it was something about her manner, the way she threw her head back when she laughed, the way she tossed her hair. Maybe she reminded him of some movie star. He reminded himself that his future was still in God's hands.

5

The next morning when Dash came out of his room, he heard the sweet voice of his sister singing in the kitchen.

"Seek ye first the kingdom of God, and his righteousness, And all these things shall be added unto you..." Dari sang.

"Hallelujah," sang Zaqui, in her little Smurfy voice.

That confirmed his plans. God was giving him a message. He would continue to let God be in control while he took care of his business, and God would bring everything together in His plans, and in His timing.

"Who's home?" Dash called as he came up the stairs.

"Unco Dasssshhhh!" Zaqui squeaked, an improvement over "Unc Da" the last time they visited. She ran and jumped into his arms. At 16 months, she was only a couple of feet tall, with a huge smile, enormous laughing brown eyes and dark brown springy curls all over her head, like Dash's curls only shorter.

"Hey, my little Kwee-Kwee!" he said as he picked her up to hug her. Dari joined them in the hug. Dari was petite and very pretty, although not as glamourous as their mother. Dari and Dash looked as if they could be twins, if Dash weren't a foot taller than she was. Dari's hair was also curly, yet the curls were softer, not quite as tight as Dash's.

"Big hug! Hi, T!" she said, using one of her nicknames for him. As children, they had taught themselves Morse code, an obvious offspring of having the name Dash in the family. The letter 't' is represented by a dash; therefore, Dash became T. The next logical step was that Dash had begun calling Dari 'Dot', or simply 'E,' to the confusion of anyone who might be listening.

"E! How's it going?" They hugged for a minute. Dari's husband, Pastor Wright, came and joined the group hug, a joyful reunion after not seeing each other for several months.

Pastor Luther Wright was an Afro-American Baptist preacher from Tennessee, a trim man about six feet tall with black hair with a white stripe down the middle, He was the most friendly and concerned person Dash had ever met. They had spent many evenings discussing spiritual things, as well as working through any problems or questions Dash had had. Pastor Wright was a great listener. Dash had known him for years before he had married Dari, and Dash had great respect for him. Dash still was not comfortable calling him by his first name. He always addressed him as Pastor Wright.

"How was the trip?" Dash asked, as they disengaged from their hug. They had traveled about two hundred miles across the state.

"It was beautiful," Pastor Wright answered, "sunny all the way."

"It's a four-mountain day," Dari added.

"Cool!" Dash responded. They had begun using the phrase 'four-mountain day' as children, whenever they took a family trip south through Washington State. At one specific point overlooking the Goldendale valley, on a clear day, four mountains could be seen: Mt. Hood, Mt. Adams, Mt. St. Helens and Mt. Rainier. Usually it was clear enough to see Mt. Hood and Mt. Adams, but the tallest, Mt. Rainier was much farther away and hard to see if any clouds were in the distance. Since the eruption of Mt. St. Helens in 1980, it was very hard to see from that point these days since it was so short now, and the top looked almost flat from that angle. On a four-mountain day, the skies were completely clear to the north, south and west of that viewpoint.

"How's my brother-in-law?" Pastor Wright asked.

"Good, good, everything is going well," Dash answered.

"How's business?" Pastor Wright asked. They had prayed together that God would bless Dash financially, and He had and still was.

"We are keeping busy, and the band is doing great too," Dash replied. "We have been playing every week since the state fair. We're the house band at a night club."

"Well, that's a blessing," Pastor Wright stated joyfully.

"Zaqui," she said, pointing to herself. "Z-a-q-u-i."

"Good girl! You can spell your name!" Dash said enthusiastically, as the doorbell rang.

Dash heard his mother greet O.K. and direct him to the kitchen.

"Hi, O.K.," said Dari, giving him a hug. "Are you O.K.? Or Knott?"

"Both, Dare-to-be-right," O.K. said, greeting Dari with his nickname for her.

"Hey, my friend," Pastor Wright said, giving O.K. a hug. Since Dari had married Pastor Wright, she had become a hugger like he always had been.

"How's it going?" O.K. asked him.

"We're blessed," Pastor Wright responded.

"How was the drive?"

"It's a four-mountain day," Dash and Dari answered together.

"Whoa, stereo!" O.K. remarked, since he was standing between them.

"Dude, can you take me to pick up my car?" O.K. asked Dash. "It's at Frank's Tire Shop."

"Now?"

"Yeah, I need to get it so I can take my mom to her hair appointment at Sally's," he explained.

"Sure, let me get my keys," he said, then to Dari and her family, "I'll be back in a minute."

"Do you want some breakfast?" Dash's mom asked, coming into the kitchen.

"No, not now, I need to take O.K. to Frank's Tire to get his car."

"Mm-kay," Victoria said, then, as an afterthought, "Can you go by the new Albertson's and get some potatoes? They have the ten pound bag on sale for seventy-nine cents."

"Okay," Dash replied.

"Do you need some money?" she asked.

"No, I have a dollar," he said with a smile.

Dash dropped off O.K. at his car, then he stopped at the new Albertson's. It was actually about six years old, but they still called it the new Albertson's. After Dash bought the bag of potatoes, he got in the car and it wouldn't start. He tried several times to start it then went to the phone booth to call home. His mom answered.

"Mom! The car won't start," he told her.

"What's the matter with it?" she asked.

"I don't know, I'm not a mechanic," he replied.

"Where are you?"

"At the new Albertson's. I went in to get the potatoes and when I came out, it wouldn't start."

"Was it acting funny before you stopped?"

"I don't know, I'm not a mechanic," he repeated.

"Was it making a funny sound or anything?"

"I don't know, I'm not a mechanic. Is Dad there?"

"No, the men had some errands to run. They went to the hardware store and then they were going to stop at that church over on Tieton to talk to the pastor there."

"Oh. Can you come and get me?"

"You don't think you can get it started?"

"No, I tried a hundred times already, and it won't start."

"I have a roast in the oven. I'll see if Dari can come and get you."

"Okay, thanks, Mom," he said.

"Mm-kay, love you," she answered, and then she hung up.

A few minutes later, Dari arrived in Mom's car, a sporty red Nissan.

"The men took our car, so Mom let me drive hers," she explained.

"Ah, now we are getting somewhere," Dash said.

"So what happened to your car?" Dari asked, looking at it as if she could see something wrong with it.

"I don't know, I'm not a mechanic," he replied.

"Are you out of gas?" she asked, getting out of the car to look more closely.

"I don't know, I'm not a mechanic," he repeated again.

"Well, the gas gauge looks pretty low," she observed. "It looks like it's right on E. Maybe you're out of gas."

"No, it's always low like that," he said.

"Okay, get in," she instructed. Dash grabbed the bag of potatoes and they both got in Mom's car and went home.

Later, when his Dad and Pastor Wright returned from their errands, Dash told them that his car was in the new Albertson's parking lot and wouldn't start.

"What happened?" his dad asked.

"I don't know, I'm not a mechanic," Dash repeated yet again. His dad was really good with cars, but Dash had never had an interest. He had never looked under the hood of any car and wouldn't even know what the battery looked like, or where to put the oil.

"Did it turn over when you tried to start it?" his dad asked.

"I don't know, I'm not a mechanic." He didn't know what difference it would make. The car wouldn't start.

"Did it make a clicking sound, or go r-r-r-r-r when you tried to start it?" his dad asked.

"I don't know, I'm not a mechanic."

His dad realized this conversation was fruitless so he stopped asking Dash about it. Pastor Wright offered to go with them to see if they could get it started. His dad brought jumper cables and a gallon of gas.

When they arrived at the car, his dad took one look in the window and then poured the gas into the tank. He and Pastor Wright did something under the hood and in a couple of minutes they had the car running again.

"You were out of gas," his dad told him. "Does your gas gauge work?"

"I don't know, it's always on empty," Dash said.

"Well, follow me to the gas station and we'll fill it up," his dad said. "You shouldn't let it get this low."

"My dad used to tell us boys, 'It's just as easy to keep the top half full as the bottom half,'" Pastor Wright said, "so I have always made it a practice to not let it drop below half a tank."

"That is an excellent idea," Dash's dad agreed.

That evening at Brubrack Moons before the band began to play, Dash immediately spotted the blond girl with her friend, sitting at the same table as they had the night before. He had that feeling that something about her was familiar, but he couldn't place her. She waved at him and motioned for him to come to their table.

"How's it going?" he asked, smiling pleasantly. This close, her friend did remind him of a giraffe, so he tried not to stare at either one of them. "I'm Dash."

"It's nice to finally meet you," the blond girl said. "I'm Shelley, and this is my best friend, Jessie." Her voice was sweet and clear.

"Nice to meet you," Dash said.

"Nice meeting you," Jessie said politely.

"We've been best friends since we were babies," Shelley said. "She's visiting from Spokane for the weekend. Last night, Mama and I came to hear The Others, and Jessie drove down and met us here. You guys are really good."

"Thank you, that's nice of you to say," Dash said.

"You're really something on that guitar," Jessie said.

"Do you want to sit with us and have a drink or something?" Shelley offered.

"Thanks, but I need to get up on stage. We're going to get started in a minute. It was nice meeting both of you. Maybe we can talk more later," he said, feeling unusually awkward.

"Come back later and autograph my napkin," Shelley said with a smile.

"I'll do that," Dash promised.

During the first set, the three men who had joined Shelley and Jessie the previous night arrived and sat with them again. Dash tried to concentrate on his music, and he suggested to the band that they play "Rock You by the Fireside," one of his original love songs from last year. The Others had dropped it from their regular set because Dash always became so emotional every time he sang it, reliving the pain of his last relationship which had inspired it.

He began the haunting ballad and The Others joined him. Although they hadn't practiced this song in months, they played it flawlessly. Dash sang, not looking in

Shelley's direction. His deep, clear voice sincerely conveyed his message to each person individually.

> *"If you'd take the time to look inside,*
> *You'd see what you always knew.*
> *Baby, there were times so long ago*
> *When it was only me and you.*
> *I know, I know, I know,*
> *I used to wipe away your tears,*
> *And rock you gently*
> *By the fireside,*
> *And chase away your fears.*
> *'Cause, Babe, I used to rock you, rock you, rock you*
> *By the fireside, by the fireside.*
> *I used to rock you, rock you, rock you.*
> *I used to rock you, rock you, rock you,*
> *Baby, by the fireside, by the fireside.*
> *I used to rock you, rock you, rock you."*

Dash and his guitar were one as he brought the song to life. The audience felt the ache of his heart with each note, with each word. He took a deep breath to stabilize his voice for the next verse.

> *"Though I don't remember what it was*
> *That took me away from you.*
> *Whatever it was, Baby,*
> *There was nothing that I could do.*
> *I look in your eyes and I see the light*
> *Of a hundred thousand years,*
> *And missin' you for oh, so long*
> *Has brought a thousand tears.*
> *'Cause, Babe, I used to rock you, rock you, rock you*
> *By the fireside, by the fireside.*
> *I used to rock you, rock you, rock you.*
> *I used to rock you, rock you, rock you*
> *Baby, by the fireside, by the fireside...*
> *I used to rock you, rock you, rock you."*

Dash went into a beautiful lead on the guitar and The Others had never sounded better. Dash avoided looking at Shelley, instead concentrating on his music.

> *"I just know I've held your hands*
> *Baby, all through time.*
> *So, how can you tell me now*
> *That you're not mine?*
> *Well, we've been through so many a-time,*
> *Baby, good and bad together,*
> *I know, I know, I know, I know,*
> *It's been you and me forever.*
> *'Cause, Babe, I used to rock you, rock you, rock you*
> *By the fireside, by the fireside...*
> *I used to rock you, rock you, rock you.*
> *I used to rock you, rock you, rock you*
> *Baby, by the fireside, by the fireside...*
> *I used to rock you, rock you, rock you.*
> *I used to rock you, hold you, hold you,*
> *Every day and night, holdin' you so tight*
> *Rockin' you...*
> *Rock you."*

The crowd was extremely emotionally involved with the music when Dash finished the song. Usually they weren't paying this much attention to the band, they were just comfortable with the music as background noise. Tonight the bartender was suddenly busy filling orders for drinks to counteract the effect the song was having on the audience. The rest of the evening went well musically, and even though Shelley kept looking up at him, Dash was feeling disappointed and somehow betrayed. The three men stayed with Shelley and Jessie until the band left.

"So, you just met her and she dumped you already?" O.K. asked, in his not-so-gracious manner, when they got into his car.

"She didn't dump me," Dash denied.

"She rejected you," O.K. said.

"No, just because someone else sat with her, that doesn't mean anything. I don't even know her," Dash said.

"Bummer," O.K. said.

"We just met," Dash said.

"Bum rap, man," O.K. said.

"Bum rhapsody," Dash said. "Hey, do you have any Queen in here?"

"Yeah, in the box under the seat," O.K. said.

Dash found "A Night at the Opera" and they listened to "The Prophet's Song," with Dash and O.K. each singing a part during the round portions. The line kept repeating in Dash's mind, "Love is still the answer, take my hand," and he was reminded God still had plans for him. They went to O.K.'s house for a late night snack and found some lasagna in the refrigerator.

O.K. had moved back with his mother a few months ago, after his dad had left her for a girl who was O.K.'s age. O.K.'s mother was a fastidious housekeeper, who freaked out about one little thing out of place. She was also a very heavy sleeper, so O.K. liked Dash to visit him late at night after his mom went to bed. They finished their lasagna and Dash stood up to put his dishes in the dishwasher.

"No, don't put them in there," O.K. warned.

"Why not?" Dash asked.

"Mom keeps it organized in her own way. No matter how you arrange things or try to follow her pattern, she'll take them out and rearrange them," he explained. "Just leave them in the sink. She likes it better that way."

Dash and O.K. played video games for awhile, then O.K. took Dash home.

The next morning, Dash got up early so he could spend some time with Dari and her family before they left. Zaqui was so excited to see him. She babbled on and on, and Dash carried on a conversation with her, pretending he could understand her. He was amazed at how fast she was growing. He could see the Farrah family resemblance in her and he briefly longed for the day when he would see a daughter or son of his own who looked like the rest of the family.

Hpsyloughehe came in the room and jumped on Dash's lap, not happy to have his attention stolen by this little person.

"Kee-ee," Zaqui said, pointing to Hpsyloughehe. "Niiiiice."

"Yes, it's a nice kitty, and we are nice to the kitty," Dash said, demonstrating how to pet him. Zaqui didn't reach out to Hpsyloughehe, and Dash knew it was because Dari's cat, Tundra, was not very friendly. Dari had probably taught Zaqui not to touch Tundra. Dash had been scratched and bitten by Tundra many times, but Hpsyloughehe didn't bite.

"Niiiice," Zaqui repeated.

"Who's ready to eat?" Dari called.

"We are," Dash's dad called from the family room, where the men were watching the football game.

"So are we," Dash answered as he grabbed his niece's hand and pulled her to her feet. Hpsyloughehe jumped to the ground, swishing his tail unhappily.

"Wheee!" Zaqui added.

The family gathered around the dining room table for their favorite breakfast, which was Mom's specialty: fried eggs with bacon, hash browns and toast. Pastor Wright blessed the table and everyone started to eat.

"Normally, when we are at home, we are in church at

this time on Sunday," Pastor Wright remarked.

"Yeah, it feels kind of strange not being there," Dari said.

"Do you think God has a specific plan for everyone?" Dash asked.

"I know He does, because it's in His Word," Pastor Wright replied. "In the book of Jeremiah, God said, 'I know the plans I have for you, plans for good and not evil.' And He has a plan for each and every one of us, individually."

"Really? He said that?" Dash asked.

"Yes, in Jeremiah, chapter twenty-nine, verse eleven," Dari verified.

"Does he make things happen, or are we suppose to make things happen?" Dash asked

"Without Him, nothing can happen," Pastor Wright explained. "We are suppose to seek Him and then follow His leading."

"'Seek ye first the kingdom of God, and his righteousness; and all these things shall be added unto you,'" Dari quoted. "Matthew chapter six, verse thirty-three," she added.

"He promised that those who seek Him will find Him," Pastor Wright said.

"How do we seek Him?" Dash asked.

"In His Word, the Bible," Pastor Wright said. "He gave us instructions for living, and He tells us how to grow closer to him."

"I believe the New Testament," Dash's mother said, "but the Old Testament was written so long ago, by so many different people, and has been translated so many times. And some of the stories in there are so far-fetched, you can't possibly believe them."

"The Bible was written by many different men, but they wrote it under the inspiration of God," Pastor Wright explained. "The Bible that we read today is exactly what God wants us to know about Him, and about Jesus."

"I believe the whole Bible," Dari said. "The Old Testament paved the way for the New Testament, with the prophecies of the coming Savior, which Jesus fulfilled. The prophets predicted just about everything that would happen to Jesus. When you read the whole Bible, you can see the parallels between the Old and New Testaments. In the New Testament, in first Corinthians, chapter ten, says that one reason the Old Testament was written was so the people who lived during those times can be examples to us. So we can learn to please God the way they pleased Him, and also, we can learn from their mistakes. We don't have to make the same mistakes they made."

"You've got to take the whole Bible together," Pastor Wright said. "It's like when my mother used to bake a loaf of bread, and I always liked the end, or we called it the 'butt' of the bread, best. If you take a loaf and cut off the ends, you don't have the whole loaf. You have most of it, but something is missing, and that's my favorite part.

"It's the same with the Word of God. You can't just take part of it and leave the rest. You have to take the whole thing, together, to get what God has for you. Some people just pick out the verses they want and ignore the rest, but that is not how God intends it to be. He wants us to have the whole thing.

"God has great plans for your life, greater than you can imagine. Ephesians, chapter three, verse twenty, tells us that God is able to do greater than anything we could ask or think," Pastor Wright said.

Dash thought about everything he had said. He wondered how it applied to his situation with Shelley, if he had a situation with her. He wanted an answer, but he wanted to do it God's way, which must be better than his own way, which wasn't happening at all. He decided to just let God take over, and if God wanted something to happen with Shelley, it would happen. Dash didn't have to try to make anything happen. If he did make something happen and it wasn't God's plan, it wouldn't work out anyway. If God didn't want it to happen, then He must have a better plan.

6

Shelley came to Brubrack Moons every night for the next three weeks. Sometimes she came with Jessie and sometimes with the older lady, whom Dash discovered was her mother. Dash smiled and said hi a few times, but he didn't approach her or treat her differently than any of the other people who were there. Some of his fellow band members talked to her sometimes, but none of them were interested in her. Dash, on the other hand, was very interested, but didn't want to start anything unless he had some kind of confirmation from God. She was so attractive, and her voice was so sweet and gentle. Dash was very patient, waiting to find out what God wanted him to do.

One evening after the show, as O.K. and Dash were loading his equipment into the car, Shelley approached them.

"Can you help me?" she asked Dash. "My car won't start."

"Well, I'm not a mechanic," Dash said, glancing at O.K., who had as much experience with cars as he did, "but I'll look at it."

The three of them walked across the parking lot to a little white 1983 Toyota wagon.

"Try to start it," Dash told Shelley.

"Shouldn't you look under the hood or something?" she asked.

"Well, let's listen to it first," Dash suggested, wondering how to open the hood.

Shelley got in and turned the key. The car made a clicking sound. Dash tried to think what that could mean.

He remembered his dad had mentioned a clicking sound when his car wouldn't start, but he had no idea why he had said that.

"Are you sure you're not out of gas?" he asked her.

"No, I'm not sure," she confessed. She looked so helpless as she looked to Dash for aid. He wanted to assist her.

"Well, if you're out of gas it won't help to look under the hood," Dash stated. O.K. smiled, undoubtedly understanding Dash's reasons for coming to this logical conclusion.

"Where's your friend?" O.K. asked. Jessie had been with Shelley earlier.

"She had a headache so she had to go," Shelley explained.

Dash and O.K. exchanged glances. O.K. gave a little nod. Dash thought this might be the sign from God for which he had been waiting.

"We could give you a ride home," Dash said, offering her O.K.'s car and chauffeur services, "if you want to leave your car here overnight. Where do you live?"

"In the lower valley, with Mama. I used to live in Spokane, but I moved back with Mama a few weeks ago."

"Where in the lower valley?" O.K. asked. The lower valley was at least sixty miles long and thirty miles wide.

"Just about twenty-five miles from here," she said.

Dash and O.K. each lived across town in the other direction, on the north side, so this trip would take them more than an hour out of their way. Dash realized this would give him a chance to have a conversation with Shelley; a safe conversation with O.K. driving and available to rescue him so he wouldn't get trapped in a situation with her.

Dash didn't look forward to riding in the small back seat of O.K.'s Subaru with his long legs, but he offered the front seat to Shelley anyway. They all got in the car and O.K. started driving. As soon as they got on the freeway, Shelley began to give O.K. directions to her house. Then she turned to Dash.

"So, Mama tells me you are the leader of The Others. She saw you on TV. When did you form the band?"

"I'm not the leader, I'm only twenty percent of the band. We are all in it equally," Dash explained.

"Oh, well, how long have you been together?"

"At least ten years. We formed The Others when we were in grade school."

"Really? So you have been friends for a long time."

"Ever since we were in first or second grade."

"That is so cool, being loyal to your friends for all that time."

"We are all friends, we all wanted to be in a band, so we all learned to play instruments and started practicing together."

"Who came up with the name 'The Others?'"

"That was my idea," Dash said. "Ever since I can remember, I wanted to have a band with that name."

"So, do you have a job? Or do you just play in the band?"

"Playing in the band is my job, then I also have a part time job working with one of my other friends and O.K. here."

"That is so cool."

"What about you? Do you work?"

"Not now, I'm going to school. I'm taking accounting classes and I am enrolled in a program that will eventually lead to a CPA job."

"CPA? Is that like CPR?" Dash asked.

O.K. and Shelley both laughed.

"Certified public accountant," O.K. explained. He had wanted to take the CPA program but he couldn't afford it. He had not been able to get a grant or a scholarship, nor had he been eligible for a student loan. He was making a living working with Dash and Goliath, and also doing some accounting for individuals, mostly at tax time. Dash was planning to hire O.K. full time as his personal assistant, as soon as he got famous.

"So..." Shelley said tentatively, "...are you seeing anyone?"

"Who, me?" Dash asked. "No, not at this time. I'm concentrating on my career right now."

"Me too," O.K. added. "I'm not seeing anyone either."

Dash wanted to ask Shelley the same question, since she had brought up the subject, but then he remembered the Hispanic guys who joined her almost every time she came to Brubrack Moons. He hadn't seen any interaction taking place besides conversation, but he felt there was something more going on between them.

"So, what about you?" O.K. finally asked, after a moment of silence. "Are you seeing anyone?"

"No, not me," Shelley said. "A few months ago, I got divorced, and so I'm very careful about who I meet," she said.

"But what about..." Dash began, then decided not to finish his sentence.

"What about what?" Shelley asked, truly concerned.

"Nothing, I was just thinking about something," he said.

"I'm not saying, I'm just saying," O.K. said.

"What are you taking about?" Shelley asked, not following the line of conversation.

"That's just a saying we have," O.K. explained.

"If you're wondering about the guys who are always sitting with us at the club," Shelley said, "the big one is my brother and the other two guys are his friends. They are working here for a couple of months before they go back to Spokane."

"Oh, your brother," Dash said, relieved, yet confused. She was blonde with very fair skin, and they all were obviously Hispanic, with their black hair, tan skin, and their Mexican accents. Her cute little turned-up nose was not at all Hispanic-looking.

"Well, Manny is my half brother," she explained. "Mama has been married a few times, and she married her fourth husband, Manuelo, Manny's dad, and then Manny was born, and then they got divorced and then she married Daddy, and then they had a perfect child, my sister Desdamonia, who died at birth, and then they had me. Desi was perfect in every way, and they wanted me to be perfect too. Mama and Daddy stayed married for 18 years, then they got divorced, then Mama remarried three more times, then her last husband died, so now Mama is a widow. Daddy and I were always really close, and I sat by his bedside for the last nine months of his life when he was dying. Ever since Daddy died, I haven't been the same. Part of me is missing. After he died, I knew I couldn't stay with Herbert -- he's my ex-husband, and he's an accountant, and he's so boring -- so I divorced him and moved back with Mama."

"So... does that mean you're not seeing anyone?" O.K. tried to clarify the conclusion of her explanation.

"That is correct, I am not seeing anyone now," she said. "But I know God has a plan for me, and I am just waiting for Him to find the right person for me," she said.

"Yes, God has a plan for each of us, individually," Dash quoted Pastor Wright.

"I knew it! I knew you were religious," Shelley said.

"I wouldn't call myself religious, but I do believe in God," Dash said.

"Same thing," Shelley said.

"My sister is married to a pastor, and he helps me keep my faith on track," Dash explained.

"Oh, that is so cool! Do you have any other brothers or sisters?"

"No, just the one, my little, older sister, Dari."

"I just have one brother, Manny, except my baby sister who died," Shelley said.

"I have twin brothers who are two years younger than I am," O.K. added.

"So, how old are you?" Shelley asked Dash. She was now fully turned around in the front seat, facing him.

"I just turned twenty-three on Saint Patrick's day," he said.

"Oh, that is so cool, you were born on Saint Patrick's day," she said. "You must be really lucky."

"Not really lucky, but I do believe that God is watching over me and He doesn't want anything bad to happen to me," Dash said.

"I believe that too!" Shelley agreed. "Well, I turned twenty-seven just a couple of weeks ago, on the fifteenth." Dash nodded. He had been curious, but hadn't wanted to ask her age.

"I'm twenty-two," O.K. said, trying to stay in the conversation. "My birthday is in August."

"Oh, you just passed the turn," Shelley said, suddenly aware of their surroundings and turning around to face the front of the car. "Turn back and go right - no, left now - on Lateral A."

They were surrounded by orchards, the main business

in this part of the valley. Many of the trees were in blossom at this time of the year, illuminated by the headlights of O.K.'s car.

"Which way?" O.K. asked at the intersection.

"Go straight here, then follow the turn to the right, and then it's the second driveway on the left," she explained.

"Second driveway?" O.K. asked.

"Yeah. Mama owns this orchard and all this land, and those apartments over there," she said. The night was too dark to see any of it.

"Here we are," O.K. said, turning into the driveway.

"Go all the way back, it's a long driveway," Shelley said.

O.K. stopped the car at the end of the driveway next to the house and Shelley turned back to Dash.

"I'll see you again soon," she promised.

Dash stepped out of the car, relieved to stretch his cramped legs, and opened the car door for Shelley. As soon as she got out of the car, the door of the house opened. Shelley's mom, smoking and coughing, came outside.

"Oh, it's you," she wheezed, through her cough. "Where's your car?"

"It wouldn't start, and Jessie and Manny had already left the club," she said. "Mama, this is Dash, the leader of The Others, and this is his friend, O.K. They took the time to bring me all the way home."

"Well, that is very nice of you," her mother said to them, softening a little.

"Nice meeting you," Dash said, approaching her and extending his hand.

"Suzie, Suzie Bovine," she said, holding the cigarette with the side of her lips while reaching out to shake his hand.

"Nice to meet you," O.K. added, also shaking Suzie's hand.

"We'll be seeing you, I'm sure," Dash said to Shelley.

"Oh, and thanks so much, guys, for the ride. Can I give you some money for gas?"

"No, thanks, it was our pleasure," O.K. said, as he and Dash returned to the car.

"Bye!" Shelley called.

"See ya," Dash responded, closing the door.

"She seems pretty nice," O.K. said, when they got out of her mother's driveway.

"Yeah, she's really nice," Dash agreed.

"Her mom's a little strange, though," O.K. said.

"A little," Dash said.

"She's been married - how many times?"

"I lost count."

"Me too," O.K. said.

"I think she said eight, or was it nine?" Dash asked.

"Does it matter?" O.K. asked.

"No, not really, but it is interesting."

"Just a warning, man," O.K. said. "They say if you want to know what a woman will look like when she gets older, just look at her mother."

"AAAHHH!" Dash joked.

"But I'm sure her mother looks like that mostly because she smokes. Have you ever seen Shelley smoke?"

"No, never," Dash said. "You know, that's not always true. Dari will never look like Mom, even when she's old."

"Not unless she bleaches her hair blond, changes her eye color and gets plastic surgery on her face," O.K. laughed.

"And grows another few inches," Dash added.

"So, do you like her?" O.K. asked.

"Dari or Mom?" Dash teased.

"Seriously," O.K. said.

"Seriously! I'm just kidding."

"No, seriously."

"I'm just kidding."

"No, seriously."

"No, seriously, I'm just kidding."

"So do you like her?"

"Shelley? She's okay," Dash said, then added quickly, "but she won't ever replace you. Even if she becomes a CPR, you've still got your place with me when we're famous."

"I'm not jealous of her, I just wondered if you like her," O.K. said.

"I'm not saying you're jealous, I'm just saying you don't have to worry."

"I'm not saying, I'm just saying."

They drove in silence for a few minutes as Dash thought about the things Shelley had told them. He was surprised at how relieved he felt to learn that she had been meeting her brother at the club, and not a boyfriend.

"So, that was her brother," O.K. said, reading Dash's thoughts.

"They don't look at all alike," Dash said.

"Not all brothers and sisters look as much alike as you and your sister," O.K. said.

"That's true," Dash agreed.

"Most brothers and sisters don't look alike," O.K. said.

"And they have different dads," Dash added.

"That's a fact," O.K. agreed.

"And it's a factor," Dash said.

"Is it a factory rebate?" O.K. asked.

"No, but I had to figure out the greatest common factor."

"I want a factory rebate."

"Different dads make a big difference."

"All the difference in the world," O.K. stated.

"In the whole, entire, United States world," Dash added, using one of their childhood phrases.

7

The next weekend at Brubrack Moons, Shelley and her brother arrived before The Others started to play. Dash approached their table.

"Dash, this is my brother, Manny," she said, "and Manny, this is Dash, the leader of The Others."

"Manuelo Miguel Martinez," he said, reaching out to shake Dash's extended hand. He was a big man, large but not too tall, with delicate features, almost pretty, with his shiny black hair, extremely smooth skin, arched eyebrows and full, red lips. His eyes had a feminine quality about them, and Dash realized that his eyelashes were unusually long. Manny had a soft-spoken manner about him.

"Nice to meet you, but I'm not the leader," Dash tried to explain.

"Oh, Dash is just being modest," Shelley said to her brother. "You've seen him on stage. Anyone can tell he's the leader."

"You and your band are great," Manny said.

"Thanks, I'm glad you like us," Dash said, deciding not to push the point that it wasn't his band.

"Where did you learn to play the guitar like that?" Manny asked. Dash noticed that although he had often heard Manny speak in Spanish, he didn't seem to have an accent at all when he spoke English.

"I've been playing ever since I was a kid," Dash answered.

"Did you take lessons?" Manny asked.

"Yeah, for awhile. I had taken piano, so I learned how to read music, but God has given me the gift of being able to play by ear too."

"We do serve a wonderful God," Manny stated.

"Yes, we do," Dash agreed. He liked the fact that Shelley and her family were religious.

"Dash!" Lenny called from the stage.

"Gotta go, we're getting ready to start," Dash said. "Nice meeting you."

"You too," Manny said.

"See you later, Shelley," Dash said.

"See YOU during the show," she teased.

Dash joined The Others on stage for their first set. He frequently made eye contact with Shelley now, and felt that God was answering his prayer by starting something between him and Shelley. His senses felt more alert. His heart was pounding so hard that he could feel it. He was drawn to Shelley, and he wanted to be closer to her. He wanted to know all about her. What was her favorite song? What did she like to do? What were her dreams? Was she interested in him, or was he wasting his time thinking about her?

From the way she was looking and smiling at him, he thought he had the answer to the last question. Every signal she gave him said she was interested in him. During the first break, he approached her table just as her friend, Jessie, was arriving. Dash had wanted a few moments alone with Shelley, but that opportunity was not arising tonight.

"How's it going?" he asked the group at the table.

"Great," Shelley answered. "Do you want to sit down for a minute?" Her voice was so kind and tender.

"Well, just for a minute," he said.

"I'll be right back," Jessie said, heading for the ladies' room.

"Me too," said Manny, as he went over to the bar.

"Did you plan that?" Dash asked jokingly.

"What's wrong? Don't you want to be alone with me?" Shelley asked in reply.

"I kind of wanted to have a few minutes alone with you, in the midst of a huge crowd," he said, referring to the full house of people.

O.K. passed the table as he was coming from the men's room and stopped for a minute.

"Double-dash, dot, triple-dash?" O.K. said, speaking in Morse code to say 'go.' This was one of their childhood signals he used to be sure Dash didn't need to be rescued.

Dash shook his head slightly, smiling. "No thanks, man."

"What was that all about?" Shelley asked, as O.K. walked away.

"He was just kidding."

"Are you serious?"

"Seriously, he was just kidding."

"What do you mean?"

"Nothing, he was just joking around," Dash explained, still smiling.

"Is he your best friend? He's always here with you."

"We have been friends since the second grade. Yeah, he's one of my best friends."

"Do you have other best friends?"

"I have lots of friends, and they are all good friends."

"Are any of them..." she paused, "...female?"

"No," he laughed, "none of my good friends are female."

"So... you're not gay or anything?"

"No! Not at all," he said with a laugh.

"Well, I just wondered," she said. "You said all of your friends are guys."

"Friends who are guys are not the same as boyfriends."

"I know, I just wanted to be sure."

"Couldn't you tell, by the way I've been looking at you?"

"Well, I was hoping, but I just didn't know. Now I know."

"Do you want to go get something to eat after the show tonight?" Dash asked her.

"Um, Jessie is here again from Spokane, so would it be all right if she came too?"

"I guess so, because, actually, I'm riding with O.K., so he'd have to come too."

"That sounds nice. I'd like that," Shelley said sweetly.

"What sounds nice?" Jessie asked, as she returned to the table.

"Dash wants us to go with him and O.K. after the show, to get something to eat."

"Oh, sure, that sounds great," Jessie said, looking around for O.K. Dash remembered his remark about her resemblance to a giraffe, and he did notice that her teeth were stubby and separated, not unlike the teeth of a giraffe. He kept smiling as he stood up.

"See ya after the show," he said.

"We'll see YOU during the show," Shelley said. Dash kind of hoped that wasn't going to become a phrase of hers, since she had used it twice in one night.

Later, at the Donut Hole, which served great home made meals in addition to fresh donuts daily, they each ordered chicken fried steak and mashed potatoes. They enjoyed good conversation, and although O.K. was not attracted to Jessie, he was polite and funny, and she was very nice to him.

"I have been asking God to put the right person in my life," Shelley announced when they finished eating. "I'm not capable of making the right decisions without Him."

"I feel the same way," Dash said. "I've made enough mistakes on my own to know that I need to let Him be in control of every part of my life."

Jessie and O.K. took this as a signal for them to leave the table for a few minutes.

"I'll be right back," Jessie said, getting out of her seat.

"Me too," O.K. said, following her.

"I think God put me in your life," Shelley said to Dash when they were alone.

"I think you could be an answer to one of my prayers," Dash said.

"Don't you just feel, like, I don't know, like, God wants us to be together?" she asked.

"I do believe that is a distinct possibility," Dash said.

"I really feel like you are special, and, um..." she stopped.

"And what?" he asked.

"Well, um, I just feel inside my soul that God has made a path that we should follow together."

"How can you tell?"

"Well, what do you feel inside, right now?" she asked.

"I feel great. I feel comfortable, and natural, like I can be myself around you."

"What about in your soul, how do you feel?"

"I'm not sure I follow you."

"Do you believe in soul mates?"

"I'm not sure about soul mates, but I do believe that God has made a special woman for each man, like the Bible says."

"The Bible says that?" Shelley asked.

"Well, it says that in the beginning when God made man, He saw that it was not good for man to be alone. Everything else He made was good, but He couldn't find an appropriate match for man among all the creatures He had made, so He made a woman for him, from man's own flesh."

"Do you read the Bible a lot?"

"No, not really, but my brother-in-law is a preacher, and we discuss it quite often."

"That is so cool. But what do you feel in your soul? About me?"

"I think you are really great, and I--"

"No, but what do you feel about me?" she interrupted.

"I feel like you are becoming someone special in my life," he blurted, not intending to say it, but he couldn't contain it.

"I feel the same way about you. Ever since I first saw you at the club, I felt God was leading me to you."

"I noticed you that first night too," he confessed.

"Do you remember how I kept looking at you?" she asked, laughing that sweet laugh. "I didn't want to look at anyone else."

"Yeah, I remember. And I avoided you because I thought you were seeing someone."

"Seeing someone? Who?"

"Well, every night you came to the club, there were guys sitting with you at your table. That's why I didn't come over to talk to you.'

"Oh, you mean Manny and his friends!" she laughed. "That was probably God's way to let us see each other before we really talked to each other, to test our patience."

"It worked," Dash said.

"Now God has let us come together, and I think He has plans for us."

Dash could feel something, deep inside himself, and he was drawn to Shelley. He scooted close to her on the bench, so close that he could smell her perfume.

"I have something very important to ask you," Shelley said.

"What?" Dash asked, with his usual smile.

"This is serious," she warned.

"Okay, what?" He stopped smiling on the outside, but was still beaming within himself.

"This is one of the most serious questions I have to ask you, before our relationship goes any farther," she said.

"What is it?" he asked, his curiosity piqued.

"Are you a Christian?" she asked.

"Yeah," he answered tentatively. "What else would I be?"

"I mean, have you accepted Jesus as your personal Savior?"

"I don't know. I guess not. I'm not sure what that means."

"It means if you have, you will go to heaven when you die. Before we get any more involved with each other, it is very important that you accept Jesus as your Savior."

"I have to find out more about it, because I really don't know what it means."

"Didn't you say your sister is married to a preacher? They are Christians, aren't they? They should know."

"Yeah, Dari did say something about it before. I'll talk to her about it."

O.K. and Jessie returned to the table.

"About ready to go?" O.K. asked. "I took care of the tab."

"Thanks, man, I'll get the tip," Dash said.

"Sounds fair enough," O.K. said.

"Thanks so much for inviting us," Jessie said.

"Really, thanks, it was nice of you," Shelley added.

"We'll have to do it again some time," O.K. promised.

The guys walked the ladies to their car and said goodnight.

The next evening, Dash called his sister.

"Dari, how's it going?"

"Dash! Great! I'm blessed! How are you? Is everything all right?"

"Yeah, I met someone."

"A girl? I mean, a young lady?"

"Yeah, her name's Shelley, she's actually about your age... she's young! Anyway, I have a question for you. You're religious. You should be able to help me with this."

"I'm not religious, I'm a Christian," she said.

"What's the difference?" he asked.

"A religious person is one who goes through rituals and different religious practices, but a Christian is a person who has taken on the character of Jesus Christ," she explained.

"That sounds like a religious person to me."

"A religious person can be Jewish or Hindu or Buddhist or Moslem, or any other religion, who might believe in God or different gods, but none of them believe in Jesus Christ. A Christian believes only in Jesus as the Son of God and that He is the only Way to heaven."

"So, what does it mean to accept Jesus as your personal Savior? Shelley said it is important for me to do that before we can have a relationship."

"Oh, so she's a Christian too! That's good! Well, if you believe in your heart and confess with your mouth that Jesus is the Son of God and that God raised Him from the dead, then the Bible says, you are saved. You turn away from this sinful world and turn to God, through Jesus Christ, and Jesus becomes your Lord and Savior."

"And then what?"

"That's it. Do you believe Jesus is the Son of God?"

"Yes, I've always known that."

"So you believe it, in your heart?"

"Yes, I do," Dash said sincerely.

"And do you believe that He was crucified, died on the cross, and on the third day God raised Him from the dead?"

"Yeah, that was on Easter, right?"

"Right! So you have just confessed with your mouth that you believe in Jesus in your heart, so you are saved."

"So... Jesus is my personal Savior now?"

"He's the One who died for you. He's the One who saves us from our sins."

"So how come He is my 'personal' Savior? Didn't He die for the sins of the world?"

"Yes, He did, but now you have accepted that He died for you individually."

"I don't have to do anything else?"

"Well, you are saved now, and the Bible says in Acts, chapter two, verse thirty-eight, that the next step is to be baptized."

"But Jesus is already my Savior?"

"Yes, He is! Do you have a Bible?"

"No, I don't think so. Mom has one, though."

"I'll get one for you. We are coming home next weekend and I'll bring it - unless you want to start reading it sooner than that, I could mail one to you."

"No, that's okay. Next weekend is fine."

"Hey, Bro."

"Yeah?"

"Now you are my spiritual brother and my natural brother! Praise God!"

"Wow, huh? I'll see you next weekend. I can't wait to tell Shelley."

"Okay, and I look forward to meeting her!"

"Love ya."

"Love ya."

"Bye."

"Bye."

While he slept that night, Dash dreamed about playing a new song on his guitar. The words and music were flowing out of him naturally, and he was suddenly singing it in front of a huge crowd in a stadium. The audience knew the song and joined him during the chorus. He looked offstage and saw Shelley smiling at him. He turned back to the crowd and was slowly lifted above them as he finished the song. Everyone began screaming and shouting for The Others, and the crowd began to push toward the stage until the entire stage rose into the air.

Dash woke up with a start and scrambled to find a pen and some paper to write the words to the song God had just given him. He didn't see any meaning to the dream, but he knew the song was from God. He titled it, "Are We Each Other's Angels?"

During practice the next evening, Dash played the song for the band. They picked it up easily, and Ham naturally sang the backing vocals. The Others sounded the same in real life singing the song as they had in the dream.

On Friday evening at Brubrack Moons, Dash stood on stage and quieted the crowd.

"We have a new song I just wrote this week, and I would like to dedicate it to a special lady who is here tonight." The crowd began to look around. O.K. grabbed a spot light and turned it on Shelley. She smiled shyly, keeping her eyes on Dash.

"For Shelley, this song is called, 'Are We Each Other's Angels?'"

Dash began with a beautiful guitar intro, and the rest of the band joined in with their parts. Dash looked directly at Shelley as he sang the already memorized lyrics.

> *"Do I know you from somewhere?*
> *You say you know me too.*
> *You kinda look familiar to me*
> *But I know that I don't know you.*
> *How did you know that I need you?*
> *How did you know what to do?*
> *I want to do what you did for me*
> *And I want you to know that I'm true.*
> *"Are we each other's angels? (watch out for ourselves)*
> *Or should we lend a hand? (to someone in need)*
> *Are we suppose to help each other? (help each other)*
> *Or just let it end? (like we know it's gonna end.)"*

Dash went into the intricate guitar solo, and when he looked at Shelley again, she was in tears. He steadied his voice to continue with the next verse.

> *"How can I help you grow*
> *If I don't understand?*

But then, someone will come and talk to me
And without even knowing it, he'll lend a hand.
Times are strange when you don't know who you
can trust,
Though it may be a friend.
But I know where I can put my faith and I know
it's safe
And I know you can put yours there too.
"Are we each other's angels? (watch out for
ourselves)
Or should we lend a hand? (to someone in need)
Are we suppose to help each other? (help each other)
Or just let it end? (like we know it's gonna end.)"

After the show, Shelley came up to Dash on stage.

"You are right," she said.

"What? Right about what?" he asked.

"We are each other's angels. That is the reason God has put us together," she said confidently.

"God gave me that song in a dream, and I believe it's true," Dash agreed.

When Dari and her family arrived in town the next afternoon, Dash brought Shelley home to meet them and his parents.

"Shelley, this is my mom, Victoria, my dad, Daniel, and this is my sister, Dari, and her husband, Pastor Wright, and their daughter, Zaqui," he said.

They all liked Shelley immediately. She was a refreshing change from Dash's often-hysterical former girlfriend.

"I am very happy to meet you," Pastor Wright told Shelley graciously, giving her a hug.

"Nice to meet you, Shelley," Dari said, also hugging her.

"Dash has told us so much about you, I feel like I already know you," his mother said.

"And I have heard so much about you too," Shelley said. "I think I've seen you at Brubrack Moons before. Do you ever go there?"

"We go sometimes when Dash is playing," his mom answered.

"And how old are you, Zaqui?" Shelley asked.

"Zaqui Victoria Wright," she said proudly.

"Can you tell Shelley how old you are?" Dari asked.

"No," she said, without explanation. "Zaqui Victoria Wright," she repeated, pronouncing each word precisely.

"Yep, you're my little Z-bug," Dash teased, as he lifted her above his head.

"Z-bug?" Shelley asked.

"Yeah, her initials," Dash said.

"Her initials are Z-bug?" She looked confused.

"Yeah, Z.V.W. Get it?" Dash explained.

"Z-V-W?" Shelley repeated.

"V.W. Volkswagen? Bug? Get it? Zaqui Victoria Wright, Z.V.W."

"Oh, I see," she said, as if she still didn't understand.

"So, you live in the Lower Valley?" his mom asked Shelley, changing the subject.

"Yes, right now I am living with Mama, and she has a farm and an orchard and some apartments there, just off Lateral A."

"That's some nice farming country," Dash's dad remarked.

"I'm glad to finally meet you, all of you," Shelley said. She then turned to Pastor Wright.

"One of my best friends is Black," she told him.

"I think that's wonderful. Where is she from?" Pastor Wright asked.

"No, not a she, a he, MaYohimbi. He's from Jamaica, but he's older than you. He was our neighbor for a long time. As a matter of fact, he lived with us for awhile. He's has been one of my close friends, and he was really there for me when Daddy died. Daddy and I were so close, I sat by his bedside in the hospital for nine months, until he died. I still miss Daddy so much, but MaYohimbi helped me get through it. You would really like him."

"I hope I have the opportunity to meet him sometime," Pastor Wright replied with a smile.

"If it's in God's plan, you will," Shelley said.

"Now, that's a fact," said Pastor Wright.

As Shelley and Dash left the group to sit on the patio, Shelley said, "Your mom looks just like Victoria Principal, except with blond hair. It's funny that her name is Victoria too."

"Yeah, everyone says that," Dash said.

Dash began to visit Shelley on the nights he didn't play or practice with The Others. Usually he went to her house after dinner time, with his acoustic or twelve-string guitar, and they sat on the big porch swing all evening, talking about their lives as he provided the background music. Fluffy, Shelley's big, gray, fluffy cat, stretched across the porch whenever Dash was there, happy to be in their presence. Shelley fixed pitchers of real lemonade and she baked giant chocolate chip cookies, which Dash didn't think went very well with the lemonade, but he accepted them together anyway, because she made them just for him. He discovered she loved the Beatles, animals, children and music. She was always encouraging him to do his best, and she wanted to help him achieve his goals, which were becoming her goals. She was supportive of him in every way. Suzie stayed inside and didn't disturb them while they were having their life-revealing conversations, but sometimes Dash had the feeling that she was just on the other side of the window, listening. It made no difference to him, though, because he was always polite and proper. He respected Shelley. He felt as if he might be falling in love with her.

One warm October evening while swinging, Shelley stopped the swing and looked directly into Dash's eyes. Dash stopped strumming his guitar.

"Is something the matter?" he asked, searching those beautiful brown eyes for a clue.

"There's something I need to tell you," she said.

"What is it?"

"Something important, something that I should have told you a long time ago," she said, looking down, away from his gaze.

"What?"

"This is really serious," she said.

"What is it?"

"Ummmm, it's just that I have..." she began, then didn't finish.

"You have what? A disease? Are you sick?" he asked, suddenly worried.

"No, nothing like that," she assured him. "I have..."

"What? What do you have?"

"I have..." she said slowly, "...a daughter."

"Oh! Is that all?" he asked, relieved. "I mean, you had me worried for a minute. Where is she? Is she inside?"

"No, she lives in Spokane with her dad, my ex-husband, Herbert, and his new wife, Camille, but she's coming down tomorrow to celebrate her birthday, the same day as John Lennon's birthday. She'll be seven."

"What's her name?"

"Britney Emily Ahrdart."

"Why didn't you tell me about her earlier?"

"I was afraid if I told you, it would chase you away," she said.

"Don't you know me well enough to know that something like that would never chase me away?" he asked.

"I do now, but I just didn't know how you would react," she explained.

"If she's anything like you, she must be wonderful, and even if she is nothing like you, she must be wonderful, just because she is your daughter," he assured her. "She's a part of you."

"Some guys would just--"

"I'm not some guys," Dash interrupted. "I'm me, and I love you," he said without thinking.

"You do?" she asked, surprised.

"Did I say that out loud?" he asked, smiling. "I hadn't meant to tell you yet."

"What were you waiting for?" she asked.

"The right moment."

"I guess that was it."

"I guess so."

The next day, Dash met Shelley's daughter, Britney Emily, a self-assured little girl with long blond hair. She looked a lot like her mother, with the same pretty brown eyes and the same turned up nose. Dash thought she seemed to be very immature for her age, clinging to her mother and having difficulty reading simple labels in her environment.

"Hi, I'm Dash, happy birthday, Britney Emily," he said, handing her an ice cream cake he had brought from Dairy Queen. "Your mother told me all about you."

"Wow, an ice cream cake, just like on TV! Can we have some, Mom?" Britney Emily asked Shelley.

"It's your birthday, and you can celebrate it however you want to celebrate," Shelly replied.

"Let's everybody have some ice cream cake!" she insisted. They all ate the ice cream cake with Britney Emily and watched as she opened the huge mound of birthday presents from her mother and grandmother, as well as the pile of gifts she had brought with her from Spokane from her dad and his wife, his parents, his wife's parents, and from her Uncle Manny and Jessie. She separated everything into two stacks: clothes and toys. The stack of toys, which included thirteen different Barbie dolls, was much larger than the stack of clothes. Dash was glad he had chosen the ice cream cake: she only received one of those.

Dash continued to see Shelley throughout the winter, although the evenings were much too cold to sit on the porch. They went inside her mother's big farmhouse and spent their evenings in front of the fireplace. Shelley cooked wonderful dinners and they ate by candlelight. Dash saw O.K. and his friends less frequently, and Jessie didn't come to visit Shelly at all that winter. By the time spring came, Dash had known Shelley for nearly a year, and they had decided they were in love, and that they were following God's plan for them.

8

Exactly one year after they first met, Dash planned to propose to Shelley. He had bought a beautiful engagement ring with the largest diamond he could afford, which wasn't enormous, but it was a nice size. He arrived at her house with his guitar on Saturday afternoon, which had become a regular meeting time for them. The weather was warm enough for them to sit on the porch swing again. Dash began to serenade Shelley. She smiled at him as he played and sang a new song he had written for her.

> *"Something was missing*
> *Before I met you*
> *You came along*
> *And knew what to do.*
> *God gave what I needed.*
> *You needed me too.*
> *His plan is perfect*
> *For me and for you.*
> *A force deep within*
> *That I can't control*
> *Draws us together*
> *From within my soul.*
> *I'd like you to be here*
> *For the rest of my life,*
> *My beautiful Shelley,*
> *Will you be my wife?"*

He stopped strumming and pulled out the ring. Tears began to run down Shelley's face.

"Hey, don't cry, you're suppose to be happy," he said.

She didn't answer.

"What? Is it that bad? Does this mean your answer is no?"

"No," she said, sobbing.

"No?" he asked.

"No, it's yes," she said.

"Yes?" he asked.

"Yes, I will," she confirmed. He slipped the ring on her finger.

"This is the most gorgeous ring I have ever seen," she said, still crying. "I'm just crying because I'm so happy. I never thought this would happen."

"It looks a lot better on your finger than it did in the box," he admitted.

She threw her arms around his neck, taking care not to smash his guitar between them.

"I've got to tell Mama!" she shouted, jumping out of the swing and running into the house. "Mamaaaaa!"

A few minutes later, Suzie came outside with Shelley.

"Congratulations," she said, with her constant cigarette bobbing at the side of her mouth, as she winked against the smoke going into her eye.

"We met exactly one year ago," Dash said, "so I thought this would be the perfect day to ask her to become my wife."

"So when's the wedding?" Suzie asked.

"We haven't even talked about a date yet," Shelley said.

"Maybe at the end of the summer?" Dash suggested. "That would give us a few months to plan."

"No, let's make it in December," Shelley said, "because that's my favorite time of the year. We could have everything decorated in red and green. Oh, that would be so beautiful."

"Can you wait that long?" Suzie asked with a laugh. "Or do you plan to move in together, now that you are engaged?"

"We can't live together before we get married," Suzie replied, before Dash could say anything, "because how would that look to Britney Emily? We need to set a good Christian example for her."

"Are you sure you want to wait until December?" Dash asked.

"Oh, yes! It takes time to plan a wedding. We have so much to do! You need to get me a list of all your relatives and friends, so I can get the invitations ordered."

"Shouldn't we decide on a date first?"

"Yeah, of course, oh, I'm just so excited! I want to have a beautiful wedding!" she said, giving Dash another hug.

"Does it have to be a big wedding? I mean, all my relatives and friends? All I need is you there."

"We can talk about that later. Oh, I love you so much!" Shelley exclaimed.

"Are you sure you want to spend the rest of your life with a musician?" Dash asked.

"Yes. I love you," Shelley insisted. "You're a musician, and that's part of you. I love every thing about you."

"Life might not always be easy."

"That's okay. I just want to be with you."

"Musicians don't have normal lives, you know."

"Oh, I know. I don't want a boring, normal life."

"When we get famous, I might be moving around a lot."

"I don't care. I just want to be with you."

"I don't even have my own place right now."

"I would live anywhere with you."

"It might take a long time before things really start

happening," he warned.

"I would live in a cardboard box under a bridge with you."

The next afternoon, Dash called Dari.

"Dari, we're getting married! I proposed to Shelley!"

"Dash, that is wonderful!" Dari exclaimed. "I am so happy for you! So, when is the wedding? You will invite us, won't you?"

"We haven't set a date yet, but Shelley wants it to be in December. And yes, you will be on the top of the list."

"December? Why December?"

"That's her favorite time of the year, and she wants to have everything in red and green."

"Oh, well, that's great. Did you give her a ring?"

"Yeah, yesterday."

"Bro, is she the one? Did you seek God about this?"

"Yeah, I'm pretty sure she's the one God has for me."

"Dash and Shelley are getting married," he heard her say, not to him.

"Let me say something to him," he heard Pastor Wright say.

"Hey, Brother-in-Law! Congratulations! When's the happy day?"

"It's going to be in December, but we haven't set the date yet.'

"Have you prayed about this? Together with your intended?"

"No, we haven't prayed together, but I have been praying," he confessed.

"Let's pray about it right now," Pastor Wright suggested.

"Okay," Dash agreed.

"Father, in the name of Jesus, we ask that You bless this union, even before it comes to pass. Bless every plan, every invitation, every person who will be involved, and most of all, bless the bride and groom. We know that You put a man together with a woman to fulfill Your plan, and we believe that my brother-in-law and his fiancé were drawn together by Your divine plan. We praise and thank You in advance for what You are going to do in this joining of man and woman. In Jesus' name we pray, Amen."

"Amen," Dash said. "Thank you for that prayer."

"Let me know if you want me to do the wedding," Pastor Wright said.

"Yeah, sure, we might," Dash said. He hadn't thought about that before.

"I'll put your sister back on the line," Pastor Wright said.

"Okay, thanks."

"We all love you and we'll be praying for you," Pastor Wright added, " and keep us in your prayers as well."

"I'll do that," Dash promised.

"So let us know if there's anything we can do to help," Dari said, when she got back on the line.

"Whatever Shelley decides. She is so excited, she is already making plans," Dash said.

"Dash, is she the girl of your dreams? Does your heart skip a beat just to hear the sound of her name? Is she all you'll ever need, all you want to know?"

"She really is."

"Are you each other's angels?"

"Yeah, we are."

"Okay, then. I'm so happy for you."

"Me too!"

9

One warm night in July, Dash's parents took Dash and Shelley out to dinner at the Red Lobster.

"So how are the wedding plans coming along?" Dash's mother asked, as they reviewed the menu.

"Everything is going great!" Shelley said. "We have it figured out, who we want in the wedding, and I already have my dress."

"You do?" Dash asked, surprised.

"Yeah, I thought, to save money, I'll use my same wedding dress again," she said.

"Don't you want a new one?" Dash wondered.

"No, this one is really beautiful," Shelley said. "You are going to love it. Is anyone having the salmon?"

"I'm not," Dash's dad said. "I'm having the roast beef."

"Crab legs," Dash said.

"What?" Shelley asked.

"I'm having the crab legs," he said.

"I think I will too," said his mother. "Or the lobster."

The waiter approached the table.

"Would you care for a bottle of wine?" he asked.

"What do you think?" Dash's mom asked his dad. "Maybe a bottle of house wine?"

"None for me, I'm driving," Daniel said.

"That sounds good." Shelley said. "I haven't had a glass of wine in a long time."

"We'll have a bottle of the house wine," Dash's dad told the waiter.

"Very well. I'll return in a moment to take your order."

"I'm not going to make the mistakes I made at my last wedding," Shelley said.

"What mistakes were those?" Victoria asked.

"Marrying the wrong guy?" Dash suggested, and everyone laughed.

"That too!" Shelley agreed, laughing. "Dash and me, we were made for each other, we are soul mates, and God let us find each other. No, I mean, I'm not going to wait until the last minute, and this time, I'm going to invite everyone who wants to come. Last time, lots of our family members and friends got mad because we didn't invite them. We don't want to start out a marriage with lots of people mad at us."

"Well, this is your wedding, not theirs, and you should make it the way you want it, and not how someone else thinks it should be," Dash's mom said.

"Exactly!" Shelley said. "And another thing, we are not going to spend too much money on this wedding. We don't want to start out in debt."

"That's for sure," Dash said.

"Good thinking," Dash's dad said.

The waiter brought the wine and took their dinner order. Dash's dad poured a glass of wine for his wife and a glass for Shelley. Dash covered his glass with his hand.

"None for me, Dad," he said.

"Do you know where you are going to have the ceremony?" Dash's mom asked.

"I want to have a church wedding. I want to get married at that big church over on Chestnut Avenue. I've already talked to Pastor Brown, the pastor there, and he can do the wedding any Saturday in December, " Shelley said with excitement in her voice, "as long as it's not December 8."

"December 8? What's wrong with December 8?" Dash's dad asked.

"That was the day John Lennon was shot," Shelley said. "It would be bad luck." she said.

"You already talked to the pastor there? You didn't mention it to me," Dash said, slightly disappointed.

"Why don't you just ask Pastor Wright to do your wedding?" Dash's mom asked.

"I don't want some Black guy to do our wedding," Shelley explained.

"He's not 'some Black guy,' he's my brother-in-law," Dash said. "I thought you liked him."

"I do like him, I love him, he's your family. But this is my wedding and I want it to be perfect," she insisted.

"It's my wedding too," Dash reminded her.

"I know, and I want it to be perfect for you too," she said.

"And one other thing I wanted to mention," Shelley said. "Because since Daddy died, and I don't have anyone to walk me down the aisle, I want to ask my dear friend, MaYohimbi to give me away."

"MaYohimbi?" Daniel asked. "What's that?"

Shelley laughed. "Not what, who. MaYohimbi is a dear friend of my family, and we have known him forever. He lives in Spokane, but I know he'll come down for the wedding. He is about the same age as Daddy was, or maybe a little younger. He's the only person I can ask to give me away."

"That sounds nice," Dash's mom said.

"Oh, and Pastor Brown said we need to come in for premarital counseling," Shelley said, pouring herself another glass of wine.

"What for?" Dash asked.

"He said it's required for all couples, before he will marry them."

"Okay," Dash agreed.

The food arrived and the conversation died down for a few minutes. As Shelley poured her third glass of wine, she giggled.

"What?" Dash asked.

"Nothing," she said, still giggling.

"What's so funny?" he asked.

"I was just thinking that this will be my best wedding, and that is so funny."

"Why is that funny? You said Herbert was so boring, so of course ours will be your best wedding," Dash said.

"Well, yeah, but I didn't tell you about Jose yet," she said, snickering.

"Jose? Who is Jose?" Dash asked.

"When I was seventeen, Daddy kicked me out of the house and I had nowhere to go and I didn't have any money. Manny had a friend named Jose who was madly in love with me. I didn't want to live with a guy and not be married, so he asked me to marry him so I would have a place to live, and I said yes. We were only married for three weeks, and nothing happened between us. Then Daddy said I could come home so the marriage was over."

Dash and his parents didn't say anything. Dash couldn't think of anything to say, so he busied himself with his dinner, which he suddenly didn't want. He was surprised at this old news, since Shelley hadn't mentioned it in any of their history-revealing conversations. His mom broke the silence.

"So, how is your mother?" she asked.

"I'm really worried about Mama, because she smokes so much. I think she has cancer," Shelley confessed.

"Oh, I'm sorry to hear that," Dash's dad said.

"It will be hard to lose her, after losing Daddy," Shelley said glumly.

"Well, it's just the right time to be thinking about your new family-to-be," Dash said, trying to encourage her. "In just a few months, we will be your family too, so you won't be left all alone."

"Oh, I'm so thankful for that!" she said, pouring the rest of the wine into her glass. After taking another drink she said, "Herbert was so boring that I had to divorce him. He promised that we would have this wonderful life and do all these exciting things, and then he became an accountant and wanted everything in our life to be ordered, you know, like, wearing the same clothes to work every week, having dinner at the same time every night, you know, always saving a certain percentage of our money for the future and for Britney Emily's college fund and stuff, and every year taking a two-week vacation in Hawaii or Disneyland or somewhere like that. He wouldn't do anything without planning it first. We couldn't just go somewhere just because we felt like going. He always liked to listen to the same kind of music and watch the same TV shows. He got upset if he couldn't find something in its regular place at home, and he always made Britney Emily do her homework at the same time every night. He just settled into his boring job and boring routine, and I just didn't want to settle. I don't want to be a boring housewife. I want an exciting life."

"But did he ever hurt you?" Dash asked.

"Yes! He hurt me with his boringness!"

Dash wondered if 'boringness' were a real word.

"You won't have that problem with Dash," his Dad said. "He is as far from boring as a person can get."

"Oh, I know, that's why I love him so much! Our life together will be exciting and spontaneous and not boring," she said, smiling at Dash. "And we'll have Britney Emily," she added.

"Oh, she's going to live with you?" Dash's dad asked, surprised.

"Yes, once we have our home established, she wants to come home to live with me, so we will be able to spend some quality time together," Shelley said. "She can't live with me at Mama's house because she has asthma and Mama's smoking aggravates it."

This was news to Dash. Shelley hadn't mentioned anything to him about Emily Britney living with them. However Dash was happy about it, because she was Shelley's daughter. He thought it would be good for all of them to share their lives together, of course, after the honeymoon and some time alone together in their new residence.

At last, at the end of August, The Others had a recording date at the studio. Since there was only one recording studio in the county, a recording date had to be reserved six months in advance, and the cost of a session was enormous. They planned to record two songs, or three, if they had time: "Go For It" and "Rock You By the Fireside," both written by Dash, and "Baby Be True or We're Through," written by Hamhocks. Dash had that excited-nervous feeling all week, knowing this could be the break they needed to help launch their career. O.K. had already organized some publicity packets and contacted dee jays at the local radio stations, who were anxious to play some of the popular songs of the most famous local band.

On Saturday morning, Dash was gathering his things together so he would arrive at the studio by noon. The Others had a four-hour block of time reserved. O.K. had tried to get them more time, but it just wasn't available. Dash had all his guitars, amplifiers, cords, cables, guitar toys and all the accessories he would possibly need and was just getting into his car when his mom came running out of the house.

"I know you are about to leave, but Shelley is on the phone. She says it's an emergency."

Dash's heart skipped a beat. He said a quick prayer that she was all right. He ran into the house and picked up the phone as his parents left in their car.

"Oh, Dash, I'm so glad I caught you," Shelley sobbed. Dash could barely understand her.

"What? What is it? Are you all right?" he asked frantically.

"It's Mama. She was just rushed to the hospital," Shelley cried. "She's dying!"

"What happened?"

"I don't know, the hospital just called me and said that there was an accident and she is there, and that I should come right away," she said, "but my car won't start and I don't have any way to get there."

Dash looked at the clock on the microwave. His mind raced. He had just twenty minutes to get to the recording studio, but Shelley lived nearly forty minutes away in the opposite direction. The hospital was more than a half hour from her house, and nearly an hour from the studio. He wasn't a math whiz, but he could figure out that if he went to Shelley's house and then took her to the hospital, he would miss most of the recording session, even if he didn't go inside the hospital with her. The Others couldn't record any of the planned songs without his lead guitar and vocals, and most likely, they all had already left to go to the studio. On the other hand, what if he chose to go to the studio, and then Shelley's mom died before Shelley could get to the hospital? He couldn't think of anyone else who could take Shelley to the hospital: O.K. and Goliath had gone to Seattle for supplies for their business, and his parents had just left to go to the slow-pitch softball regional tournament where his dad was the main pitcher on his team and his mom was the official scorekeeper for the afternoon.

"Dash? Are you there?" Shelley asked. For a split second, Dash wished he had left a moment earlier so he hadn't been home to receive this call, but now he had to make a decision: his career and his friends, or his fiancé and her mother? He couldn't win either way.

"Do you have to go right now?" he asked.

"Yes! They said I should come right away."

"Okay, I'll be there as soon as I can," he said, feeling not only his own disappointment, but that of his fellow band members. They all needed him, but they had each other. Shelley didn't have anybody else.

He hung up the phone and looked up the number for the studio so he could tell The Others he was going to be late. The line was busy. He tried again a minute later, and it was still busy. He looked up the number for the hospital and called to check on Shelley's mother.

"I'm calling to check on the condition of Suzie Bovine?" he asked.

"I'm sorry, we don't have anyone here by that name," the receptionist with a nasally voice told him.

"B-o-v-i-n-e?" he asked.

"Nope, no one by that name," she repeated.

Dash dialed the recording studio again, and the line was still busy. He dialed Shelley's number and her line was busy. The clock on the microwave now said eleven fifty-five. He couldn't waste any more time.

He got in his car and began speeding to Shelley's house. He figured that if he went very fast, he could make it to the studio by one-thirty or two o'clock. Just after he pulled onto the freeway, traffic was stopped. He slammed on his brakes and got in line with the other hundreds of cars. He wondered what time it was. He wasn't wearing his watch, and the clock in his car didn't work. The next off-ramp was at least fifteen miles down the road. Why was this happening, today, of all days? Was God trying to tell him something?

Dash noticed that no traffic at all was on the other side of the freeway. Something must be going on, he thought. He got out of the car as an older Native American was walking down the freeway.

"What's going on?" Dash asked him. "Was there an accident?"

"No," the old man laughed, "it's the annual burro races."

"The what?" Dash asked.

"Are you new around here?" he asked, smiling.

"No, I live up on the north side of the valley," Dash said.

"Oh, well, everyone in the lower valley knows that on the last Saturday of August, they have the burro races on the freeway, about ten miles down. They close the road from noon until about two o'clock. They've been doing it for at least fifty years."

"So how can I get off the freeway? It's an emergency," Dash said desperately.

"You can walk," the old man said, smiling, and continued walking toward the burro races.

Dash felt like crying. He was stuck in a huge traffic jam and nobody knew where he was. He briefly wondered if Shelley knew about the burro races, but quickly decided no, she didn't know. He couldn't get out of his car and walk because all of his equipment was in the back seat and trunk, and he couldn't leave it there; besides, he was still nearly twenty miles from Shelley's house. Even if he started to walk back to town, it was a good ten mile walk.

He sat in the car and waited, thinking about how mad his friends would be at him, and about how Shelley would think he wasn't coming to get her. He wondered how her mother was doing, and why they didn't have her name at the hospital. He was so disappointed in himself for letting the recording opportunity slip through his fingers. He had tried to take control of everything and now realized that he had control of nothing.

More than an hour later, car engines began to come to life, and a few minutes later, traffic started moving, Dash finally made it to Shelley's house just after two o'clock.

"Dash! I was so worried! Are you all right?" she asked, her face full of concern.

"Yeah, I just got caught in traffic, stuck for more than an hour on the freeway because of the burro races," he said in a resigned manner.

"Oh, was that today? I forgot all about that!" she said.

"How's your mom?" he asked.

"I don't know, I haven't been able to get any answers from the hospital. They just say I need to come right away."

"Before I left from home, I called to check on her, and they said they didn't have anyone there by the name of Suzie Bovine," Dash said.

"You called the hospital?" Shelley asked, taken aback.

"Yeah, right after I talked to you. I thought I'd check on her condition, but they said she wasn't there."

"Oh," Shelley said, obviously upset. "Well..." she paused for a few seconds, "...what hospital did you call?"

"Memorial, where else would she be?"

"Oh! Well, she's in... she's at the Sunnyside hospital."

"Sunnyside? That's almost an hour south of here," he said.

"Yeah, I know, so we better get going," she insisted.

They got in his car and he started driving toward

the Sunnyside hospital. Dash didn't feel like talking. His concern for Shelley's mother was blending with his disappointment over not making it to the recording studio.

"What's wrong?" Shelley asked, after a few minutes of silence.

"Oh, nothing," he answered. "I'm just concerned about your mom."

"I really appreciate you taking the time to take me to see her. I mean, it's taking up your whole afternoon."

"I hope she's okay," Dash said.

"Me too," she said.

Shelley looked in the mirror on the passenger's visor and arranged her hair. She then glanced at the back seat.

"Oh! You're going to the recording studio today! What time are you going?"

"Well, we have it scheduled from noon to four," Dash said, "but it doesn't look like I'm going to make it." He was sure he had mentioned the time to her, but then, she was so upset about her mother, she must have forgotten.

"I'm SO sorry! Do you think you can still make it?"

"I doubt it," he said, then he added, "but this is more important."

"I love you," Shelley said, leaning over onto his shoulder.

"I love you, too," Dash replied.

When they arrived at the hospital, Dash turned into the parking lot entrance.

"Just drop me off at the front door," Shelley instructed.

"Where will you be?" Dash asked.

"With Mama," she said.

"I mean, how will I find you?"

"Oh, you don't need to go in with me. Only family can visit her now."

"Is she in intensive care?"

"I don't know, but only family can visit her. I'll probably stay here with her all night," she said. "You go to your recording session."

"I doubt that I'll make it on time," he said. "I'd rather just stay here with you, now that we've come all this way."

"No, go on," Shelley said firmly. "I insist. I'll be all right, as soon as I get to Mama's room."

"Call me and let me know how she's doing," Dash said.

"Yes, I will," Shelley promised. "I love you."

"I love you, too," Dash said.

Dash reluctantly left Shelley at the front door and drove to the studio. He arrived just as The Others were walking out the door.

"Dude! Where have you been?" asked Lenny.

"Oh, man, you wouldn't believe my afternoon," Dash began.

"We recorded two of my songs and one of Joe's," Lenny said.

"Man, Shelley's mom is in the hospital and I had to take her because her car broke down," Dash explained.

"Whoa, is she all right?" Hamhocks asked.

"I don't know, I left Shelley there and then came here," Dash said.

"You didn't stay with her?" Lenny asked.

"She insisted that I try to make it to the recording session."

"You just missed it. Joe was pretty mad that you didn't show up."

"Dude! Why didn't you call?" Joe asked.

"Man, I tried, but the line was busy, then I had to go.

She called me just as I was leaving to come here. Then I got stuck on the freeway waiting for the burro races. And then we had to go all the way to the Sunnyside hospital."

"Oh, man," said Lenny.

"Yeah, man," Dash said.

"Man!" Ham said.

"Mansville," said Joe.

"Man, oh, man," Lenny said.

"What an m-and-m head," Joe said.

"So, you guys recorded a few songs?" Dash asked.

"Yeah, the only ones we could do without you," Ham said.

"You know, 'Waiting for the Rain,' it has no vocals, we did that one, and then we did 'Don't Smash It,' and Joe and I both sang," Lenny said. "It's not as good without your guitar lead, but we improvised with the keyboards."

"You said you did three songs?" Dash asked.

"If you pay attention, you might accidentally learn something," Lenny said, in an authoritative voice.

"LaBissonaire!" they all shouted, referring to their seventh grade math teacher who had used that phrase on a daily basis.

"Yeah, we did 'Nothing Greater than Love,' and I did the vocals," Ham said, "and we added extra bass to fill in for the missing guitar leads."

"Did you mix them already?" Dash asked.

"Yeah, we just went with the standard mix, nothing fancy because of the extra fees they charge," Lenny said.

"Yeah, what a rip-off," Joe said.

"Man! Can I hear it?"

"The dude, Max, he's burning copies on CD for us right now," Lenny said.

"Right on," Dash said, unable to hide his disappointment at having missed the recording session.

"They have an opening next February, if we want to schedule it now," Ham said.

"We probably should," Dash said, and they all went back inside to schedule their next recording date.

When Dash arrived home, he found his parents in the family room, reading and watching TV.

"Shelley called a few minutes ago," his mom said.

"She did? How's her mom?" Dash asked.

"She said to tell you they were back home and her mother is okay now."

"What happened?"

"She didn't say."

Dash dialed Shelley's number, but the line was busy. He went to his room and played his guitar. Shelley didn't come to Brubrack Moons that night, and he didn't hear from her the next day. By the time he finally talked to her on Tuesday, her mother was fine and what had seemed like questionable events on Saturday were in the distant past. He knew her too well to suspect that she would even think of doing anything contrary to their goals.

10

Shelley and Jessie kept busy taking care of all of the wedding plans. From September until December, Shelley and Dash were scheduled to meet with Pastor Brown four times for premarital counseling. Dash wasn't really excited about it, but Pastor Brown required counseling for all couples he married.

"Shelley, Dash, the first thing I need to know is, why do you want to get married?" Pastor Brown asked at the first session.

"Because we love each other," Shelley said.

"Can you define love?" Pastor Brown asked.

"Love is... caring for the other person, wanting all the best, supporting the other person, taking care of the other person," Shelley said.

"What do you think, Dash? What is love to you?" Pastor Brown asked.

"Well, I agree with all those things," he said nervously. He knew he shouldn't have any reason to be nervous, but these were things he sang about, not things he talked about, especially to a pastor. "Love, to me, is also not being able to contain yourself when you see your loved one. You just want to wrap your arms around her and hold her close to you. It's when your heart leaps when you think about her or just hear her name, when you can't wait to see her again." He looked at Shelley, sitting across from him, so sweet and lovely. "You want to take care of her for the rest of her life. You want to share your dreams with her, and you want them to come true together, with her. You feel a part of her is deep inside of you, in your heart, and part of your heart is somehow within her."

"Those are good definitions," Pastor Brown said, "but I was thinking of the Biblical definition of love. In the Bible, in First Corinthians, chapter thirteen, love is defined this way: 'Love is patient and kind, love does not envy; love does not parade itself, love is not puffed up. Love does not behave itself rudely, love does not seek its own,' in other words, love does not seek everything for himself or herself, 'love is not provoked, love thinks no evil. Love does not rejoice in inequity, but rejoices in the truth. Love bears all things, love believes all things, love hopes all things, love endures all things. Love never fails.'

"Love always thinks of the other person before thinking of one's own self. In marriage, in a Christian marriage, God is at the head of the relationship and the husband and wife are two equal partners, working together with each other and with Him. Before I go any further, I need to ask, are you both saved? Have you each accepted Jesus Christ as your personal Savior?"

"Yes, I made sure of that before we ever got involved," Shelley said. Dash nodded in agreement.

"That is going to be the key to your relationship together. You will be able to love one another, care for one another and forgive one another in a way that the average person, the non-Christian person can't do, because he or she has not the love of Christ within. Christ forgave you so that you may forgive others, and especially each other, in that same way.

"God made woman for man, that they would be partners. Now, it won't always be a fifty-fifty relationship. Sometimes, it will be ninety-ten or eighty-five-fifteen or eighty-twenty. In other words, it won't always be fifty-fifty. When one of you is sick, the other will need to give more. When one is working hard outside the home, the other may need to work harder inside the home. When you have children together, which I am guessing you will..."

Dash and Shelley looked at each other and both nodded.

"...you both may feel like you are giving a hundred and ten percent. Love is not an equal opportunity employer. Love is giving freely of yourself to your spouse, and thinking the best of your spouse, defending your spouse, and caring for your spouse, not only when things are going well, because that's easy, but especially when things aren't going well, when the chips are down, so to speak."

Dash felt a swelling in his heart that he had never felt before. He knew this was the type of love he had for Shelley.

"And one more thing," Pastor Brown added. "You are not in this marriage alone. You have your friends and family to support you, and most of all, God is in this with you. When you are struggling or just need some extra help or guidance, ask the Lord to help you. He is there for you. He is just waiting for you to ask."

"I'm glad you reminded me of that," Dash said. "We can't really do it all on our own."

"One more thing," Pastor Brown added. "Have you discussed your finances, your current financial situations?"

"Yes, a little," Shelley said, at the same time Dash said, "No, not really."

"Well, let me just ask this one question," Pastor Brown said. "Are either of you in debt?"

"No, not at all," Dash answered.

"Me neither," Shelley added. "I don't owe anybody anything."

"Well, then you're in good shape in that area," Pastor Brown assured them.

"Thank you, Pastor Brown. We really appreciate your help in this, and we are hoping to have the wedding on December fifteenth," Shelley said.

"I'm putting it on my calendar right now," Pastor Brown said.

"It was nice meeting you, and thanks so much," Dash said.

"You two should come to our Sunday services," Pastor Brown suggested. "We're here every Sunday. We have an eight o'clock service for the early birds and an eleven o'clock for the traditional crowd. Hey, do either of you play the piano or organ?"

"Dash plays the guitar," Shelley said. "Haven't you ever heard of him?"

"No, I'm afraid I'm not too much up with the new culture," Pastor Brown said, "but maybe you could bring your guitar and play a couple of songs, if you can read music. Our piano player just had surgery and will be out for a couple of months."

"I don't know how to play any religious songs," Dash said.

"Well, you are welcome to just come, and if you want to play, you are welcome to do that too," Pastor Brown said with a smile.

A couple of weeks later, Dash and Shelley attended Sunday service at Pastor Brown's church. Dash didn't bring his guitar, and once the service started, he was glad that he hadn't. The songs were too easy, too repetitive. He could have easily played all of the songs, but they were too simplistic for him. Shelley seemed so distracted during the service, as if she were looking for someone. After the service, she decided they didn't need to attend church to worship God.

"It was nice, but we don't need all that," Shelley said.

"Well, it's up to you. I haven't ever really gone to church before," Dash said.

"I can't stand that one song they sang," she said, as they got in the car.

"Which one?" Dash asked.

"That one about being blind."

"You mean 'Amazing Grace?' That's the only song they sand that I knew."

"I just can't stand it," she repeated.

"Why not? I like that song."

"But I don't like the part about the 'wretch like me.' That line really bugs me. I don't want to be associated with a wretch. I've always been a good girl."

"I think the point of the song is that God will accept anyone, no matter how bad they are."

"Well, I don't care. I'm a good girl."

"And I'm thankful for that," Dash said, putting his arm around her.

By the beginning of December, the wedding plans had fallen into place perfectly. More than three hundred people had already responded to the R.S.V.P. on the wedding invitation. Jessie had scheduled a caterer and ordered the food and helped Shelley select the cake. The dresses for the ladies and girls in the wedding party had been made, and the men had all been fitted for their tuxedos.

Dash and Shelley began looking for a house to rent. They wanted it to be ready by the first of the year when they returned from their two-week honeymoon in Hawaii, which Shelley had scheduled. Dash appreciated the fact that Shelley was good with budgeting and money management, like Dari was, since that was not his forte. Shelley had everything computed to the penny, and had figured their finances so they would not start their life together in debt. Dash was impressed that she was able stay within their budget. She was incredible in so many ways, and this was just one of them.

On a Saturday afternoon, they had seen at least twenty houses by two o'clock. Dash knew an affordable house meeting their qualifications had to be somewhere, but they couldn't find it. Dash liked several of them, but his requirements were not as strict as Shelley's.

"So what was wrong with the one on Avalanche Avenue?" he asked, when they had seen every house on their list.

"It doesn't have a fenced yard," Shelley reminded him. "We need a fenced yard."

"And ... why?"

"We want to get a dog, don't we?"

"Well, we don't have to get one right away. We already have two cats."

"I just didn't like it. The bedrooms were so small."

"What about the one on Franklin?"

"Oh, no, we can't live in that neighborhood."

"But it's a really nice house, with a big yard."

"I'm not living in that neighborhood, I don't want Britney Emily living in that kind of neighborhood."

"It's not that bad."

"It's that bad."

"How about the one on Englewood?"

"Too busy. The street is way too busy."

"But the house sits way back from the road."

"I don't want to back out onto a busy street every day."

"Okay, how about the very first one we saw? I like that one."

"It is nice..."

"It's in a good neighborhood."

"But it only has a one-car garage."

"It has a carport on the side."

"No, one of our cars wouldn't be safe."

"It is really reasonable."

"No, we need a two car garage. It's too bad we aren't moving to Spokane. There are so many nice houses there, and they are much more affordable."

"But I don't have a job in Spokane."

"You can do your job anywhere. You could start a new business of your own, and not have to depend on Goliath any more."

"But I do depend on him. He gets our jobs, he does the scheduling. I can't do any of that. Besides, a lot of my income comes from the band."

"You could join NorthStar. They are looking for a lead guitarist."

"NorthStar? Featuring Janeena? That's a country band. I play rock."

"I thought you said you can play any kind of music."

"I can play any kind of music, but I don't want to play country. It's so depressing."

"You would be good at it."

"Well, you can listen to any kind of music, too, but don't you prefer to listen to your favorite kind?"

"I have lots of favorites."

"Shell, why are we even talking about this, anyway? The Others are depending on me, Benny is depending on me, Goliath and O.K. are depending on me. I can't just go off and leave them hanging. All my friends are here. My family is here. Your mom is here. Why would we even think about moving to Spokane?"

"You're right. I was just thinking of all the nice houses we would be able to get into up there. And we would be close to my two best friends, Jessie and MaYohimbi. And Manny lives there too. And I could finish school up there, because I have already taken all the junior college accounting courses offered here. And we'd be near Herbert and Camille, so it would be easy for us to get Britney Emily to their house on the weekends."

"Yeah, your friends are there. But our income is here. My life is here. Everything we need to start our lives together is here."

"I'm sorry, Dash-honey, I didn't mean to make you mad."

"I'm not mad, I'm just saying -- in a calm voice -- that everything we need is here. God has made a place for us here."

"You're right. All we really need is each other, and here we are," she agreed. "Our home is here ... at least until you get famous," she added.

II

That night at Brubrack Moons, Dash was surprised to see the entire club decorated with streamers, banners and balloons. About two hundred people jumped out and shouted, "Surprise!" when Dash stepped up to the stage with his guitar.

"We wanted to give Dash a righteous party - before his bachelor party, that is," O.K. announced into the microphone. "Shelley? Where's Shelley?"

"She's coming later, with her mother," Dash said.

"Oh, great, well, we'll do the dedication when she gets here," O.K. said.

"Dedication?" Dash asked.

"Never mind. But now, Benny says, first drink is on the house!" O.K. shouted. His announcement was answered with whoops and screams as everyone scrambled to place their orders.

The Others began to play and the crowd was unusually excited tonight. Dash was having a great time, enjoying himself with his music and his friends. Shelley arrived, looking radiant, with her mother and Manny, and they sat at a table near the band, which had been decorated and reserved for them. At the end of the set, when Dash stepped off the stage to greet Shelley, Joe took the microphone to make an announcement.

"Can we have your attention, everyone? Attention, please! As most of you know, in just two weeks, our own Dash will become Mr. Shelley," Joe joked.

The crowd roared.

"No, seriously, Dash will be giving up his freedom to become the husband his lovely fiancé, Shelley -- right over there beside him -- so the rest of The Others want to dedicate this song to them. Dash, you two have the entire dance floor, and this time, we'll sing."

The remaining Others played the first song Dash had written for Shelley, "Are We Each Other's Angels." They did not sound as good without Dash's dynamic voice or his intricate guitar lead, but they were sincere. They nearly brought a tear to Dash's eye as he danced with Shelley, looking into her trusting eyes, as he realized that this person, this girl, this woman, would be depending on him for the rest of his life. He didn't feel that as a burden, though, he felt it as a complete joy. The warmth from her body seemed to envelope him. She rested her head against his chest when they slow danced.

All evening, friends from junior high, friends from high school, acquaintances from around town, people he had met on jobs, and just about everyone he had ever met came up to Dash and congratulated him. Some promised they would be at the wedding, while others gave him their reasons for not being able to come.

At the end of the evening, after the crowd had left, Manny came over to Dash to shake his hand.

"Hey, man," Manny said, "I'm confident that you will take good care of my sister."

"Sure, thanks, man," Dash replied.

"She couldn't find a better man," Manny said, almost wistfully.

"I promise I will do the best that I can," Dash said.

"I'm sure you will," Manny said, and threw his arms around Dash in a big bear hug, holding him there for at least a minute.

"Come on, Dash, time to dash," O.K. said, carrying some of Dash's equipment to his car.

"Dash, I'm taking Mama to the restroom," Shelley called

across the dance floor, as Manny finally released Dash. Suzie looked quite tipsy, stumbling and leaning on Shelley.

"Shell, O.K. needs to leave now, and he's my ride," Dash said.

"That's fine, I'm riding with Mama and Manny. Love you and I'll see you tomorrow," she said, helping her mother into the ladies' room.

"Love you too!" Dash called.

"Love you too!" O.K. mimicked.

"We all love you too!" Benny said, as he ushered everyone toward the exit.

"Benny, Shelley and her mother are in the restroom," Dash told him, as he stepped outside.

"She's a smart girl, she can find her way to the door," Benny said. He had become quite fond of Shelley. "I'll wait here for her and be sure they make it out, if it will make you happy."

"I know she can get out, but, you know, her mom and stuff, she might need help," Dash said.

"I'll have the car warmed up and ready for them," Manny said from across the parking lot.

"Okay, they are in good hands," Dash admitted.

"Thanks for letting me know," O.K. said, starting his car. "Man, I'm starving."

"I could eat," Dash agreed, as he got in O.K.'s car.

"Arby's has the five-for-five dollars deal," O.K. said.

"Sounds like a deal," Dash said.

"Shall we get them to go?" O.K. asked.

"Yeah, I think the dining room is closed anyway. Just go to the drive up window," Dash said.

O.K. drove to Arby's and pulled the car into the parking

lot, where they discovered that quite a few people had the same idea. O.K. drove to the end of the long line.

"Hey, Shelley's brother was giving you quite the hug tonight," O.K. teased.

"Are you jealous?"

"No, but his sister should be."

"Yeah, he has quite the grip."

"He just wrapped himself all around you, didn't he?" O.K. laughed.

"Man!"

"No, Manny."

"Mansville!" Dash laughed.

"Arizona."

"Oh, man," Dash said.

"What, man?"

"What are you ordering, man?"

"I can eat five," O.K. confessed.

"I can't eat five. Maybe two or three."

"Okay, we'll order ten and we can take the extras home. I'm starving to the max, man."

"Hevi-starvation head?"

"Starvation City, USA."

"Totally hungry, huh?"

"Massively."

After nearly half an hour, they got their order and O.K. parked in front of the restaurant.

"Dude! I don't want to eat here, in the car," Dash said.

"Well, you can eat where ever you want, but I can't wait," O.K. said, putting half of one sandwich in his mouth.

"Scarfsville, Arizona, man."

"I'm starving halfway to death!" O.K. said, with his mouth full.

The sound of sirens pierced the cool December air. O.K. and Dash watched three fire engines pull out of the fire station next door to the restaurant.

"Must be a fire," Dash observed.

"Yes, Inspector, it must be a fire."

"That's Chief Inspector," Dash corrected.

"Chief!" O.K. shouted.

"I don't see any smoke," Dash said.

"Where there's not smoke, there's not fire," O.K. commented.

"It is pretty dark," Dash added.

"Pitch," O.K. said.

"Slow pitch?"

"No, fast pitch."

"It's so pitchy."

"Totally."

After O.K. finished his second sandwich, he started the car and took Dash home. They looked for smoke, but didn't see any.

The next morning, Dash's mom woke him up early.

"Dash! Dash! Are you awake?"

"Hmmm?"

"Are you awake?"

"I don't want to be."

"You'll want to be now," she said. Dash heard the phone ring.

"What?"

"Brubrack Moons burned to the ground last night."

"What?!?" he said, sitting up in bed.

"They suspect it was arson."

"No, it couldn't -- we were just there."

"It's gone now," his mom said. "I'm so sorry."

"How--?" he asked.

"They don't know. A fire started just after everyone left. Luckily, no one was hurt."

"Luckily?" Dash said.

"If it had started just a half hour or forty-five minutes earlier, nearly three hundred people could have been trapped inside."

"Man!" Dash said. "Poor Benny."

"You didn't leave any of your equipment there last night, did you?"

"Just my big speaker. I always bring everything else home."

"What about the rest of the band's equipment?"

"They usually leave most of it there. I -- I didn't notice last night, though."

"Honey, I'm so sorry."

"Yeah, I guess The Others won't be able to play for awhile," Dash realized.

"And if it was arson, Benny's insurance might not pay to replace the equipment."

"That place was all that Benny had!" Dash said.

"Poor Benny," his mom said.

"Dash, Shelley is on the phone," Dash's dad called.

Dash picked up the extension. "Hello?"

"Dash! Did you see the news?" Shelley asked.

"No, but Mom just told me."

"About the fire?"

"Yeah."

"Dash, what are we going to do?"

"We?"

"Yeah, that was a good part of your income."

"We'll talk about it later. I can't talk right now."

"Okay. I love you."

"Love you too, Shell."

The investigation pointed to arson. The Others didn't have a place to play and couldn't even practice. Except for Dash's guitars, all their best equipment had gone up in flames. Benny suffered a heart attack two days after the fire. He couldn't replace any of the band's things; he couldn't even take care of himself. The Others had to look for real jobs, since they were suddenly without any income. Joe and Ham went to job interviews in Seattle. Goliath couldn't give Dash any more work; as a matter of fact, business had slowed and they were getting less work.

Dash worried about money. How was he going to hold up his end of the wedding budget? The wedding was just days away. How could he find a job? Shelley said they couldn't get a refund on their airline tickets to Hawaii, and she had gotten a bargain on a honeymoon suite. Dash didn't feel like he could enjoy a honeymoon right now, but they couldn't postpone the wedding or the honeymoon.

"Remember what Pastor Brown said, about good times and bad times, sticking together?" Shelley said.

"Yeah," Dash answered.

"Well, maybe we are just starting out with some bad times, but then things will get good. We've waited all this time to get married, and God has always had just the right plans for us. Do you still trust God, even though things aren't going your way?"

"Yes, of course I still trust Him," Dash said.

"Well, maybe this is His way of telling us we should move to Spokane," Shelley suggested.

"How can you say that?" Dash asked.

"Well, we haven't been able to find a house, your two jobs have just shut down, and this whole town right now is going through an unemployment slump."

"Not really."

"Yes, really. I think this is God's way of leading us to Spokane. As soon as we get back from our honeymoon, we should look for a house there."

"Let's not make a decision right now. I'm not ready to move."

"You're right. We have time to decide later. Let's just get through the wedding first." She held Dash close, and he could feel that things were going to get better.

12

On the day of the wedding, Dash was surprisingly nervous. They had been planning this grand event for months, and now all the people he loved were coming together to celebrate Dash and Shelley coming together. O.K. was his best man, and Goliath, Hevi-Kevi, Frankly, Watermelon and Manny were all groomsmen. Dash had never been to a wedding so large. Jessie was Shelley's maid of honor, while Dari and Frankly's girlfriend, Melody, were two of the bridesmaids. Dash didn't know the other bridesmaids in the wedding. Zaqui was the flower girl and five other little girls who were daughters of Shelley's friends were "little ladies of the bride," as Shelley described them.

The wedding rehearsal on Friday night had gone perfectly. Zaqui had led the procession, with her mother and her Uncle Manny following a few steps behind, as a couple. Then Jessie and O.K. followed another little girl, and the bridesmaids and groomsmen were paired up, each couple following a little girl. The huge chapel in the church had been empty except for the wedding party, with chairs set up at the ends of the pews for the expected overflow of guests. When the entire wedding party had completed the procession, before Pastor Brown could say anything, Zaqui spoke up.

"Uncle Dash?" she said, looking up at him with her big brown eyes open wide.

"What, Kwee?" Dash answered, too amused to be angry.

"I'm the flower girl," she told him, beaming.

"Yes! You are, aren't you? And tomorrow you are going to be carrying the flowers for the wedding," Dash said.

"Actually, you're going to be carrying a basket of flowers," Shelley corrected. "And Sweetie, you need to be quiet during the wedding, okay?"

"Okay," Zaqui said, then added, "Shelley, tomorrow are you going to be my Aunt Shelley?"

"Yes, Sweetie, I will be after the wedding."

"Then you can call me Kwee, like Uncle Dash," Zaqui told her.

"Oh, thank you, I will," Shelley said, smiling. She turned to Pastor Brown. "You can start now."

Pastor Brown then described what would happen during the wedding as Dash tried to pay attention. He still couldn't believe this was happening to him, and he was in a bit of a daze.

"Earth to Dash," O.K. whispered, jabbing him lightly with his elbow.

"Hmm? What?" Dash answered.

"Would you like to have a candle lighting ceremony at the end?" Pastor Brown asked.

"Yes, we want one," Shelley said. Dash didn't know what it was, so he just nodded in agreement.

"All right, in that case we will have the candle lighting after the vows. Then I will introduce you as husband and wife, and you will go down the aisle in the reverse order as you came," he explained. He addressed the rest of the wedding party.

"Wait until the bride and groom get to the end of the aisle before the rest of you begin to exit," he instructed.

Dash and Shelley walked down the aisle as Frankly hummed the closing portion of the wedding march. The other couples followed. They all went out to the rehearsal dinner at a beautiful restaurant, and everyone had a wonderful time.

Now, in the dressing room alone, before any of his friends arrived, Dash had an extreme stomach ache. He didn't feel the excitement he usually felt before a show. He felt something different, indescribable. It's just nerves, he told himself. He wondered if he should have eaten something today. He hadn't eaten anything, so why did his stomach hurt? He was concerned about the cost of the wedding; he and Shelley were paying for all of it. She had purchased things at a discount when she could, but Dash knew the tuxedos and the dresses and the piano player and the photographer and the caterer and the rental of the church and fellowship hall and the cake and the flowers must be costing them a fortune. Shelley hadn't said exactly how much, and Dash was worried about it now, when it was too late to do anything about it.

O.K. opened the door. "Ahh, there you are," he said in his Head Blue Meanie voice. He stepped inside and immediately perceived that something was wrong with Dash.

"Dude, what's the matter? Are you okay?"

"No, you're O.K."

"I'm O.K., you're okay. Aren't we?"

"You're Knott!" They both laughed nervously at that old joke.

"Cold feet?" O.K. asked.

"No, hot stomach," Dash replied.

"Maybe if you hadn't had seventeen glasses of wine with dinner last night you'd feel better now," O.K. teased.

"Man! I should have stopped at sixteen," Dash joked. He hadn't had any wine. "Why didn't I know better?"

"Man, you didn't have the Supreme Mondo Extreme Burrito, did you?" O.K. asked, "because I did, and it gave me supreme mondo extreme heartburn."

"No, I had the sirloin tips with the baked potato, Shelley

insisted, but I didn't really eat much," Dash said, bending over in pain.

"Man, you need to get it together. Everyone is going to be arriving immediately, if not sooner," O.K. warned.

"Yeah, maybe I'll go to the restroom again," Dash said.

"Take a deep breath," OK. suggested, "but don't hyperventilate."

Dash took a deep breath.

"Okay, that didn't help," Dash said.

"If you really do have cold feet, I'd be happy to sneak you out the back and go and make the announcement that you are stuck in a snow storm in Alaska," O.K. suggested.

"Tempting as that sounds, it's too late to turn back now," Dash said. "I really do love her, and I know this is the right thing to do. I prayed about it, and we both know God has put us together."

"Is she really the girl of your dreams?" O.K. asked.

"Yes! Well, my dream has changed a little, but she's the one," Dash insisted.

"Do you think about her when you are apart? Do you long for the moment you will be together again?"

"Of course! I wrote that song, remember?" Dash said. He was starting to feel a little better. Shelley knew all about their finances, and she wouldn't overspend. The wedding would be beautiful, they would begin their life together, and travel the journey to stardom together. She was already his biggest supporter and she encouraged him every day.

"Man, we better get dressed," O.K. said.

The door opened and the groomsmen entered. They each hugged Dash.

"So, today's the day!"

"You're giving it all up for a woman!"

"No more freedom!"

"No more lonely nights!"

"Tonight's the night!"

They put on their matching tuxedos, black with dark green cumber buns and dark green bow ties. They all had matching black shoes and socks, all purchased together at the Bon, and they checked each other for hairs out of place, teasing about the penguin look. The door opened and Dari entered with her camera. Dash tried not to laugh at her huge green dress with the enormous puffy sleeves. He hadn't seen the dresses yet and had no idea what to expect. He hadn't expected the ridiculous.

"Dash! I want to take some pictures of all of you before the wedding," she said, out of breath. She gave Dash a hug.

"Were you running?" Dash asked.

"That mean lady wouldn't let any of us leave the room, so I said I was going to the bathroom. I had to hide my camera under my dress, then when she was turned the other way, I sneaked out the back door and ran around the church so I could get in here without her seeing," she explained.

"What mean lady?" Dash asked.

"Shelley's mom?" Goliath asked.

"She's not that mean," Dash said.

"No, not Suzie, I don't know who she is, but she's running the wedding," Dari said. "I noticed that the video camera is set up in the wrong place, but she wouldn't let me go out to the sanctuary and fix it. She doesn't want anyone to see my dress before the wedding."

"I can see why," O.K. said jokingly, and they all laughed.

"Yeah, I know, I feel like a Christmas tree with big puffy branches!" Dari exclaimed, flapping her arms up and down.

"Oh, Christmas tree, oh, Christmas tree," Frankly sang.

The door opened again and a lady quickly entered and slammed the door. Dari dashed behind Dash before the lady saw her.

"Now, I don't want any of you to leave this room until I say you can leave," she said sternly. "You can't be seen until the wedding begins," She examined each of them and reluctantly nodded her approval. They stood in a line at attention, not daring to breathe.

"We can't have the guests seeing you too early," she warned, shaking her finger at them, "or you will spoil the entire wedding." She frowned as she took one last look at them, then she left as quickly as she had entered, again slamming the door.

"Whoa! Wedding Nazi!" Frankly said, as if he were really scared. Dari came out of her hiding place.

"No doubt!" said O.K.

"Who is she?" asked Goliath.

"I have no idea," Dash answered. "I have never seen that woman before in my life."

"Let's all go out and see what she does," Hevi-Kevi suggested.

"Let me get a few pictures first," Dari said. "Everyone get around Dash, line up, yeah, like that, tallest in the middle," she said. They gathered around Dash and Dari snapped a few pictures.

"Say 'Please!'" O.K. shouted. Dash's friends all lifted him up sideways and held him over their heads. Dari took a few more pictures until they finally set him on his feet again.

"Dash?" Dari said. "Congratulations." She smiled and gave him a big hug. He was so glad to have her for a sister.

"Thanks, guys, now I need to sneak back," Dari said.

"We only have 45 minutes or so before we start, and we can't be seen," she warned.

"I'll distract the Wedding Nazi so you can get back to your room," O.K. suggested.

"No, that's okay, O.K. I can do it. I'll just pretend I'm one of the Christmas trees," she said, slipping out of the room.

The guys all laughed and joked until the Wedding Nazi returned and told Dash it was time for him to join Pastor Brown. She instructed the others not to open the door until she came back to give them their cue. As he left the room, Dash heard Frankly remark, "What if I have to use the bathroom?" The Wedding Nazi snapped, "Hold it!"

As Dash entered the sanctuary, he could not believe the transformation of the church. Everything was decorated in red and green. Hundreds of poinsettias lined the aisles, the altar and the borders of the room. Several Christmas trees had be strategically placed, and Dash smiled to himself, thinking that Dari could have been camouflaged as one, if she had a star on her head.

Every seat was filled, and Dash recognized people he hadn't seen in years. Family members and friends were smiling at him. His heart was so full of thankfulness, he had to hold back the tears. He walked to the front of the church and stood beside Pastor Brown. He had the advantage of the best view of the procession, and he realized that his stomach had settled. He remembered to breathe. He was filled with anticipation. He felt as if he must be the happiest man on earth right now. On his face he could feel the biggest smile, filled with joy and satisfaction of this wonderful occasion.

The piano began to play, and Dash could see the couples lined up at the back corner of the church. Zaqui, in her miniature Christmas tree dress, led the group of attendants, carrying a basket of flowers with little bells. She was so cute, with her little springy ringlets arranged neatly around her head. Dari, as the first of the Christmas tree ladies, and Manny, stretching the seams in his tuxedo, followed arm in arm a few yards behind Zaqui, stepping slowly, as they had rehearsed. The other couples began to follow at the appropriate distance.

When Zaqui reached the far end of the aisle, the spectators all turned in their seats to look at her. She froze. Dari and Manny caught up to her, and Zaqui grabbed onto her mother's leg. Dash continued to smile. Zaqui wouldn't let go. Dari kept smiling as she tried unsuccessfully to shake Zaqui loose. The next little girl and Jessie and O.K. bumped into Dari and Manny. The other couples, unaware of what was happening in front of them, all bunched up at the end of the aisle as Dari tried to free herself from Zaqui's terrified grip. Finally, Dari took a step, with Zaqui still clinging to her leg. Dari held her leg stiff so she could move. Manny, trying to act as if nothing were unusual, slowed the pace as he looked straight ahead. Manny and Dari made the long hike to the altar in that fashion, with Zaqui clinging to her mother's leg the entire way. Dari walked as if she were wearing a leg cast. Dash didn't want to start laughing, because he was afraid he wouldn't be able to stop. He glanced at his parents in the front row and saw his mom trying so hard not to laugh that she was dabbing her eyes. The guests were all attempting to suppress their laughter. Dash quickly focused on the people coming down the aisle toward him. He was glad Shelley wasn't in the room yet, so she didn't see the potential for disaster at her perfect wedding. Finally Manny and Dari finished their unusual walk and Zaqui released her mother's leg. Zaqui looked up at Dash and smiled proudly, unaware that she had done anything wrong. Dash smiled at his niece.

The remainder of the wedding party joined Dash at the altar without any problems. The music changed and Pastor Brown asked everybody to please stand in honor of the bride.

Dash's beautiful bride came around the corner, her white dress sparkling and flowing. Dash was surprised when he saw her escort, MaYohimbi, in his white tuxedo and white bow tie. His hair was in four-inch dreadlocks all over his head, and his broad smile revealed several gold teeth. Dash got over his initial shock and returned his eyes to Shelley, the most beautiful girl he had ever seen. She seemed to be glowing, gliding down the aisle. Dash felt a swelling of his heart, and thanked God for bringing this wonderful girl into his life, and for permitting this wedding.

MaYohimbi brought Shelley to Dash, and Pastor Brown began to speak. Dash knew what he was saying, but couldn't hear through the buzzing in his ears. He felt slightly dizzy and wondered if he were having a stroke. He saw faces in the distance looking at him. He looked over Shelley's shoulder to Dari and Zaqui. Zaqui had two fingers in her mouth and was looking at her distorted reflection in the grand piano, rocking back and forth to watch as it changed shape.

Focus, Dash thought, I've got to focus. He felt like laughing. He kept smiling as Shelley smiled up at him. All voices stopped, and Dash realized this was his time to say, "I do." The words escaped his lips of their own accord, and Dash glanced again at Zaqui, who was now lying on the floor, still sucking her fingers. She was looking up over her head at Dash with her big, round, brown eyes. He held back the laughter and then it was all over: he was kissing Shelley, Pastor Brown was introducing them as husband and wife, the music was playing and they were leading the procession back down the aisle. Actually, he felt as if he were floating.

Dash was now married to Shelley, the love of his life. She had become Mrs. Dash Farrah. Their life together had just begun.

13

To Dash, the honeymoon in Hawaii was all a blur. They were whisked off to the airport after the wedding, and Shelley had insisted that they begin to celebrate by drinking on the plane. Dash wasn't used to drinking alcohol, so his mind felt dull. They landed and were chauffeured to a hotel. At one point during the honeymoon, Dash realized he hadn't brought even one guitar with him to Hawaii; but then he was so busy with his new bride that they didn't leave the champagne-stocked honeymoon suite more than twice the entire time they were there. Dash felt as if they could have been in Dallas or Chicago, for the amount of scenery they had a chance to see. He was so happy with his bride. His problems were literally thousands of miles away.

Shelley was sweet, loving, constantly serving Dash and attending to his needs. She massaged his shoulders frequently, whispering to him that this was just another benefit of marriage. He completely relaxed and they both enjoyed their honeymoon to the fullest extent.

During the plane ride home, reality began to hit him. They didn't have a place to live. Dash was not comfortable bringing Shelley to his parents' house to live, and he couldn't live with a chain smoker, so her mom's place was not an option either. Suddenly, they didn't have the income they had just a month ago, so they couldn't rent a house. They couldn't stay with any of Dash's friends. Where were their options?

"Maybe we could stay with MaYohimbi for a week or so, until we figure out what to do," Shelley suggested.

"MaYohimbi? I just met him at the wedding, for about two seconds," Dash said.

"He has a big house, and he lives all alone. He has told me many times, if I need a place to stay, I can stay with him."

"I don't think that invitation includes your husband," Dash said.

"Sure it does! MaYohimbi is like another father to me," Shelley said.

"I don't know about that," Dash said.

"Let's call him when we get home -- oh, we don't have a home -- I mean, let's call him when we arrive and see what he says."

After staying with Dash's parents for two nights, Dash found himself with Shelley at MaYohimbi's home in Spokane, unable to find another place to stay.

"Are you sure it's all right for us to be here?" Dash asked doubtfully.

"Da house of MaYohimbi always open to Shelley, and open to you as well," MaYohimbi said kindly.

"We really appreciate it, man, just for a few days," Dash said apologetically.

"It is no problem for me, whatever da Lord say," MaYohimbi said.

"I'm going to go over to Jessie's and let her know we are here," Shelley said.

"Why don't you just call her?" Dash asked.

"Silly goose! MaYohimbi doesn't have a phone," Shelley explained, as she rushed out the door, leaving the two men to their own devices.

"So... Shell says you're from Jamaica?" Dash asked.

"Ya, mon, I and I live here 'most twenty year now," MaYohimbi answered.

"So, you used to live next door to Shelley when she was young?"

"Ya, we neighbors for a few month, den she move, but we stay friends. She always come back an' visit wit' MaYohimbi, and some time stay."

"I understand you were involved with her mother, Suzie?"

"I would not touch dat."

"Oh, sorry, man, we don't have to talk about it."

"No, MaYohimbi mean to say, I would not touch she mama."

"I guess I misunderstood what Shelley said, but I thought she said you were very close to the family, that you lived with them for awhile."

"Not wit' dem, I and I live next door to she and she husband."

"Oh, you know Herbert?"

"Not dat husband, she first husband."

"Oh, Jose. Yeah, she said they were married for three weeks when she was just seventeen."

"No, not dat husband either, she first husband."

"Jose wasn't her first husband?"

"No, Rico she first husband, when she just a chil', just sixteen. She come over to visit MaYohimbi every day when she husband at work and tell MaYohimbi all about da problems she having, and MaYohimbi teach da chil' to cook and convince she go back to school."

"She dropped out of school?"

"Jus' for a year, den she go back. Den she marry Jose. And she keep coming to visit and we stay friends all dese sixteen years. And den she finish school, and den she go to college, and she remain friends with MaYohimbi, even after she get married again, dis time to He-bert, and move away. Den she bring she baby to show MaYohimbi, an' I and I bless da baby."

"Wait, sixteen plus sixteen is thirty-two. She told me she's only twenty-seven."

"Ah, MaYohimbi learn a lesson, and I and I teach it to you: never discuss da age of a woman."

"So she's thirty-two and she's been married three times before she married me? She hasn't been completely honest with me."

"Ah, MaYohimbi say to you, both da deceiver and da deceived is in da hands of Jah."

"What does that mean?"

"Da Lord, Jah, He have everyone in His hands and dere's no ting He don't know. He know all da secrets and He still forgive. He know da hurt and He heal. It all dere, in da Bible. She a good girl. She make da mistake and Jah forgive. MaYohimbi forgive. And you forgive too. You drink da tea, and you forget da conversation with MaYohimbi."

Dash took a sip of the tea and wondered how he could ever forget this conversation. His new wife, whom he trusted, had lied to him about two important things. What else had she lied about? How could he believe anything she said? Dash could hear O.K.'s voice saying in his head, "You've got to believe me! Everything I told you is a lie!"

14

After living with MaYohimbi for two months, Dash knew he had to do something. For the first time in his life, he was away from his friends and away from his family. He was out of a band and out of a job. He missed Hpsyloughehe; MaYohimbi was allergic to cats. The Others had split up, after being together for more than twelve years, and the rest of the former band members had gotten real jobs, most of them in the Seattle area. Dash had Shelley and he had his guitars, but he had nothing else. He had hoped to audition for a local band, but he hadn't been able to locate any rock bands in town; they were all country-western bands. That was the only kind of music the clubs in this area wanted.

Shelley often told Dash that everything would work out for the best, according to God's plan. She was spending most of her time at Jessie's house, where she could take a shower, use the phone, and watch cable TV, leaving Dash in an unfamiliar town without any contacts. MaYohimbi's home was old but well-kept and very clean. The plumbing was outdated, and he had only a huge claw-foot bathtub without a shower. Each room had only one electrical outlet; MaYohimbi didn't need more. Dash couldn't plug in his guitar without blowing a fuse. MaYohimbi spent much of his time in the rocking chair on the front porch, which was enclosed with storm windows for the winter. When he wasn't rocking, he was cooking greens and cornbread, or beans with ham hocks. Dash enjoyed the time he spent with MaYohimbi, and appreciated the wisdom he shared.

One evening in early March, Shelley came home from Jessie's in a flurry of excitement.

"You'll never guess what I've been doing!" she said,

beaming.

"By the fresh smell of your hair, I'd say you've been taking a shower?" he guessed.

"Well, yeah," she laughed, "but, I mean, work!"

"What do you mean?"

"I mean, I found out how to get us a business license, and we can start our own business!"

"Doing what?"

"The same thing you were doing with Goliath."

"I can't do that myself," Dash said.

"Not by yourself, I'm going to help you!"

"You are going to help me wire buildings?"

"No, I'm going to get the jobs and do the scheduling and the accounting, the business part of it."

"I don't think I can do the wiring alone," Dash said. "I've always done it with Goliath and O.K."

"It will be better this way. You may take a little longer, but you won't have to split the profits with anyone. We'll get it all," she said.

"I don't know how to draw the diagrams or make the plans," Dash said. "Goliath did all that. I just helped him pull wire and attach the ends."

"Don't sell yourself short! You can do it, I know you can," Shelley encouraged. "We can do anything together. Didn't you tell me that one time?"

She was quite convincing. Maybe she was right. Dash hadn't actually done all the work, but he had seen Goliath do it. As long as Shelley took care of the scheduling and paperwork, he thought her plan just might work.

Britney Emily came to visit on Dash's birthday. They had wanted her to move in with them, but MaYohimbi's house didn't have room for her. They decided to wait until they moved into a place of their own.

"How is da favorite chil' of MaYohimbi?" MaYohimbi asked, as he let her in the door.

"Fine," she said, pushing past him.

"Britney!" Dash said, reaching out for a hug as she came in the kitchen, where he was just about to cut his birthday cake. Dash could not recall a birthday with so few people celebrating with him, but he was satisfied with his new family. He was slightly surprised that he was enjoying this mellow occasion.

"It's Britney Emily," Shelley corrected.

"Brit!" Dash said.

"It's Britney Emily," Shelley repeated.

"Brit-Em!" Dash said, always seeking a nickname for everyone.

"It's Britney Emily," Shelley said again.

"Can I just call her Bee-Em?" Dash asked, laughing.

"Her name is Britney Emily," Shelley said.

"What about Brit-ly?"

"No, her name is Britney Emily," Shelley insisted.

"Ne-Lee?"

"Dash! Just call her Britney Emily, like everyone else."

"I don't call everyone else Britney Emily," he joked. "As a matter of fact, I don't call anyone else Britney Emily."

"You know what I mean," Shelley said, sounding irritated.

"I know, and you are so cute when you are mad," he said, leaning over to give her a kiss.

"I'm not mad!" she shouted.

"No, she's not mad," Britney Emily agreed. "You don't want to see her when she's mad."

"I am not mad," Shelley said calmly.

"That's why I have to live with Dad and Camille," Britney Emily said.

"Why?" Dash asked.

"Ours is not to question why," MaYohimbi said.

"That's enough about that," Shelley interrupted. "Let's all sing 'Happy Birthday' to Dash!"

After the small group sang to Dash, Shelley handed him a birthday card. He opened it and was touched by the romantic message, his first card from his new wife. He gave her a big kiss of thanks.

"Oh, there's something else in the envelope," Shelley said excitedly, reaching into it and pulling out a piece of paper.

Dash looked at it but didn't comprehend what it meant.

"Happy birthday! I got you an audition!" she beamed. "That's the number for you to call, on that paper!"

"An audition? For what?" Dash asked.

"NorthStar! The hottest band in the Northwest!"

"NorthStar?" Britney Emily asked, her eyes wide. "Really?"

"NorthStar?" Dash repeated. "The country band?"

"They are really big! They play all over, the big places!" Shelley said enthusiastically. "You can really make it big with them."

"And Janeena is so pretty," Britney Emily added.

"But I don't want to play country music," Dash protested. "I play rock music."

"Well, you have to do something while we work on our business and get it going," she said.

"I don't know any of their songs, and I really don't want

to play that kind of music," Dash said, sensing he was fighting a losing battle.

"Think outside the box," Shelley insisted. "Just call them and go and meet them, then see if you want to play with them or not. At least give it a chance. You'll never know unless you try."

Dash considered his options. He realized that he didn't have any other options. He would call the number and make an appointment for an audition.

Three days after his birthday, Dash stood in a warehouse, waiting for his audition for NorthStar. They had a practice hall here, along with an office and storage space for their equipment and a bus. Dash looked at the hundreds of photos of the band covering the wall of the office, trying to recognize some of the famous country performers. He knew which ones were NorthStar, from the giant poster on the door: Janeena, the lead singer, who really was pretty, just as Britney Emily had said, with large blond curls and a wide smile which revealed straight, shiny, white teeth; Andy Sanderson on rhythm guitar, with fuzzy brown hair; Duane Packard on bass, with short black hair and beady eyes, and Roger Villanueva, a cute, young, blond boy on the drums. Every member of the band was wearing cowboy hats, western style shirts and cowboy boots. Dash couldn't picture himself in that type of costume. How would his curls fit under a cowboy hat without getting smashed?

"You must be Dash," a young man said, extending his hand. "I'm Walter, Janeena's husband and manager."

"Nice to meet you," Dash said, shaking his hand.

"So, you play guitar?" Walter asked.

"Yeah, lead guitar," Dash said.

"Can you play our stuff?"

"Well, to be honest, I'm new in the area and I'm not familiar with your songs."

"Can you play by ear?"

"Yeah, and I can read music," Dash said, becoming intrigued by this new challenge. He had never liked country music, but now he wanted to prove to himself that he was a serious musician who could play any kind of music.

"Is that right? That's rare these days. Most of the musicians we see can't even read English," Walter said.

"Really? Well, I've been playing since I was about seven," Dash said.

"Why don't you take this tape and have a listen to a few of our songs, then come back tomorrow at four o'clock and we'll have a listen to what you can do. Or, is that enough time for you?"

"Sure, I can do that," Dash said, shaking Walter's hand again.

"We'll see you tomorrow, then," Walter said with a smile.

Dash was surprised at the simplicity of the songs on the tape. Immediately, he was playing along with the tape, and he had no doubt that he could easily fit into their musical style, even if he didn't really enjoy it. The next afternoon, the whole band was at the warehouse to hear him audition. They were obviously impressed, and asked him to play a few songs with them. He played perfectly, without error, almost too well.

"Dash, sweetheart," Walter said, "don't get carried away with those guitar leads. Remember, always remember, Janeena is the star of this group."

"She's the NorthStar star," Dash said.

The band members exchanged glances.

"Welcome to NorthStar!" Janeena said, with a sparkling smile. "You're in!"

15

Learning the rest of NorthStar's songs was easy for Dash. He began practicing with them five nights a week. After three weeks, NorthStar performed at one of the colleges, to a huge crowd. Shelley and Jessie were right in front, leading the cheer squad for the band. The band was different, the music was different, and the audience was a different caliber of people, but the feeling Dash got when they began to play was the same as it had been on stage with The Others. Janeena sang to the audience, and then she took turns singing to each of the band members. When Dash played one of his leads, she danced beside him. The crowd loved the interaction between the two of them. Dash was the only band member taller than Janeena in her high heels, and they made quite a duo onstage. Walter had provided Dash with a western shirt to match the rest of the men in the band, and Shelley had taken Dash shopping for a cowboy hat and boots.

The next day, the local paper featured an article about NorthStar, recognizing their new member, with a nice picture of Dash and Janeena onstage. The writer had been impressed with the performance, and this brought many calls to Walter, inquiring about hiring NorthStar to play for their events. Suddenly, they had gigs scheduled for the next few months.

Shelley was successful in starting their business, which she had named Dashell Wiring. Using Jessie's phone and computer, she scheduled several small jobs, which led to a couple of larger jobs. Between Dash's work for NorthStar and Dashell Wiring, they were able to save enough for a down payment on a small house purchased directly from the owner, and to give something to MaYohimbi for the months they had spent at his home.

At the beginning of May, Dash and Shelley moved into their own house. They were ecstatic, as they sat on the floor in the living room for a picnic dinner, their first meal in the house. All they had were their personal belongings: their clothes, a few towels, pillows, blankets and various appliances they had received as wedding gifts. When Dash had ended his relationship with Demanda, he had let her have the few second hand items of furniture they had accumulated together when he moved back to the comforts of his parents' home. Shelley had let Herbert have everything they had bought during the years of their marriage; all of that boring furniture fit into his boring house and his boring life. She didn't need any of it when she returned to her mother's house.

"We need to get some furniture," Shelley said, taking a bite of her taco, over the napkins spread on the floor.

"What for?" Dash teased. "As long as we have each other, what else could we possibly need?"

"Dishes," Shelley replied, "and silverware... and a microwave,"

"I suppose some civilized people have use for those unnecessary items."

"We need furniture for our room, and for Britney Emily's room, and for the kitchen, and for the dining room, and pots and pans and cooking utensils. We need all these things."

"The Bible says, 'seek ye first the kingdom of God and His righteousness, and all these things will be added unto you.'" Dash said.

"We seeked God already, before we even got married, so now He has to give us all these things," she said. "He promised."

"I think it's 'sought,'" Dash said.

"You think it's hot?" Shelley asked. "Are you hot?"

"Not 'hot,' 'sought,' instead of 'seeked.'"

"What are you talking about?"

"Nothing. Never mind," Dash said.

"Well, I have already ordered a phone," Shelley continued, "and we need to get a computer for the business. It's a write-off."

"How can a computer be a write off?" Dash asked. "You don't write on a computer. How can it write off?"

"You're so silly!" Shelley laughed. "I mean, a tax write-off. Next year at tax time, we are going to have so many tax advantages, we'll get a ton back on our refund."

Dash had no idea what she meant by that. O.K. had been taking care of Dash's taxes for years. He was comforted by the thought that Shelley was strong in the area where he was weak: accounting and finances.

"Let's make a list of what we need, and then when the money comes in, we can work it in to purchase them," Dash suggested, in the most budget-minded brainstorm idea he had ever had.

"Do you have any credit cards?" Shelley asked.

"Nope, I don't believe in them," Dash said, " or checking accounts either. Show me cash, so I know how much I have. One time I opened a checking account. I wrote four checks, and then all my money was gone. But I still had a bunch of checks left. It didn't make sense to me. I went to the bank and they explained to me all about balances and keeping a record of your checks, and deposits and sequential numbering. But it didn't make any sense to me. I still had all those checks. Why didn't I have any money? Whenever Mom needed money, she would cash a check. But they said I couldn't do that, my money was all gone.

"I didn't like it. I closed the account and have just worked with cash ever since. That way, I know what I have. And what I don't have," Dash said.

"I can see, that's why I need to take care of all of our finances and budget," Shelley said, to Dash's great relief. "We need to get a credit card, for the business. We need to establish credit. That way, we can get the things we need now, and pay for them over time. We are getting a pretty good income now, between the band and the business. We'll be able to pay off everything we buy on credit in a year or so. I know all about making budgets and credit and payments and accumulated interest and everything."

"That's great, because that is not my strong point," Dash said. "That's why God has put us together. We're good for each other."

"Make that great, my wonderful husband," Shelley said, popping a tater tot in his mouth.

One evening about two weeks later, Dash came home from doing a job at a small business, and was surprised to see the living room full of furniture: a new couch, two recliners, a coffee table, two end tables, three lamps and a TV with a built-in VCR. Three paintings which complimented the furniture hung on the walls. In the corner stood a computer desk with a brand new computer and printer on it. Dash glanced in the dining room and saw a new, large, cherry wood dining table, too big for the small room, with six matching chairs.

Dash peeked in the bedroom they had planned to be Britney Emily's room. The entire room had been decorated with Beatles memorabilia: curtains covered with yellow submarines, bunk beds with Magical Mystery Tour pillows, comforters decorated with the faces of the Beatles, framed photos of several Beatles album covers, a Blue Meanie clock, an Apple Bonker lamp, street signs that said "Penny Lane" and "Abbey Road," and strawberry fields wallpaper.

"Shelley?" Dash called, as he backed out of the room, dazed.

"Oh, Dash, you're home!" she said happily, appearing from nowhere. She wrapped herself around him and gave him a big kiss.

"Where did all this come from?" he asked, puzzled.

"I went shopping! We couldn't leave the house bare any more. We might have guests coming over soon!"

"How did you get all this? We haven't received our credit cards yet."

"At the furniture store, you don't need a credit card. They have their own financing." She took his hand. "Wait 'til you see our bedroom."

She led him to their tiny room which was now crowded with matching furniture: a king-size bed, two chests of drawers and a dresser with a large mirror.

"How can we open the drawers on these things, when there's not any room in here?"

"Oh, you're so funny," she said, pulling a drawer out halfway, stopping it before it hit the bed. "See? Plenty of room."

"How much did all of this cost?"

"Now, remember, you do the work, and I take care of the finances. It's worked into our budget."

"I thought we were going to select our furniture together."

"Don't you like it?"

"Yeah, it's really nice, but--"

"I went to all this work to get all the furniture, to surprise you when you came home from a long day at work, and this is the thanks I get?" Her voice was getting higher with each sentence.

"No, seriously, it's really nice. You did a good job," he admitted, giving her a big kiss and hug.

A week later, Dash came home to find Shelley in the laundry room surrounded by piles of clothes. She was stuffing a huge wad of his clothes into the steaming washer.

"Shell, I think you are suppose to separate the clothes," he said.

"I did. These are all yours. Mine are over there," she said, pointing.

"No, I mean, lights and darks, so the colors don't run."

"Dash, I've been doing laundry since before you were born. Do you think I don't know what I'm doing?"

"No, but you can't just mix colors together. You have to separate them."

"You don't have to do that any more with these new washers," she explained. "They are really amazing."

Dash wasn't so amazed the next day, when he put on his faded blue jeans over his light blue, dirty-looking underwear and slipped into his light blue, dirty-looking t-shirt.

16

In June, Dash and Shelley traveled back home for the first time since they moved to Spokane, for his dad's birthday. Dash hoped to see some of his friends, but most of them had moved to Seattle, including O.K. However, Dari and her family had also come for the weekend, and Dash was so happy to see them. He couldn't believe how much Zaqui had grown. She had turned three while they were in Spokane.

"Uncle Dash!" she said, leaping into his arms when she saw him.

"Hi, my little Kwee-Kwee!" Dash said, hugging her. She was bursting with excitement, and she wanted to tell him something.

"Uncle Dash, what did Grandma say?"

"I don't know, what did Grandma say?"

" 'I love you, Sweetie,'" Zaqui said.

"Did Grandma say that?" Dash asked.

"What did Grandpa Dan say?" Zaqui asked him.

"I don't know, what did Grandpa Dan say?" Dash said.

"'Hi, Rascal Lady,'" Zaqui told him.

"That sounds like Grandpa, all right."

"What did Daddy say?"

"I don't know, what did your daddy say?"

"'The Lord is GOOD!'"

"Is that what he said?"

"What did Mommy say?"

"I don't know, what did Mommy say?"

"'Oh, yukky!'"

"What did that lady say?"

"That lady? What lady?"

"That lady."

"I don't know, what did that lady say?"

"'I see, I see, I see it!'" Zaqui said proudly.

"Hey, Bro! Zaqui is collecting sayings from everyone," Dari explained, giving Dash a hug. "She likes to remember what she has heard people say, then she keeps talking about it. We saw a lady coming out of a store, and that's what she shouted when she saw her car. Zaqui has been repeating it ever since."

"So you said, 'oh, yukky,' huh?"

"Out of everything she's heard me say, I don't know why she has to remember that one phrase I used once."

"That's why we have to be careful what we say around children," Dash's mom said, "because the one time you say a bad word, they will hear it and repeat it forever."

Pastor Wright and Dash's dad came into the room, and everyone joined together for a big group hug.

"So, how are the newlyweds?" Pastor Wright asked.

"Wonderful!" Shelley exclaimed. "Dash is the best husband anyone could ever have."

"Yeah, things are going really well," Dash said, suddenly realizing how much he had missed his family, his friends, and his hometown. He tried not to feel homesick, by focusing on his new life and the positive things that were happening now.

"We are in our new house, and after school gets out, Britney Emily will be coming to live with us," Shelley said.

"How's your job going?" Dash's dad asked.

"Which one?" Dash answered. "They're both going

great, anyway, the band and the business. This is the first weekend we've had off. It's Janeena and Walter's anniversary, and they wanted to spend some time alone for a change, so they didn't book us for this weekend."

"And since we have our own business, I was able to keep the weekend free for us, so we could come and be here for your birthday," Shelley added. "We're going to visit Mama too, while we're here."

"Dash, you can have the TV that's downstairs if you want it, and the VCR," Dash's mom said. "And I have some dishes and a few other things we're not using, that you can have if you want. Shelley, come and look at these things and see what you need."

"Let's all sit down and relax," Dash's dad said, as Shelley and Victoria left the room.

"So have you found a church in Spokane?" Pastor Wright asked.

"No, we haven't really had a chance to look," Dash said.

"I have a couple friends who are pastors up there. I can give you their numbers."

"Thanks, but I don't think Shelley would like that kind of church," Dash said, laughing.

"What do you mean?"

"Well, you are so energetic and enthusiastic during your services," Dash explained. "Shelley likes something more mellow."

"Well, you're enthusiastic during your performances," Dari said, "so maybe she would like it."

"Yeah," Dash laughed, "that is true."

"So, have you been baptized yet?" Dari asked. "You had mentioned about a year ago that you and Shelley were going to be baptized together."

"No, we haven't really talked about it."

"The Bible tells us in Acts, chapter two, that after they had heard about Jesus, the people asked Peter what they needed to do, and Peter told them to repent and be baptized," Pastor Wright said.

"Well, I accepted Jesus as my personal Savior a couple of years ago, when I first met Shelly," Dash said.

"I am so glad. That was the first step," Pastor Wright said.

"At the end of the book of Mark, it says 'he that believes and is baptized shall be saved,'" Dari said. "So that's the next step."

"Yeah, I really do want to be baptized," Dash admitted.

"You can come down to Vancouver and be baptized in the Columbia River like I was," Dari suggested.

"He is NOT going to be baptized in the river!" Shelley shouted, as she came into the room.

"But he just said he wanted--" Dari began.

"Nobody should never force no one to do nothing they don't want to do," Shelley interrupted.

"I agree completely," Pastor Wright said.

"Wait, Shell, did you just use a quadruple negative?" Dash asked. "Or a quintuple negative? Doesn't that cancel itself out? Do you mean that everyone should always force someone, or no one should ever force anyone not to—"

"Don't be stupid, you know what I mean," Shelly said angrily.

"You're right," Dash said, too seriously. "No one is forcing anybody to do anything, or nobody to do nothing."

"We worship God in our own way," Shelley explained, her voice again calm and under control. "We read the Bible together at home on Sunday mornings and have our family worship time then."

That was news to Dash. He couldn't remember ever reading the Bible with Shelley, and on Sunday mornings they slept until at least noon or one o'clock, after their late Saturday nights with NorthStar.

"We're going down to see Mama, then we'll come back up here to visit for a while this evening, then we're going to stay with Mama overnight, since you already have a full house," Shelley said. She and Dash got up to leave.

"You just got here," Dari said.

"We'll be back," Shelley said.

"Will you be back in time for dinner?" Dash's mom asked.

"We might, but we probably won't," Dash said, as they left.

"We'll save you some of Dad's birthday cake," his mom said.

When they arrived at Shelley's mother's house, she was on the porch, smoking. She lit another cigarette and put it in her mouth before crushing the old one under her feet, to join the hundreds of butts that were covering that area of the porch.

"Here's your mail," she said in her scratchy voice, pointing to a huge stack of envelopes with a rubber band around them. Some of the envelopes had been opened.

"Hi, Mama! I missed you so much!" Shelley greeted her mother with enthusiasm.

"Hey, Suzie," Dash said.

"You call me Mama too," she told Dash, her perpetual cigarette bobbing.

"What is all this?" he asked, indicating the bundle of letters.

"It's probably nothing, just a bunch of junk mail," Shelley said.

"No, it's your bills!" Suzie screamed at Shelley. "You said you had money to pay for your wedding!"

"Mama—" Shelley cried.

"Shelley! How could you? You didn't never say one word about putting nothing on credit!" Suzie yelled, then coughed, attempting to clear her throat.

"Credit?" Dash asked, puzzled.

"Have you paid for any of it?" Suzie screeched at her daughter.

"Of course we did--" Shelley started, but her mother interrupted her again.

"What? What did you pay for? Here's the bill for the cake, the caterer, the food, the photographer, the flowers, the dresses, the shoes, the tuxedos, the honeymoon, the flight, the church, the minister! You didn't even pay the minister? Don't you know that's bad karma, not to pay the minister who married you?"

"I didn't —" Dash began.

"Mama, we were going –" Shelley tried to continue.

"We! Are you using the royal 'we'? Don't you go blaming Dash! I can see your handiwork all over the place. This is all your doing, isn't it? Dash didn't know nothing about it, did he?"

"We were going—"

"Three thousand dollars for poinsettias?" Suzie barked.

"You opened my mail!" Shelley shouted. "That's none of your business! It's a federal offense to open someone else's mail! I could have you arrested!"

"You used my name! That bill was in my name!" Suzie said, shaking a letter at Shelley.

Dash was extremely uncomfortable with this outburst of emotion. His family did not yell or scream at each other.

He didn't know what to say.

"You know you are never going to get to see your wedding pictures," Suzie said sharply.

"Mama—" Shelley cried.

"Don't you talk back to me!" Suzie screamed at her.

"I'm not!" Shelley screamed.

"There you go again!" Suzie yelled.

"Just leave me alone! I thought you would be happy to see us!" Shelley yelled.

"If you woulda called me, we coulda discussed this over the phone! We coulda worked something out! I'm not paying any of these bills for you!" Suzie growled.

"We just got our phone," Shelley whined, "and we can't afford to make long distance calls right now!"

"You bet you can't! You've got over twenty thousand dollars in bills, right here, and that does not include the eight hundred for the pictures you will never see!"

"We'll take care of it," Shelley cried.

"You sure will, and without any help from me!" Suzie said angrily.

"We'll work it into our budget," Dash added, although he had not the foggiest notion about their budget at all.

"Now, get out!" Suzie screamed at Shelley. "Take your bills! And don't you come back here! Ever!"

Shelley grabbed the bundle of bills and stomped over to the car. Dash paused, wanting to say something to Suzie, but she gave him a threatening look as she lit another cigarette. Dash followed Shelley and got in the car.

Shelley calmly said, "Shall we go back to your parents' house for dinner? Or should we just go home?"

"Shell, I think you should apologize to your mom before we go," Dash suggested, before starting the car.

"Me, apologize? She's the one who was screaming at us."

"I don't want to leave with this between you," Dash said.

"Forget it. No way. There's nothing between us. I'm never speaking to her again. She can just die of cancer and I'm not coming back to take care of her."

"Let's go back for Dad's birthday party. That's why we came here, anyway. Then we'll decide what to do from there."

"Okay, whatever you want to do. It's your trip from now on."

"What do you mean by that?"

"I mean, we came for YOUR dad's birthday. We are through with Mama. So whatever YOU want to do, that's fine. I'm out of it."

"You're not out of it. You're part of my family now. They all love you, just like another daughter."

"Okay, fine."

They rode in silence for a few minutes, until Dash had to get some answers from Shelley.

"So... if we paid for the whole wedding on credit, or, I mean, we haven't paid for the wedding yet, what happened to the money we had budgeted for it? The cash I gave you?"

"You only gave me two thousand dollars, and I couldn't do much with that."

"Two thousand dollars? You couldn't do much with two thousand dollars?"

"I had to pay a cash deposit on the flowers, and a cash deposit on the tuxedos, and a deposit to the caterers. And we had a LOT of other expenses that had to be paid in cash. I didn't know you wanted to check every receipt to be sure I wasn't wasting your money."

"No, that's not what I mean at all. I just wonder what happened to all that money. And it's not MY money, it's OUR money. It WAS."

"It was all spent on the wedding, and I didn't want to ask you for any more."

"I had no idea everything was going to cost so much. Couldn't we have cut down on some of those expenses?"

"We wanted to have the perfect wedding, didn't we? And it was perfect, wasn't it?"

"Yeah, it really was perfect. But it was way too expensive."

"We'll be able to pay it off. We're making lots of money now. It won't take us too long."

They enjoyed the evening celebrating Dash's dad's birthday. Victoria made a delicious dinner of pork chops with rice, and they all gave gifts to Daniel. Zaqui helped him blow out the candles on the cake.

"Now are you four?" she asked, as they ate their cake.

"I'm a little more than four," her grandpa said.

"You're FIVE?" she asked, her eyes wide.

"Yeah, Grandpa Dan is five now," Dash said, smiling.

The family had a peaceful evening, with no mention of the incident with Shelley's mom. Dash and Shelley had planned to stay with her overnight, since Dari and her family were with his parents, but now they had to change their plans.

"Let's just go home," Shelley said, when they had a moment alone together.

"We can just stay here. They have plenty of room."

"I feel left out," she confessed.

"Why? You are included in everything."

"But it's your family, your house, not mine."

"Shell, when we got married, everything I had became yours, including me and my family."

"I don't feel comfortable," she said. Dash remembered how uncomfortable he had been at her mother's house that afternoon.

"It's a four hour drive home, and it's so late," Dash said.

"The roads are fine, it's summer," Shelley said. "I'll do some of the driving."

He could see he couldn't win, so he agreed with her.

"Okay, let's go home," he said.

They said goodbye to their disappointed family, put Hpsyloughehe in the car, and prepared to leave. Dash had to look away from the tears in Zaqui's eyes.

"Bye, Uncle Dash," Zaqui said, sobbing. "You didn't play your guitar for me."

"I will next time, Kwee-Kwee, I promise."

Throughout the summer, Dash continued to play with NorthStar, as they traveled around northeast Washington state and Idaho, to perform at colleges, large weddings and in stadiums with other bands. The income was steady, and working a couple of days per week for Dashell Wiring brought in extra cash to help Dash and Shelley begin to pay their bills. Shelley took care of the finances and she told Dash she now had their budget under control.

They had another wonderful, blissful summer, enjoying their new home and learning about each other, settling into a life together. Britney Emily did not come to stay with them, instead choosing to go with her dad and stepmother to a villa in France for the whole summer.

One hot afternoon Dash came home early and found a lovely, flowered note from Shelley, saying that she was with Jessie, and she would be bringing home dinner. He smiled to himself and considered how nice his life had become with her to help him, encourage him, and love him. He missed talking to his friends and the camaraderie they had shared since childhood, but things were going well in his new life. He was just checking the refrigerator with Hpsyloughehe to see if they had anything good for a snack when the phone rang.

"May I speak to Mrs. Farrah?" a woman asked.

"She's not here right now. Can I give her a message?"

"Is this Mr. Farrah?"

"Yes, it is."

"Well, she had called to ask why your application for a credit card had been denied, and I told her I would call her back."

"It was denied?"

"Yes, because of your outstanding bills. Even with your income, they exceed our limit of twenty thousand dollars. If it were just a little over, we could probably push it through, but you're more than double our limit."

"Our bills aren't that high. They might be around twenty thousand, but I'm sure they can't be double of that."

"Well, the student loan itself is twenty-five thousand dollars, and nothing has been paid on that loan in more than five years."

"Student loan?"

"Yes, your wife's student loan that she took out nearly eight years ago."

"I wasn't aware of that loan."

"Well, it's there, unless it has been paid in the past three weeks."

"No, I'm sure it hasn't."

"Well, when you get your loans paid down, then you may reapply for a credit card with us. Is there anything else I can do for you today?"

"No, thanks. I appreciate your call."

Dash couldn't believe it. They were deeper in debt than he could imagine. He couldn't comprehend how they would be able to pay their house payment, their furniture payment, the wedding payments and the student loan, even with the money he was making.

Shelley came bursting in like a wave of sunshine, with a big pan in her hand.

"We made lasagna at Jessie's! I know how much you love lasagna."

"Shell, I just got a call from a credit card company, saying they can't give us a credit card because of our outstanding bills."

"We don't owe that much," she said, shrugging.

"Shell, you didn't tell me you had a student loan for twenty-five thousand dollars."

"What?" she asked, surprised. "Oh, I forgot all about that! They told me I didn't have to pay it back."

"Doesn't the word 'loan' mean that you have to pay it back?"

"Well, yeah, but I didn't spend it on going to college."

"You what?"

"I mean, I spent it on college, but I didn't complete the course."

"You didn't complete the course? Which course?"

"Any of them. I signed up for the CPA program, and I took some accounting classes but they were so boring, so I quit. They said when I took the loan, that if I didn't take the classes, I could get a refund on the class and I didn't have to pay it back."

"You always have to pay back loans."

"No, you weren't there. You don't know what they said. They explained it all to me, and that is a loan that doesn't have to be paid back."

"What do you mean?"

"Just LEAVE ME ALONE! Don't criticize me! You don't know anything!"

"Shell, you don't have to yell. I'm just trying to figure it out."

"Don't underestimate me," she warned.

"What?" he asked, wondering what she meant.

"Oh, you don't know ANYTHING."

"Yes, I do."

"You don't know a single THING."

"I know things."

"Did you go to college?"

"I took some music classes."

"But did you go to college?"

"Yes, I took music classes."

"That's not going to college, that's just taking classes."

"I took them at the college."

"But you didn't go to college. I went to college, so I know."

"I don't have to go to college to know stuff."

"What kind of stuff do you know?"

"Stuff."

"What kind of stuff?"

"All kinds of stuff. Mass! I know mass! I know lots of stuff."

"You don't know anything."

"Shell, you just told me you didn't go to college."

"Yes, I did. I registered and I went to classes, and I studied."

"But you just told me you dropped out."

"I am NOT a dropout!"

"Did you take the courses to become a CPA?"

"Don't turn this around to be MY fault! Why is EVERYTHING always MY fault?"

"What are you talking about?"

"See, you don't know anything."

"Shell, I just want to know if you have any other debts that I don't know about?"

"Why is it always about the money? Is that all you care about? You don't even care about me, just about the money."

"What are you talking about?"

"You're obsessed with money, all you want is money."

"What I want is the truth."

"Oh, so now you're calling me a liar?"

"I just want --"

"What about ME? What about what I want? Don't you ever think about ME? Am I NOTHING to you now?"

"I'm going for a drive while you cool off. I don't know what is the matter with you."

"NOTHING is the matter with me. You are just freaking out over nothing. COME BACK HERE!!!"

Dash went out to his car and started to drive. He didn't

know where to go or what to do. He wanted to talk to somebody, but who? He was friendly with the guys in NorthStar, but he didn't want to bring them his personal problems. He didn't want to call his parents or Dari. He wanted to talk to O.K. or Goliath, because they might understand, but he had been out of touch with them for so long, he didn't even have their phone numbers in Seattle. He would have to call their parents to get their numbers, and he didn't feel like doing that. He thought about going to visit MaYohimbi, but he was really Shelley's friend, not Dash's friend.

Dash went to Dairy Queen and ordered a large hot fudge sundae. The girl working there kind of flirted with him and gave him extra hot fudge in his cup. He remembered how nice most people were to him, and he thought about his wife. What had happened to her? She had started acting strangely for no reason at all. She was behaving as if she were a completely different person than the woman he had married.

He finished the sundae and drove back home. The house looked dark, but when he opened the door, he could see that Shelley had lit candles all over the living room and dining room. The house smelled good, like a meal had been cooked: lasagna.

"Aren't you hungry?" Shelley asked sweetly, as he came in the house. The anger was gone from her voice. She had changed into a silky robe.

"A little," he answered, noticing that his stomach had become accustomed to eating dinner each night.

"Well, let's eat. Everything is ready for us," she said, as if they hadn't just been arguing earlier.

Dash sat down at the table, not sure what to expect. Shelley served their dinner and joined him. Just as they were about to eat, the phone rang. Shelley got up to answer it.

"Hi! Yes, we're fine. Everything is fine, going good. Well, we are just about to eat dinner. Sure! Later this evening, or tomorrow would be fine. I love you too. Bye."

"Who was that?" Dash asked.

"That was Mama," she answered.

"I thought you were never going to talk to her again."

"What are you talking about? Of course I'm going to talk to Mama, silly. She's the only Mama I have."

Dash was puzzled by Shelley's behavior. His family didn't argue and fight, and they didn't scream and shout at each other. He was quiet during dinner while Shelley babbled on about one thing after another. He got ready to go to band practice and tried to put their earlier argument out of his mind.

NorthStar had several big performances scheduled, so they started practicing and playing seven nights a week. They would be sharing the stage with a few really big bands during the rest of the summer and fall, so they wanted to perfect their own songs. They were being paid quite well now, and they were getting to be very well known in the area. Walter had scheduled them to go into the studio and record several songs he had written for Janeena to sing. They had even been practicing a couple of Dash's songs, with a country flavor added to them.

Shelley and Jessie attended every performance, and were two of NorthStar's biggest fans. They sat at the table with the wives of the other band members, and they all got to be friends. Shelley didn't seem to mind that Janeena interacted with Dash on stage more than with the other band members; it just made sense that the lead singer would pay more attention to the lead guitarist than to the other band members. Janeena and Dash had an onstage presence that the audience loved. The fact that they were both married kept their relationship on a professional level.

One Sunday afternoon, Dash looked over the work schedule Shelley had made for him for the week.

"Shell, can you call these people and reschedule these jobs for the afternoon? After one or two o'clock."

"But they wanted you to come in the morning," she said.

"Three of them are just for estimates. They won't take that long. We are practicing late every night this week, and I need to sleep in the mornings."

"Why do you have to be so lazy?"

"Lazy? I'm working twenty hours this week, and with the band for another thirty or forty."

"But you don't want to get up until eleven or twelve o'clock every day."

"I'm not going to bed until four or five o'clock in the morning. I need to get some sleep."

"Okay, I'll fix your schedule so you can be lazy," Shelley reluctantly agreed.

17

As their first anniversary approached, Dash and Shelley settled into married life. Dash hadn't realized what a drastic change it would be for him, but now he was getting used to his new life in Spokane. He was a lot more quiet than he had ever been, and he wasn't surrounded by friends like he had always been. He and Shelley were working together establishing their business, and getting some of their bills paid. Britney Emily came to stay with them sometimes on weekends, but Shelley didn't want her to live with them because she wasn't satisfied with the school in that neighborhood. Herbert lived in an area with a much better school, so they all decided it was better for Britney Emily to keep living with him and Camille.

MaYohimbi invited them for Thanksgiving dinner, along with Jessie and Manny. They had enjoyed a great meal of ham and mashed potatoes and greens and sweet potato pie. Now they were making plans for Christmas. Dash was hoping to see O.K., since they hadn't had a chance to talk to each other in nearly a year. If everything worked out as planned, they would both be visiting their parents at the same time and could get together again.

"We have to work it out so no one will get mad," Shelley said.

"Mad about what?" Dash asked.

"We have to see everyone equally," she explained.

"What do you mean?"

"We have to see your parents, and we have to see Mama. Mama wants to see Britney Emily, so we have to take her down there, and Britney Emily needs to get to know your family too. But she also has to spend time with Herbert and Camille, and Herbert's parents and Camille's parents. Herbert and Camille can't have any kids, so Britney Emily is the only grandchild either of their parents will ever have."

"Does she have to see them all on Christmas day?"

"Well, no. We can split it up, between Christmas eve and Christmas day."

"That sounds like a lot to do in just two days, because, you know, we are playing on the twenty-third and the twenty-sixth."

"I've already talked to Herbert, and he and Camille are going to take Britney Emily to all of her Spokane grandparents on Christmas eve. Then in the evening, we can pick her up and take her to your parents' house, then we'll spend the night there, and on Christmas day, we can take her to Mama's. Then the day after Christmas, we can come home so you can play that night."

"It sounds like you have it all figured out," Dash said.

"This will be the best way."

On Christmas eve, Shelley woke up Dash early, even though he had been up late the night before with the band.

"Let's get everything packed so we can get Britney Emily by ten o'clock," Shelley said. "We want to travel while it's still light, so we don't have to deal with icy roads."

Dash pulled himself up and stumbled to the shower. He was so tired. He didn't feel like spending the day driving and visiting. He spent a few minutes with Hpsyloughehe, then stood in the shower to wake up enough to get started on their busy Christmas schedule.

When they arrived to pick up Britney Emily, she wasn't home. Herbert told Dash and Shelley that Britney Emily had gone with Camille to her parents' home to get her presents from them. Herbert was just leaving to meet them there. Dash and Shelley waited in the car for two hours for them to return. When they finally came home and Britney Emily saw her mother and Dash, she was excited and ready to go.

"I need to get all my presents," Britney Emily said. "Come and help me carry them."

They went inside Herbert and Camille's picture-perfect, beautifully decorated house to the giant Christmas tree in the huge living room. The tree was surrounded with at least two hundred presents for the three of them.

"All these are mine!" Britney Emily said happily, indicating the huge stack nearly surrounding the tree. "Daddy said I have to wait until Christmas to open them."

Dash and Shelley each made four trips to the car to carry Britney Emily's presents, which nearly filled the back seat.

"Leave some room for me!" Britney Emily said.

When they arrived at Dash's parents' house, Dari and her family were already there. Everyone joined in a huge group hug. Zaqui was so happy to see her new cousin, Britney Emily, but Britney Emily treated Zaqui as if she were just a baby.

"Now, don't touch any of those presents," Britney Emily told Zaqui, as soon as they had brought in all the presents from the car. "Those are all mine."

"I have some presents," Zaqui said, pointing to the tree, which was surrounded by presents for the whole family. Britney Emily's car load of presents made the rest of the pile look quite small.

"Let's count to see how many we have," Britney Emily suggested.

Dash watched as they separated the presents into piles. Britney Emily found more for herself, from Grandma Victoria and Grandpa Dan, and from Dari and her family. Zaqui was enjoying every moment with Britney Emily, who proudly announced that she had the most presents, one hundred and twenty-two, besides the big ones she had left at her dad's house.

"You only have eighteen," Britney Emily bragged. Zaqui didn't mind.

"Hey, Bro, look what I made," Dari said, pointing to a huge tray of chocolate cookies.

"Fudgies!" Dash said. They had been making fudgies, a chocolate oatmeal cookie, at Christmas time as long as he could remember.

"Our favorite," Dari said.

"Yeah, but I'm trying to cut down on sweets," Dash said.

"And I stopped eating sugar, the day after Halloween," Dari said.

"So I guess we can't eat any of them," Dash said, his mouth watering as he looked at the fudgies.

"But they do have oatmeal in them," Dari said, "a redeeming factor."

"That's a fact," Dash said.

"Oatmeal is really good for you," Dari said.

"Redeeming factor," Dash repeated.

"Maybe just one," Dari said.

"Or two," Dash said, reaching to get a few.

"Dash, O.K. called, and he's at his mom's," Victoria said, coming into the room with Shelley close behind her. "He wants you to call him."

"You don't have any time to spend with him," Shelley told Dash.

"I'm just going to call him," he said.

"We just got here," Shelley said. "Don't be rude to your family."

"I'm just going to call him," Dash repeated, picking up the phone. For a second, he couldn't remember the number he had been calling for nearly twenty years, since he hadn't dialed it in such a long time.

"Dude!" he said when O.K. answered.

"Dude! Where are you?"

"I'm at Mom's," Dash said.

"I'm there," O.K. said.

"See ya in a few," Dash said, hanging up the phone.

"So, how is married life treating you?" Pastor Wright asked.

"It's fine, great," Dash answered.

"Just this past week, I was talking to a couple who have been married for nearly fifty years," Pastor Wright said, "and they are as much in love as they were when they first got married. I asked them what was their secret, and the wife said, 'Jesus is the center of our lives,' which I knew. Then the husband told me something I shall never forget. He said, 'Every time I look at Lucille, I see that same seventeen-year-old that I fell in love with, and I fall in love with her all over again. After ten kids and all these years together, I still see that beautiful young woman I married,' he told me. His wife has gained some weight and she has lots of health problems. She has lost her sight, but he still looks at her with love, and sees her the same loving way he has always seen her. So I considered that, and I appreciate that advice he gave me. You know, if you are going to get advice, go to someone who is in a good position to give you good advice. Don't go to someone for advice who is worse off than you are."

"That;s good advice," Dash said.

"Hey, man!" O.K. shouted as he entered the room. He hadn't wasted any time getting to the house.

"O.K.!" Dash said, and they hugged.

"Hey, O.K.," Dari said.

"Dee-Dub," O.K. said, giving her a hug.

"How are you doing, my young friend?" Pastor Wright asked.

"Well, I'm doing great, now that I can finally see my best friend again!" O.K. exclaimed.

Dari grabbed a couple of fudgies and she and Pastor Wright left Dash alone with O.K.

"How's married life going?" O.K. asked, putting a fudgie in his mouth.

"Great, how are you doing?" Dash asked.

"Dude, I'm engaged!"

"No way! To who?"

"A girl I met in Seattle. Her name is Lana Lynn."

"Lanolin? You're engaged to lanolin?"

"Yeah, you're gonna love her."

"Is she here?"

"No, she's with her family at Disney World. She has a two-year-old daughter, and her parents took them all down there for a week," O.K. said.

"Congratulations, man! When's the wedding?"

"Sometime next year. We haven't set the date yet. Hey, you gonna be around for New Year's?"

"No, we're playing at the Dome that night."

"For real, man?"

"For real, man. Wanna come?"

"I wish we could, but we have tickets to The Big Jam that night."

"Oh, cool."

"Yeah, Joe and Frankly and Goliath are going too. Hey,

did you hear that Goliath is getting married in February? On Valentine's day."

"No way!"

"Yes, way."

"Whoa, to who?"

"To whom."

"To whom?"

"A girl he met in Seattle."

"So, what are you all doing, going to Seattle to meet someone to marry?"

"Just about."

"How long are you here?" O.K. asked.

"Just until tomorrow, then we go to Shelley's mom's, and then we have to go back to Spokane."

"Oh, man!"

"I know, man."

"Hey, did the police ever call you about the fire?" O.K. asked, lowering his voice.

"Fire?" Dash asked.

"Yeah, the one last year at Brubrack Moons."

"No, but we didn't have a phone until May or something."

"They called me and asked me to come down to the station and make a statement. They were asking everyone who was there that night, so I did. I told them we had gone to Arby's right after we left, and so really, you're off the hook."

"So why would they need to call me if you told them I was with you?"

"I guess they wanted to talk to Shelley."

"She didn't know where I was."

"Apparently they didn't know where she was."

"She left with her mother, right after we did."

"But nobody actually saw them leave."

"What about Benny?"

"He couldn't remember anything about that night."

"You're not saying--"

"I'm not saying, I'm just saying."

"She didn't, she couldn't..."

"But she was the last one to leave, maybe she saw someone."

"I doubt it. She would have said something if she saw something."

"Yeah, I guess."

"She would have."

"The police still don't have any leads."

"Did Benny ever get his insurance money?"

"I'm not sure. When I moved to Seattle in April, he hadn't by then. Did you know he's in a nursing home now?"

"No! No way!"

"Yep, he had a stroke."

"I thought he had a heart attack."

"He did, then a couple months later, he had a stroke. He's paralyzed on one side. He can't talk."

"Oh, bummer, man."

"Yeah, bum rhapsody."

"Really."

Britney Emily came into the room with Zaqui following her.

"Do you want to make a gingerbread house with me and

Mommy?" Zaqui asked, sitting beside her on the couch.

"No, my dad already bought one for me," Britney Emily replied.

"Do you want to play a game with me?" Zaqui asked.

"No, you're too little to play with me."

"Britney Emily, you can play with Kwee," Dash said.

"Why do you call her Kwee? Her name is Zaqui," Britney Emily said.

"But it's spelled with Q-U-I. That spells Kwee."

"But you say it Za-KEY, not Zakwee."

"But Q-U-I looks like Kwee."

"Why don't you just call her Zaqui? That's her name."

"Kwee is her nick name."

"I don't have a nick name."

"I know. Now, why don't you play a game or read a book to Zaqui?"

"I have a kitty book you can read," Zaqui said.

"Okay," Britney Emily sighed.

They sat together and Britney Emily read a story about Punkin the cat. Dash and O.K. listened, sitting across from them on the other couch. Dash was concerned that Britney Emily seemed to be struggling with such a simple book. Wasn't she in the third grade? Or was she in fourth? Shouldn't she be able to read a preschool book like that without any problem?

Zaqui was so happy to have Britney Emily read to her. She clapped her hands when the story had ended and said, "Now teach me how to read it."

"I can't teach you how to read," Britney Emily said.

"Can you teach me how to read, Uncle Dash?" Zaqui asked.

"Not right now, Kwee-Kwee. It takes a long time to learn how to read."

"If you don't teach me, how will I learn?" Zaqui asked.

Dash and O.K. exchanged glances. Neither was prepared for these kinds of questions from a child.

"Your mom will help you learn to read," Dash said. He remembered Dari reading to him when he was young. He could not recall the time when he didn't know how to read. He had learned to read before starting school, because his mom and sister had read to him all the time.

"Will you teach me how to play the guitar?" Zaqui asked.

"When you are a little older," Dash promised.

"Can you play your guitar for me?" Zaqui asked. "You promised."

"I didn't bring it with me this time," Dash said, feeling terrible about disappointing his niece. "The car was too full of presents, and it wouldn't fit."

"You actually went somewhere without your guitar?" O.K. asked. "Man, you are a changed man. Maybe I need to rethink this marriage deal."

"Oh, man."

"What, man?"

"Oh, man!"

"What, man?"

"What are you guys talking about?" Britney Emily asked, puzzled. "Why do you keep saying 'man.' anyway?"

"That's just what we say," Dash explained.

"Why?" Britney Emily asked.

"Why not?" O.K. asked.

"What?" Britney Emily asked.

"Why not?" O.K. said again, with a grin.

"Why not what?" Britney Emily asked, frustrated.

"You asked me why and I asked you why not," O.K. said.

"You guys are just weird," Britney Emily said, and left the room. Zaqui stood up and began to leave the room, then stopped and turned back.

"You are NOT weird, Uncle Dash," she said, then she proceeded to follow her cousin.

"We're about to eat," Shelley announced, coming into the room. "It was nice you could stop by for a minute," she said to O.K., dismissing him, then she turned to Dash. "You need to go and wash your hands."

O.K. looked at Dash, who was embarrassed by her comments. Dash's mom came into the room.

"Dash, do you want a glass of eggnog with dinner?" she asked, then she saw O.K. "O.K., I didn't know you were still here. Do you want to have dinner with us?"

Shelley gave Dash a stern look, which O.K. noticed.

"No, I need to--" O.K. began.

"Come on, we have plenty of food," Victoria urged. "We have room for one more. You're like part of our family too, you know."

"Great! Let's wash up!" Dash said, avoiding Shelley's reaction. "No eggnog for me, Mom. I'm not feeling noggish tonight."

"Would you like some, O.K.?" Victoria asked.

"Yeah, I'm a little noggish. How about a small glass?" O.K. said.

Christmas eve dinner was a grand affair with turkey, cornbread and bacon stuffing, mashed potatoes with gravy, yams with marshmallows, dinner rolls, cranberry sauce, corn, green bean casserole and three kinds of pies: apple, pumpkin and sweet potato pie, which was one of Pastor Wright's favorites. They all had a toast with sparkling apple cider, and Zaqui said the dinner blessing.

"Thank you, Lord, for this wonderful dinner that Grandma made for all of us, and please let us always have a Christmas like this, with the whole family together: Grandma and Grandpa and Uncle Dash and Aunt Shelley and Britney Emily and Mommy and Daddy and me. Let us always remember to thank You for everything. And thank you for O.K. being here with us too. In Jesus' name we pray. Amen."

"Thank you, Zaqui, that was such a nice prayer," Daniel said.

"This is my favorite kind of Christmas, with all the family here together at Grandma and Grandpa's house," she said.

"Mine too," Dash agreed.

"Where did you learn to pray like that?" Britney Emily asked.

"From my mommy and daddy. We always pray like that," Zaqui explained.

"We don't pray at my house," Britney Emily said.

"This is delicious," O.K. said.

"Thank you," Victoria said. "It's just something I whipped up during the past ten hours."

"Our favorite Christmas dinner," Dari remarked.

"And I helped with the pies!" Zaqui announced.

"Good job, Z-bug!" Dash said.

Although Shelley was silent during the meal, Dash had a wonderful time with his family. He didn't realize how much he had missed everyone, and just being here. He and O.K. spent the evening together, entertaining Zaqui and Britney Emily. Shelley stayed in the other room with his mother and Dari.

"Don't forget, we have to get up early to go to Mama's," Shelley reminded Dash as she was on her way to bed.

"We are usually up early on Christmas morning," Dash said, smiling at the girls.

"I'm going to bed, I'm so tired," Shelley said.

"Okay, I'll be down in a while," Dash said.

O.K. left, and Dash spent a couple of hours with his parents and Dari and her husband. He felt so happy to have such a wonderful family. He told them all about their business, his work with NorthStar, and their life in Spokane. He didn't mention their financial indebtedness. Zaqui curled up on the couch and fell asleep beside Dash. Britney Emily fell asleep on the other side of Zaqui. Dash covered them with blankets and left them to sleep there.

On Christmas morning, the girls awakened the family early.

"Merry Christmas!" they shouted.

"Let's go open our presents!" Britney Emily said enthusiastically.

"Wait, we have to wake up everyone else first," Dash said.

"Oh, just let them open their presents," Shelley said, pulling up the covers.

"In our house, we have a tradition. We all go to the living room together, so everyone is together while we open our presents," Dash said.

"I'm too tired," Shelley mumbled. "I need to get some more sleep."

"You girls, go wake up Grandma and Grandpa," Dash instructed. "Z-Bug, is your mother awake?"

"I'll go wake her up!" Zaqui said, bouncing up the stairs.

"Come on, Sweetie, let's go up," Dash urged.

"I'm too tired," Shelley complained.

"The girls are so excited. You can go back to sleep after we open our presents. It won't take long."

"Oh, all right, if you insist," Shelley finally agreed.

As they entered the living room and the huge mound of presents, Dash lit the lights on the Christmas tree. Dari had her camera in hand and was already snapping pictures.

"I have the most presents!" Britney Emily announced.

"You certainly do," Victoria said.

"I have a lot too," Zaqui said.

"Yes, you do," Dari agreed.

"I'll pass them all out to everyone, since I can read," Britney Emily said, grabbing a pile of presents. She distributed the gifts, and by the time she was finished, she was nearly buried in presents.

"Look how many are mine!" she said proudly.

"Let's open them!" Zaqui said.

For the next fifteen minutes, the family was opening presents, thanking each other for the gifts. Britney Emily was like an unwrapping machine, tearing through her presents, pausing only to tell Zaqui not to touch any of hers. Zaqui reached over to look at one of Britney Emily's new dolls, and Shelley snapped at her.

"Don't touch those! You have your OWN presents!" she said.

Zaqui looked as if she were about to start crying.

"Kwee, look at this," Dash encouraged, picking up one of Zaqui's toys. "What is this, anyway? It sure looks like a strange animal."

"That's a glow worm," Zaqui told him, stopping her tears. "See? You squeeze it and it lights up."

"That is so cool!" Dash said.

"I didn't get one of those," Britney Emily whined.

"You're too old for one of those," Dash said.

"Let's hurry up so we can get over to Mama's," Shelley said. "She'll have more presents for you there, Britney Emily."

"More presents? Let's go!" Britney Emily shouted.

"Shell, it's not even six o'clock in the morning," Dash said. "We don't have to rush off this early."

"Mama is expecting us for breakfast," Shelley said.

"I thought you said we were having Christmas dinner there," Dash said.

"We are, but Mama wants us to come early and help her."

"I hope every Christmas we can all be together like this," Zaqui said.

"Me too," Dash agreed.

"We have to get going," Shelley insisted.

Shelley helped Britney Emily collect her presents and they all somehow fit in the car. By seven o'clock on Christmas morning, they were on their way to Shelley's mom's house. Dash was a little disappointed that he hadn't had more time with his family, but he realized that a married man must make some sacrifices.

Dash drove slowly because the roads were icy. The thought occurred to him that if they had waited a couple of hours, the temperature would rise and the ice would melt. He didn't mention that fact to Shelley, though, because he didn't feel like arguing with her.

When they finally arrived, Suzie's house was dark. Britney Emily knocked and knocked on the door, until finally her grandmother opened it.

"Whaddya want?" she barked.

"Merry Christmas, Grandma Suzie!" Britney Emily said.

"Shelley, what're ya doin' here so early?" Suzie yelled from the door.

"You said you wanted us to come over early on Christmas," she said.

"I said, for an early dinner," she coughed. "Well, whatever, you're here now. Get in this house so I can close this door! It's freezing out there!"

Suzie went back to bed and Shelley and Britney Emily went to take a nap in Shelley's old room. Dash sat in the living room, noticing the lack of Christmas decorations. Fluffy jumped up beside him and rubbed her head against Dash's hands, as if to say, "pet me." She laid down on his lap. They waited in the living room for several hours until his mother-in-law finally came downstairs.

"Do you want some coffee?" she asked, lighting a cigarette.

"No, thanks," Dash answered.

"I'm making it fresh," she said.

"No, thank you, I don't drink coffee," Dash explained.

"You're not one of those health nuts are you?" she asked accusingly.

"No, I just don't like coffee," he said.

"You just have to get used to it."

"Why?"

"Everybody drinks coffee."

"No, thank you. I'm fine."

"Well, okay, you're the one missing out," she said.

Shelley and Britney Emily joined Dash and Suzie in the

late afternoon. Suzie had several more presents for Britney Emily, which she opened immediately. Suzie served a cold canned ham with canned green beans for Christmas dinner. Everything tasted very salty, but nobody complained.

"Are you going back up to Victoria's to stay tonight?" Suzie asked.

"No, Mama, we have to go back to Spokane," Shelley said.

"I have to see my other grandparents and get my other presents," Britney Emily explained.

"We have to keep everybody happy," Shelley said.

"That's good, make everybody happy," Suzie said, pouring herself a cup of rum and adding a little eggnog. "And don't forget to take your cat this time," she added.

The drive home to Spokane was slow, not only because the roads were slick, but because the car was so full of presents Dash couldn't see out any of the side or back windows. Fluffy did not like riding in the car. After unsuccessfully trying every type of exit and howling continuously for more than an hour, she finally settled on Dash's lap as he drove. Dash was so hot with this radiant heater on his lap; but he couldn't turn off the car heater because then Shelley and Britney Emily would get too cold.

When they finally arrived in Spokane, it was nearly midnight. Britney Emily complained when Shelley told her she would be staying with them overnight, but Britney Emily was too tired to argue with her mother. Dash introduced Fluffy to Hpsyloughehe, and they growled and swiped a few times at each other, then went their separate ways. Hpsyloughehe stayed close to Dash, the way he always did when Dash came home. Dash stretched the cat across his shoulders, like a mink stole, and Hpsyloughehe just purred and purred, happy to have his favorite human home with him.

The New Year's Eve performance at the Dome was sold out, with NorthStar the main group playing that night. Manny and two of his friends sat with Jessie and Shelley, and MaYohimbi arrived around eleven o'clock to join the celebration. The event had brought music producers and agents, and promises of bigger and better gigs for NorthStar during the next year. At midnight, Janeena counted down the seconds to the new year, and Dash leaped off the stage to give Shelley a kiss that would last from the old year to the new. She threw her arms around him, and told him that he was the greatest guy in the world.

During the holiday season, Shelley hadn't scheduled any jobs for Dash, so he could spend more time with her when he wasn't with the band. On the morning of January tenth, after practicing until two that morning, and not getting to bed until after four, Shelley shook Dash until he awakened.

"What? What's wrong?"

"Get up!"

"What?"

"Get up! You have to go to work!"

"What time is it?"

"It's almost eight o'clock."

"In the morning?"

"Of course, in the morning."

"Why are you waking me up so early?"

"You have to go to work. Come on, don't be lazy."

"I'm not lazy, I'm tired. I haven't even been asleep for four hours, and we practiced hard last night."

"You are so lazy!"

"No, I'm tired."

"Have a cup of coffee."

"You know I don't drink coffee."

"You should, then you wouldn't be so lazy."

"I don't have to go this early," he protested.

"Yes, you are scheduled to be there at eight-thirty, and it's clear across town."

"I asked you to not schedule any jobs this early in the day."

"You can't be lazy forever. You have to get out and get to work."

"Just call them and reschedule for any day, any time after noon."

"You are SO LAZY!" she screamed at him, then slammed the bedroom door as she left. Dash immediately fell asleep again.

18

Dash continued with his routine for the next few months. He spent much of his time with the band. Shelley was with Jessie so much of the time, and he didn't like spending too much time at home alone with the cats. He enjoyed practicing for hours, and even when the rest of the band wasn't there to practice, he often went to practice alone. Dashell Wiring wasn't getting a lot of jobs, but Shelley reassured Dash that their bills were all being paid on time, thanks to his nice salary from NorthStar.

One evening Dash arrived home at about six o'clock, and Shelley ran out to meet him with an envelope in her hand.

"Dash, you've got to go pay this phone bill RIGHT NOW or our phone will be turned off."

"Right now?"

"Yes, this is the final due date."

"We can pay it one day late and they won't turn it off."

"No, this is the final due date, it HAS TO be paid today! RIGHT NOW! GO!"

"You told me that we were paying all our bills on time," Dash said.

"You have to go NOW! They close at six-thirty," Shelley insisted.

"Why didn't you pay it earlier?"

"We didn't get the bill! They didn't send it until late," she said.

"Why didn't you go and pay it today?"

"I just called them because this notice says they will

turn it off if we don't pay it TODAY! HURRY! GO!"

Shelley handed the bill to Dash, who was shocked to see the total.

"Eight hundred and twenty dollars?" he asked.

"Hurry UP, or you won't make it on time!"

"Shell, I only have about forty dollars on me," Dash said.

"You can just pay the minimum, and that's thirty-six, and they won't turn it off."

"How did this get so high?"

"DASH! HURRY UP or they're gonna close!" Shelley shouted.

Dash got in his car, wondering how this had happened. He and Shelley had both agreed not to make any long distance calls. He knew he should to pay closer attention to their finances, but he didn't know what to do or how to do it. He thought Shelley was taking care of everything. He made it to the phone company before they closed and he paid the minimum amount. The lady working glared at him, as if he should be paying all of it now.

When Dash got home, he wanted to ask Shelley about the status of the rest of their bills, but she wasn't there. He had no idea where to start looking for information. He looked around the computer where Shelley took care of all their business. Hpsyloughehe joined him. Dash found a big box on the floor, out of sight, which was full of mail. Hpsyloughehe jumped in the box, wanting to be the center of Dash's attention. Dash lifted him out of the box, gave him a hug and set him on the floor. None of the envelopes in the box had been opened. Dash dug through the pile and found mail and bills four months old. Dari had sent him six letters, and his mom had sent two. He found eleven birthday cards from friends and relatives, mailed nearly three months ago. He sat on the couch and began to read his mail, feeling guilty that he hadn't responded to any of these letters or even acknowledged them. Three birthday cards had checks in them. He opened a small package from Dari and discovered a little photo album full of photos she had taken at his wedding. Shelley came home while he was reading his letters.

"Shell, why didn't you tell me I had all this mail?" he asked, trying not to sound angry.

"I forgot," she said, shrugging.

"But this is my mail."

"You never asked about it."

"I didn't know about it."

"It's not my job to tell you every little thing."

"And what about all those bills in that box?"

"Were you going through my private things?" she demanded.

"No, I was just wondering if we had any other unpaid bills," he said.

"You just STAY OUT of my stuff! Don't go messing everything up! You do YOUR job, and I'll do mine," she yelled, stomping out of the room.

Dash slept on the couch that night and for the next two months.

19

One summer day, Dash was getting ready to go to work when he heard Hpsyloughehe meowing loudly.

"Hpsyloughehe? Where are you, boy?" he called. Fluffy ran to greet him. When Dash went into the living room he could tell the crying was coming from the front porch.

"Hpsyloughehe! What are you doing outside?" he asked, opening the door for him. Hpsyloughehe had always been satisfied as an indoor cat, never wanting to go outside. Dash and Shelley had discussed the importance of keeping both cats inside the house because the street where they lived had so much traffic. Dash wondered how Hpsyloughehe had gotten outside.

"Shelley!" he called. He looked out the window and saw that her car was gone. Hpsyloughehe and Fluffy rubbed against Dash's legs, and he suspected that Shelley had forgotten to feed them again.

"Come on, I'll get your food," he said. As if they understood, both cats raced him to the kitchen and waited patiently as he opened a can of food and put some in each of their dishes.

That evening, Dash asked Shelley about the incident.

"How did Hpsyloughehe get outside?" he asked.

"He wasn't out," she answered.

"When I got out of the shower, he was on the front porch."

"Well, I didn't let him out."

"He can't open the door."

"Are you accusing me?" she asked, her voice getting higher.

"I'm just asking you."

"Oh, so it's MY fault? Why is it always my fault?" she yelled.

"I'm just asking," he repeated calmly.

"Why are you always blaming me? It is NOT my fault!"

During the summer, Dash was becoming more and more dissatisfied with his marriage. He didn't want to fight with Shelley, but she acted like two different people: sometimes she was so sweet and loving and considerate, and other times she was yelling and screaming and demanding that he do something. She had another screaming fight with her mother, again vowing to never speak to her. Shelley and Manny had a huge argument, and she told him he was no longer welcome in their house. Four more times Shelley insisted that Dash must rush out to pay a bill at the last moment, and nearly every morning Shelley screamed at him to get up early and stop being so lazy. He had returned to the bedroom, but he wasn't interested at all in Shelley anymore. When they touched, he was mechanical, not feeling what he was doing, his mind elsewhere. He felt great relief each time he came home and she was already asleep.

He thought about his parents who had stayed together all these years. He thought about the good marriage Dari and Pastor Wright had, how they worked together as a team. He thought about O.K. and Goliath, both newlyweds, and he felt guilty for missing both of their weddings. He had made a vow to Shelley, in front of all of them, promising to stay with her, in good times and in bad. He just didn't know how to make her happy. She had promised to help him with his musical career, and lately she had begun to act jealous of Janeena. Dash needed to talk to somebody, but he didn't want his family to know he was a failure, thinking about giving up on his marriage. He asked God for a sign, to direct him in the right way.

At the beginning of November, Dash considered the upcoming holidays. He didn't want another Christmas like they had last year. Since Shelley and her mother had reconciled again, they would need to go through the same routine at Christmas, rushing around to see everyone so no one would get mad; however, he hadn't been happy with the arrangement. They had been too rushed. He heard Kwee's voice: 'I hope every Christmas we can all be together like this ... This is the best Christmas!' He pictured his mom's disappointment when he had told her they couldn't stay long, and his dad's short-lived happiness at the few hours they had spent together. He knew he had to tell Shelley that they needed to separate; he couldn't stand her ups and downs much longer. Each evening, he didn't know if he would be coming home to a sane, loving wife or an angry, paranoid, raving lunatic.

As he drove home early from band practice one evening, he rehearsed in his mind what he would say when he got home. He would tell her that things just weren't working out between them, and that he wasn't happy. That was the truth, and she should know. He imagined her yelling and screaming, and he would hang his head guiltily. He wouldn't argue with her, but he would just stand his ground. He mentally collected his few personal belongings. He would let her have everything they had accumulated together, everything she had selected without him and purchased on credit. He might be able to stay with one of the band members for a week or two until he could get an apartment of his own.

He pulled his car into the driveway and saw that the house was completely dark. Shelley's car was there; maybe she had fallen asleep on the couch watching TV. Dash quietly opened the front door and was overwhelmed by a wonderful scent of food cooking. Candles were lit all over the house.

"Shelley?" He didn't see her in the front room or in the kitchen. "Shell?"

Shelley emerged from the bedroom with an angelic smile on her face. She was wearing a sexy, silky nightgown and robe. Something was different about her, and the thought flew through his mind that she had just been with a lover in their bedroom.

"Dash, I'm so glad you're home," she said in an inviting voice.

"What's all this? What's going on?"

"Do you like it?"

"Yeah, but--"

"It's all for you, Daddy."

"What?"

"I'm pregnant."

20

Dash knew God had plans that were different from his own plans, so he took Shelley's announcement as a sign that he should stay with her. Shelley had become a different person, a loving, considerate person. She began to make plans for the baby, and decided to decorate Britney Emily's room as the baby's room. Shelley acted the part of the dedicated wife and mother. Although Dash was suspicious of her behavior, he soon fell into the role of the doting husband and father. Shelley hadn't seen a doctor yet, since they didn't have insurance, and Dash kept encouraging her to make an appointment. She waited until December, when she figured she was three months pregnant, then she asked Dash to drive her to the doctor's office. He offered to go with her to talk to the doctor, but she wanted to go in by herself. She was very self conscious about her weight, since she had already gained more than forty pounds.

Dash waited nervously in the car until Shelley finally returned.

"Well?" he asked.

"Well what?"

"What did he say?"

"He said I have a high-risk pregnancy and I should take it easy until the baby is born."

"What do you mean by that, 'take it easy?'"

"I'm not suppose to drive, and I should get as much bed rest as possible."

"Okay, what else?"

"I guess that means I can't do much cooking or house cleaning," she said regretfully.

"That's okay, I can handle it," he said, thinking that he had been doing most of it lately anyway.

"Also, he said that this type of pregnancy can make me more irritable than usual," she warned.

"Thanks for the warning," he said, wondering how much worse she could get.

"And since I'm allergic to milk, he wants me to eat ice cream every day," she added.

"He didn't say that," Dash challenged.

"He did!" she shouted.

"He told you to eat ice cream every day?"

"Are you calling me a liar?"

"You're saying that the doctor told you to eat ice cream every day?"

"Statistics show that pregnant mothers need more calcium, and statistics don't lie," she argued.

"Statistics don't lie, but liars use statistics," Dash replied.

"You need to go to the store and get some ice cream," Shelley insisted.

"Right now?"

"Of course, right now, what do you think?"

"Are you suppose to be taking vitamins?"

"He didn't say anything about that."

"Did he tell you that you should avoid any specific foods?"

"No, but he said if I have any cravings, I should eat those things because that is what my body needs."

"So, basically, whatever you feel like eating, I have to go to the store and get it for you," Dash said.

"That's what the doctor said. So go to Safeway now, because I need some of their triple chocolate fudge delight ice cream. Get one of those three-gallon tubs. And while you're there, can you get one of their deluxe deli pizzas? The one with everything on it, with the extra thick crust."

At Christmas time, Dash and Shelley had a repeat of the year before, rushing from house to house. At each house, they made the announcement to their families that they were going to have a baby in April or May. Suzie was happy to hear about her new grandchild, and she and Shelley were speaking as if they had never fought. Britney Emily was quite upset when she realized she might not be the center of attention any longer, but the rest of the family was excited. Shelley and Manny made amends and were speaking again, and Manny brought a car load of baby gifts when he heard the news. The holidays flew by quickly. By January, Dash and Shelley were on better terms, both looking forward to the birth of their child.

Shelley had gained more weight and was constantly hungry. In mid-January, she awakened Dash at three in the morning.

"Dash, wake up," she whispered.

"What is it? Are you all right?"

"I'm hungry."

"We have seven kinds of ice cream in the freezer. What kind do you want?"

"No, I don't want ice cream. I need some real food."

"Like what? Do you want me to make you a sandwich or something?"

"No, I want a taco. No, two tacos. And a grande burrito, with guacamole and extra sour cream. And a quesadilla. And a chicken fajita."

"Right now?"

"Yes! I'm starving!"

"But I just fell asleep!"

"So, it should be easy for you to get up!"

"Can't I fix you a bowl of cereal or something?"

"No! Taco Bell is open twenty-four hours!"

"Shelley! That's clear across town!"

"It doesn't take that long to drive there."

"The car is cold, and the roads are icy."

"Okay, I'll just DRIVE MYSELF!"

"No, you know you can't be driving anywhere."

"Then you HAVE TO go get it for me. Right NOW! Do you want to starve your baby? Don't you care about us?"

Dash dragged himself out of the warm bed, pulled on his long johns and his clothes, and made the long, slow, cold drive to Taco Bell and back. When he got home, Shelley was sound asleep and snoring like a buzz saw. He put her food in the refrigerator and got back in bed.

The next day, he found the Taco Bell food, untouched, in the trash.

"Shelley! Why did you throw that away?"

"It's garbage."

"That's the food I brought for you."

"Oh, it made me sick! I opened the bag and then I threw up! Oh, get it out of here! I can't stand the smell!"

"You made me go clear across town, in the middle of the night, to get this specific food you had to have, and then you just threw it away?"

"What are you talking about?"

"Taco Bell! Three in the morning!"

"You are crazy! Don't you ever bring that kind of garbage in this house again!"

Shelley wasn't scheduling Dash to work as much, so he could take care of her at home. Since she couldn't drive and couldn't spend much time on her feet, she began to spend a lot of time at the computer. She was doing all the business accounting on the computer. She told Dash she had set up an e-mail account for the business, as a way to communicate with clients. Dash spent his days cooking, cleaning the house, and going to the store to get whatever Shelley was craving that day. She had begun to drink ten or more cans of Pepsi every day, insisting that she needed it. Dash didn't think that was healthy for her or the baby, but Shelley began to scream when she didn't have any, so he made sure their refrigerator was well stocked, with a few extra cases in the garage.

One frosty February afternoon Dash came home from the store to find Hpsyloughehe lying in the driveway. Dash jumped out of the car and ran over to him. The cat was very cold, but alive. Hpsyloughehe tried to lift his head, and he opened his mouth for a silent meow. His legs were injured and he couldn't walk.

Dash rushed into the house, his heart pounding. Shelley was sitting at the computer, laughing.

"I just got the funniest e-mail from a friend of mine," she chuckled.

"Shelley! I think Hpsyloughehe was hit by a car!"

"No, he's not even outside," she said, not turning from the computer.

"I just found him lying in the driveway."

"Oh, well, he wanted to go out."

"He hates the cold! Why did you put him out?"

"Can't you see, I'm busy? I have to get some work done so we can get some money to pay our bills!" she shouted.

"I'm taking him to the vet," Dash said.

"Do you know how much that is going to cost?" she asked angrily.

"Hpsyloughehe is injured! He can't walk!" Dash said, finding a blanket and a box he could use to carry his cat.

"He'll be okay," Shelley said, uninterested.

"Are you going with me?" Dash asked hopefully.

"I have to get this work done, I told you."

"Okay, I'm going now," he said, making his way to the door.

"Stop at that Thai restaurant on your way home and bring me two orders of their Special Number Three," she instructed.

Dash fought back the tears as he drove Hpsyloughehe to the nearest veterinarian. Hpsyloughehe had been with him for nearly eight years. He was the best cat a human could have. He had never been sick, and was always so loving. He didn't like to go outside, especially in the bitter cold. He must have been forced out of the house that day. As Dash drove across town, being careful to make the ride as smooth as possible, Hpsyloughehe reached out of the box toward him.

"It's going to be okay, boy," Dash reassured him, as he touched his outstretched paw. Hpsyloughehe lifted his head slightly to look at Dash, as if to acknowledge that Dash would take care of everything.

When they arrived, Dash carefully carried Hpsyloughehe in the box into the pet clinic. The vet's assistant took one look at Dash's panicked expression and at Hpsyloughehe and ushered Dash to the back.

"What happened?" the vet said.

"I found him lying in our driveway, and something is wrong with his legs," Dash said. "Is there anything you can do?"

The veterinarian gently felt Hpsyloughehe's body and listened with his stethoscope. Then he took him to the back room for an x-ray.

"I'm afraid he has been run over by a car," the vet said grimly, bringing Hpsyloughehe back to Dash.

"Is he going to live?" Dash said over the lump in his throat.

"He has some internal bleeding, as well as several broken bones. If we operate, he might not survive the operation. If he does survive, he probably won't be able to walk, and he'll need to be on medication just to withstand the pain."

"So, you are saying..."

"In my opinion, it would be best to put him to sleep," the vet said.

"I've had him so long..."

"I know, he's a family member. You really love him, don't you? If you choose to keep him alive, should he survive the surgery, what would be the quality of his life, especially if he can't walk?"

Hpsyloughehe lifted his head and looked at Dash, giving a little nod. He blinked his eyes, as if to say good-bye, then took one last look at Dash. He put his head back on the blanket and closed his eyes.

"Good-bye, Hpsyloughehe, my good boy," Dash said, letting the tears flow. He gave him one last kiss on the forehead, and petted him gently. Hpsyloughehe did not open his eyes. Dash handed the box to the vet's assistant, who whispered something to the vet. He examined the unmoving Hpsyloughehe.

"Dash, your cat has just passed away. I'm so sorry."

Dash sat in his car in the parking lot for nearly an hour, unable to drive. He was numb, with tears streaming down his face. He didn't want to go home. He started his car. As he was driving past the mall, he decided to stop and make a collect call from one of the indoor pay phones.

"Mom?"

"Dash, what is it? What's the matter?"

"Hpsyloughehe just died."

"Oh, Honey, I'm so sorry."

"He was hit by a car," Dash said, his sobs under control.

"But I thought he didn't go outside," Dash's mom said. "He never did here."

"He did today," Dash said.

"I'm so sorry," she repeated.

"I don't know what to do," he said.

"Where is he?"

"He died at the vet. But I don't know what to do with myself."

"What do you mean?"

"I don't want to go home."

"Your wife and baby are expecting you to come home."

"Yeah."

"Take some time to pull yourself together, then go home."

"Yeah."

"Dash?"

"Yeah?"

"I love you."

"I love you too, Mom."

When Dash arrived home several hours later, Shelley was still sitting at the computer. Without looking at him, she demanded, "Where's my Thai food?"

2I

"Hey, Sweetie, I need a little, small thing to fit under this desk," Shelley said one afternoon in April, sitting at her computer and getting larger by the day.

"A little, small thing? Isn't that redundant?" Dash asked, as he was putting on his shoes to go buy another flavor of ice cream.

"What are you talking about?"

"When you say 'little,' doesn't that imply that it's small?"

"You're not listening to me," she whined.

"Yes, I am," he said, almost enjoying her irritation.

"No, you're not."

"If I weren't listening to you, I wouldn't have heard you use a redundant phrase."

"See? You're not listening."

"Yes, I am, I heard you say you need 'a little, small thing.' So what kind of a thing?"

"You're not listening! If you were listening, you'd know what I mean!"

"Yes, I am."

"I need a little, small thing to fit under this desk."

"Besides being little and small, what kind of thing?"

"Oh, just forget it."

"Okay."

"You don't even care."

"Yes, I do."

"You don't care about your own baby, your own flesh and

blood. What kind of father are you, anyway?"

"I do care."

"Forget it, I'll get it myself."

Dash brought home ice cream and found Shelley in bed, watching a movie on TV.

"I need some of that ice cream right now," she demanded.

"Coming right up," Dash said cheerfully.

"Stop that," Shelley said, enraged.

"Stop what?" Dash asked, wondering what kind of bee was in her bonnet tonight.

"That!"

"What's that!"

"That! Stop it?"

"What are you talking about?"

"You know what I'm talking about."

"No, I don't," he said, truly puzzled.

"You're doing it again."

"Doing what?"

"That."

"What?"

"Don't do that."

"Do what?"

"That!"

"I'm not doing anything."

"Yes, you are! Stop it!"

Whatever it was, he stopped doing it by leaving the room and bringing Shelley's ice cream. When he returned, she was a completely different person.

"What are we going to name the baby?" she asked.

"If it's a boy, I like Patrick," Dash said.

"No, I hate that name," she said, dismissing his first choice.

"What do you like?"

"For a boy, how about Dylan?" she said.

"That's not bad," Dash said.

"No, wait, not Dylan. I like Nicholas," she suggested.

"Nick, that's okay," he said.

"No, not Nick, no nick names... no... how about Herschel?"

"Herschel? Hershey? I don't think so," Dash said. "How about Todd?"

"No, I don't like it," Shelley said. "How about Eugene?"

"No, not Eugene. What about Warren?

"I hate that name," Shelley said. "What about Hugh?"

"No, it's too much like huge." Dash said.

"Do you like Rex?" Shelley asked.

"No, our neighbors had a dog named Rex, and he was always smelling our bottoms," Dash said. "If we name him Rex, I'll always think of Smeller-bottom."

"What about Dash, Jr.?"

"No, I'm not into juniors."

"How about Gene?" Shelley suggested.

"That's short for Eugene, and I really don't want to name a baby Gene or Eugene."

"Don't you like anything?" Shelley asked, exasperated.

"What if it's a girl?" Dash asked.

"I hope it's not another girl," Shelley said.

"I just hope he or she is healthy," Dash said.

"How about Tabitha?" Shelley asked.

"No, we used to have a cat by that name," Dash said.

"Well, how about Penny?"

"Penny? Is that short for something? Pendolyn?"

"No, it could be Penny Lynn, like Penny Lane," Shelley said.

"Well, why not Lucy-in-the-sky, or Lady Madonna?" Dash asked.

"Now you're getting ridiculous," Shelley said. "What about Beth?"

"Short for Elizabeth?"

"No, not Elizabeth, that's an old name. What about Jennifer?"

"Jennifer? You like Jenny?"

"Not if you're going to call her Jenny," Shelley said.

"What about April?"

"How about May or June?"

"We're not having Daisy Duck's nieces here," Dash said.

"What about Amanda?"

"No way, not Amanda."

"Lucinda?"

"Cindy?"

"Oh, no, not Cindy."

"I like Serena."

"No, too serene," Shelley said. "How about Jeffrey?"

"For a girl? No way!"

"No, for a boy."

"No, too preppy. How about Tyler, for a boy?"

"Tyler?"

"Yeah, that's a good name."

"Like Steven Tyler?"

"Or like Tyler..."

"Tyler, like Tyler Banks. Not bad," Shelley said. "Tyler what? Middle name?"

"Tyler ... Freeman?" Dash suggested.

"No, not Tyler Freeman Farrah. But Tyler is good for a boy."

"Tyler it shall be, if it's a boy."

"Okay, and what for a girl? We can think of a middle name later."

"How about Jana?"

"No, too close to Janeena."

"What about Trana?"

"No, too Black," Shelley said.

"What about Heather?"

"I like Heather. How about Heather Erica?"

"I think Erica means Heather, in another language, German or something."

"No, I don't think so."

"I think so. How about Heather Victoria?"

"No, then Mama will get jealous."

"I don't want Heather Suzie."

"Heather Suzanne?"

"No, Heather... Lynn?"

"How about Erica Heather?"

"Not Erica Heather, they both mean the same thing."

"No one will know."

"Yes, they will," Dash said. "I will."

"Okay, Heather Erica."

"Not Erica. Let's say Heather for the first name, if it's a girl, and decide on a middle name later."

"Okay, so we have Tyler and Heather," Shelley agreed.

"What if it's twins?"

"It better not be twins!"

The baby was to be born sometime around mid-May. Shelley was so excited, and she had a whole production planned. Of course, Dash had to be there, but so did Shelley's mom, Jessie, Manny, one of Manny's friends to videotape the entire event, and even Britney Emily, to welcome her new brother or sister. Dash was very uncomfortable about being there, especially with all those other people, but since it was so important to Shelley, he agreed.

"Am I as big as a house?" Shelley asked on the first of May.

"No, obviously not," Dash said. "You're in the house, aren't you? So how could you be as big as the house?"

"You're so mean! But seriously, I'm huge, aren't I?"

"No, you're not huge."

"I weigh more than you," she said.

"You've always weighed more than me."

"I hate you! You are so cruel! Don't you even love me? Don't you care about the baby? Do you hate the baby too?"

"I'm sorry, I didn't mean it like that."

"Why do you hate me?"

"I don't hate you, I love you."

"So, do you think I look fat?"

"No, I think you look pregnant, and you look beautiful."

The next day Shelley's contractions started, and quickly became close together. Shelley called her mom, Jessie and Manny and asked them to meet her at the hospital. Her mom had a suitcase packed, and was ready to drive to Spokane at a moment's notice. Jessie would pick up Britney Emily.

Dash put Shelley's bag in the trunk and nervously drove to the hospital, being careful to avoid the potholes and any bumps he saw in the road. Shelley cried out in pain every minute or two as Dash tried to concentrate on his driving. They arrived safely at the hospital, and Dash ran inside to get a wheelchair for Shelley. He pushed her inside, as she continued to moan.

"My wife is having a baby!" he said to the receptionist.

"You need to take her to the other entrance," she told him.

"Where is it?"

"Go out this door, follow the sidewalk to the left, and go past the emergency entrance to the maternity ward."

Dash wheeled Shelley out the door to the correct entrance in record time.

"My wife is having a baby!" he shouted, as they came through the door.

"Who is her doctor?"

"Who is your doctor, Shell?"

"Doc-tor Shrop-shire," she said between breaths.

"Dr. Shropshire!" Dash yelled.

"Bring her over here, and we'll get her checked in. Have you pre-registered?"

"Shell, have you pre-registered?"

"No, (breath-breath) it's not due (breath-breath) for

another two weeks."

"Then you'll have to fill out these forms first," the desk clerk instructed.

"AHHHH!" Shelley shouted. "I think the baby is coming!"

"Are you sure?" Dash asked.

"You just be quiet! I've done this before! You don't know anything!"

"Can I fill out the forms after she gets into a room or something?" Dash asked, as Shelley let out an ear-piercing scream.

"Okay, take this clipboard with you, and bring these pages back to me as soon as you get them filled out. Keep the two blue ones."

"Thank you so much."

"Cecile! Take this young lady and her husband into room four."

"Follow me," Cecile said to Dash, as she pushed a moaning Shelley down the hall.

Dash waited in the hall while the doctor on call examined Shelley. A nurse came to tell Dash that it would most likely be a few hours, and he could go back into the room with Shelley.

"Something's wrong, and they're not telling me, I know it," Shelley told Dash.

"What do you mean?"

"Something is wrong with the baby!"

"Nothing is wrong with the baby," Dash said, comforting her.

"It wasn't like this with Britney Emily," Shelley said.

"Every baby is different," Dash said.

"Oh, how would you know? Have you ever had a baby?"

"No, but --"

"Then you can't say anything," Shelley said. "Oh! Oh! Oh!"

"What's the matter?"

"Ow!!! OW!" Shelley shouted.

"Are you all right?"

"Of course I'm not all right! Don't you know anything?"

"Should I get the doctor?"

"He doesn't know anything!"

"What can I do?"

"Just be quiet, that's what! Just leave me alone!"

"Do you want me to go?"

"No, are you crazy? Don't you dare leave me her to suffer like this alone!"

As Dash was trying to think how to respond, Manny arrived with his friend, who had brought his video camera.

"Manny! Thanks for coming," Shelley said sweetly, with the voice of a different person.

"Dash, have you met Richard?" Manny asked.

"How's it going?" Dash asked, reaching to shake Richard's hand.

"Where do you want me to set up?" Richard asked.

"Right over there," Shelley instructed. "Dash, can you brush my hair for me? My brush is in that purple bag."

"So, this is the real thing?" Manny asked.

"The real thing?" Shelley asked, puzzled.

"Yeah, remember with Britney Emily, how many false alarms you had before she was finally born?"

"Oh, yeah, well, this is the real thing," Shelley assured

him. "Dash, go and get me a Pepsi."

"Shell, you can't have anything besides water right now."

"I need a Pepsi!" she demanded.

"No Pepsi," Dash said.

"You can't tell me what to do!" she shouted.

"I'm not telling you, the doctor told you."

"Don't listen to him, he doesn't know what he's talking about."

"Think about the baby, Shell."

"I NEED a Pepsi! That is what the baby is asking for!"

Dash went out into the hall, with no intention of bringing a Pepsi against the doctor's orders. Jessie arrived with Britney Emily as Shelley let out another huge scream.

"Is Mommy okay?" Britney Emily asked, her face crunched up with worry.

"How is she?" Jessie asked.

"Is the baby born yet?" Britney Emily asked.

"She's fine, she just wants a Pepsi," Dash said, "and no, the baby hasn't been born yet."

"I want to see the baby come out of Mommy's ear," Britney Emily said.

"Out of her ear?" Dash asked.

"That's what Mommy told me," she said.

"Okay... I'm not sure about that one... but this is my first baby," Dash said.

"Is she in labor?" Jessie asked.

"I guess. They said the baby will probably be born in the next few hours," Dash said, heading down the hall as they entered the room.

Dash was thrilled, yet nervous. He prayed that the baby would be all right, but he didn't want to go back into the room and have Shelley yell at him any more. He wanted to be present for the birth, but he was uncomfortable with everyone else in the room. He hoped to be the first to see his baby, yet he felt embarrassed that Britney Emily was there, a mere child herself.

Dash was about to become a father. Would it be a boy or a girl? Would he or she have his brown curls or Shelley's blond hair? Would the eyes be closed, like when kittens were born? Would Dash be a good father? Could he take care of the needs of a newborn baby? He couldn't leave Shelley now: they were forever bound by this child.

He returned to the room to the sound of Beatles music and chattering. If he hadn't known better, he would have thought they were having a social gathering. Everyone, including Shelley, was drinking Pepsi and eating Chili Cheese Fritos. They continued their party as he slipped into a chair and observed. He must have dozed off, because suddenly Suzie was in the room, speaking in her raspy voice, asking if Shelley would mind if she smoked. Richard was taping the whole thing. Dash looked at the clock. He and Shelley had arrived at the hospital nearly eighteen hours ago.

Dr. Shropshire arrived and ushered everyone out of the room. From the hall, Dash could hear Shelley screaming in pain once again. Dr. Shropshire left and the group moved back into the room. Shelley announced that she was in extreme pain, but that the baby would be coming soon. The tape was turned on again, and each time Shelley yelled, her mother was at her side to comfort her. A nurse returned and told them they would all need to wash up and put paper protective coverings over their clothes and faces, which they did quickly, as Shelley continued to scream. Dash stood on one side of Shelley with Britney Emily beside him, and her mother and Jessie stood on the other side.

The doctor and two nurses or assistants came into the room and began to prepare for the birth. Although Shelley kept yelling as if she were being tortured, they paid no attention to her. They kept busy with the task at hand. When Dash saw the first bit of blood, he looked away from that area and kept his focus on Shelley's face contortions. She gave a grunt, and the doctor said the baby was almost there. Shelley gave one last yell and collapsed, then turned to her mother and vomited on the floor beside her. Dash looked toward the doctor as he lifted a pink, wrinkled baby with a head covered with dark hair.

"Congratulations! It's a girl!"

"Waaa!" a tiny voice said. Dash stared at his daughter.

"Here you go, Dad." The nurse wrapped the baby in a blanket and handed the crying bundle to Dash.

"I'm your daddy," he said gently, and she immediately stopped crying. Her eyes opened to look at him, then a tiny hand with miniature fingers and fingernails grabbed at the blanket, then gripped his finger

"What are you going to name her?" Britney Emily asked.

"We decided on Heather," Dash said, examining the perfect, pure child in his arms, as the team took care of Shelley, who was panting and trying to catch her breath.

"Heather, huh?" Suzie asked.

"Yeah, we both like that name," he said, his heart full of love for this tiny being who was depending on him. He was transfixed; he couldn't look away from his precious daughter.

"Can I see her?" Shelley asked, when the doctor finished with her.

"Here you are, Mom," Dash said, handing his daughter to her mother.

"Did I look that ugly when I was born?" Britney Emily asked.

"Britney Emily, she's not ugly," Suzie said, "and you were just that beautiful. Only you were bald until you were two."

"Yuk!" Britney Emily said, disgusted.

"She looks just like you, Dash," Jessie said.

"She doesn't look like me?" Shelley asked.

"Shell, no way are you that beautiful," Manny said.

"Oh, be quiet, Manly," Shelley said.

"I told you not to call me that," Manny warned.

"But you are so manly," Shelley teased.

"Stop it! I mean it!" Manny said.

"Manly Manny!" Shelley shouted.

"Both of you, cut it out!" Suzie shouted more loudly, triggering a coughing fit.

"He started it!" Shelley yelled.

The baby cried. A nurse came into the room.

"I'm going to have to ask all of you to leave. Mother and baby both need to get some rest," she said.

"Can't my husband stay?" Shelley asked. "I really want him by my side."

"Everyone needs to leave right now," the nurse said. "You are going to get some sleep. Your husband can come back in an hour or so."

Dash gave his daughter a kiss on the forehead and tried to memorize her face before he left. He almost couldn't believe that he was a father, and that this precious baby was his daughter! She was the newest baby in the world!

"Good job, Shell," he said. "She's absolutely beautiful."

"What about me?" Shelley asked, pouting.

"You're beautiful too," he said, giving her a kiss. "I'll see both my girls soon," he promised.

"I'll stay at your house until Shelley comes home," Suzie told Dash, "if that's okay with you."

"Oh, yeah, sure. Just follow me. Where did you park?"

22

Suzie stayed at their house and took a nap while Dash returned to the hospital several hours later. As he approached Shelley's room, a nurse intercepted him.

"Your wife is asleep. Why don't you let her rest?" she suggested. "She's wiped out. But you can go see your daughter in the nursery over there."

"Thank you," Dash replied. He couldn't wait to see Heather again. He walked to the nursery and peeked through the window. Only two babies were in the nursery, so he figured that Heather was the one in the pink blanket. He saw the pink name card that said "Baby Girl Farrah" and he beamed with pride. She was lying there, so pure and innocent, moving in slow motion. He pondered her beauty. A young hospital volunteer stepped up beside him.

"Is that your baby?" she asked.

"Can you tell?" he asked, with a huge smile on his face.

"I can see it in your face. Your first, isn't she?"

"Yes. Isn't she just perfect?"

"She is," the volunteer agreed. "But how did you pick that name?"

"We discussed a lot of names, and we both like it. It fits her, don't you think?"

"I don't know, I've never heard that name before."

"You've never heard of Heather before?"

"Heather? That's not Heather. No, her name is McCartney. I helped your wife fill out the birth certificate."

"McCartney?"

"You haven't heard that name either?"

"I've heard of it, Paul McCartney of the Beatles."

"Who?"

"My wife loves the Beatles."

"Who's that?"

"You haven't heard of the Beatles?"

"No, are they famous?"

"They were. Very famous."

"I've never heard of them."

"She named her McCartney?"

"That's what I wrote on the birth certificate."

"McCartney?"

"Yeah, I thought it was weird too."

Dash was extremely upset. They hadn't even discussed the name 'McCartney.' He was about to go awaken Shelley when another nurse tapped his shoulder.

"Would you like to hold your daughter?" she asked.

His anger melted as he turned to his daughter. He slipped into the protective paper over-clothes and sat in a rocking chair in the nursery. The nurse handed McCartney to him and he held her so carefully.

"She won't break," the nurse said.

"Thank you," he said, gazing at the new human in his arms. He rocked her, and she didn't cry. She looked up at him several times. He couldn't look away from her.

"It's so nice to finally meet you," he whispered, "my little sweetheart. McCartney. Cartney. Carty. You know, you have my heart already."

He sat rocking her for nearly an hour, until a nurse told him that Shelley was awake. He carefully carried McCartney to her mother.

"Do you want to hold her?" Dash asked.

"No, just put her in the crib," she said, indicating a raised table with glass sides. Dash didn't want to put his baby in such a sterile environment. He preferred to hold her for a while longer.

"I'll hold her for a while longer," Dash said.

"You're going to spoil her," Shelley said.

"She's so beautiful," Dash said.

"More beautiful than me?" Shelley asked.

"No, of course not," Dash lied, in order to keep the atmosphere calm around the baby.

"Do you want to nurse her now?" an aide asked, as she came into the room.

"No, I can't nurse her," Shelley explained.

"You can try," the aide said.

"No, I can't. I have bad milk," Shelley insisted.

"Would you like to speak to the lactation counselor?" the aide asked.

"No, I don't need to speak to the lactation counselor," Shelley said. "I have bad milk."

"Well, your baby is probably getting hungry," the aide said.

"Well, then, bring me a bottle and some formula!" Shelley demanded. The aide scampered out of the room.

"What a miracle she is," Dash said, looking and learning his daughter.

"You know, I almost died having her," Shelley said.

"You what?" Dash asked.

"I almost died having her," she repeated.

"You didn't almost die," Dash said.

"You were right here! You saw what happened!"

"I saw you have a baby, naturally," Dash said.

"You weren't having the baby! Weren't you paying attention?"

"Yes! I was right here."

"Then you saw me almost die," she said.

"The doctor didn't say anything about it," Dash said.

"Doctor Shropshire didn't want anyone to panic," Shelley explained.

"Everything went normally," Dash said.

"Except that I almost died! Why are you so dense? You can watch it on the video, there's the proof that I almost died."

Dash knew that was the last video he wanted to watch. As he was deciding to agree that she almost died, the phone rang. Shelley reached over to answer it.

"Ouch!" she shouted; then sweetly, into the phone, "Hello?"

Dash looked closely at Carty's eyes and noticed long, tiny eyelashes. She reached up with her tiny hand, and grabbed Dash's finger. Dash could tell Shelley was talking to his mother.

"It was really terrible," she said, "and I almost died. The doctor had to do emergency procedures, and he told me I'm lucky to be alive. They almost lost me. They had a team working to keep me alive. And that's how close I was to dying... uh-huh... he's right here, do you want to talk to him? Dash, it's your mom."

"Hi, Mom!"

"Congratulations! Suzie called us and said you have a daughter."

"She's so perfect, Mom. I'm holding her right now."

"What did you name her?"

"Shelley chose the name 'McCartney,'" he said.

"McCartney? That's not a name for a baby girl," his mom said.

"Shelley loves the Beatles, you know," he said.

"Well, I loved Gene Kelly when I had you and Dari, but I didn't name you 'Gene' and 'Kelly,' you know."

"I know, but, well, you know."

"Yeah, I know. McCartney's a cute name. Dad and I want to come up and see her. When will they be going home from the hospital?"

"Just a minute, I'll find out. Hey, Shell, when can you and McCartney go home?"

"Since I almost died, they will need to keep me here for a few days for observation."

"Mom, they might have to be here for a few days," Dash said.

"How about if Dad and I come up this weekend?"

"That would be great."

"Is your band playing this weekend?"

"Yes, as a matter of fact, we are playing in the stadium at that new casino, Friday and Saturday nights."

"Then we can hear you play, too."

"Great! We'll see you then."

"Love you."

"Love you too."

"Are they coming up?" Shelley asked. "Because you know, we don't have room for them, with Mama here."

"I'm sure they will stay in a motel," Dash said.

"Oh, well, that will be all right. Now, put the baby down, before you spoil her."

The next day, Shelley and McCartney were examined and found to be in excellent condition, and were released from the hospital. Dash's parents came to Spokane for the weekend and they really enjoyed the time they spent with their newest grandchild.

23

Suzie stayed in Spokane with them for nearly two months. Britney Emily visited often, now that she was 10. Dash didn't feel like he could get a moment alone with McCartney, since Shelley and her mom were so protective of her. Suzie stayed at the house while Shelley went to visit Jessie for hours on end. Shelley and Suzie wouldn't let Dash hold McCartney for long because they didn't want him to spoil her. Shelley had Dash give McCartney her bottle, but Shelley was so restrictive on how much the baby could have. When Dash mentioned that he thought McCartney was hungry, Shelley told him to give her a bottle of water. McCartney didn't have that round, baby fat look; she was thin. Even her cheeks were thin. Dash didn't approve of Suzie smoking around the baby, but when he mentioned that McCartney was coughing because of the smoke, Shelley said McCartney probably had asthma and that cigarette smoke couldn't hurt anyone.

One evening, while Suzie sat chain smoking near McCartney's crib, Dash picked up McCartney to give her an extra bottle of formula.

"Have you had children before?" Shelley yelled at Dash

"No, but--"

"Then you don't know anything!" Shelley shouted.

"I can tell when someone is hungry," Dash said.

"Look, I've been doing this since before you were born! You can't tell me anything!"

Dash was torn by his love for McCartney and his hurt and frustration over his relationship with Shelley.

Although Suzie usually stayed out of the arguments, she was there to back up her daughter so that Dash could never win. Dash felt as if he had no support at all; his family and friends were too far away.

One evening in July, after finishing a job, Dash stopped at the store to pick up baby formula and a few more cases of Pepsi. He saw a pay phone and decided to call home to see if Shelley needed anything else. The phone rang four times, then the answering machine came on.

"Hi, Shell, I'm at the store, and I just wondered if we need--"

"Dash?" Britney Emily said quietly.

"Hey, Britney Emily, how's it going?"

"Dash, I'm really hungry. I can't find anything to eat. Can you bring me a hamburger or something?"

"Where's your mom?"

"She and Grandma Suzie left early this morning, right after you left."

"Where's McCartney?"

"She's in her crib. She was crying a lot, then she finally went to sleep."

"Did you feed her?"

"I don't know how to feed her," she cried.

"I'll be right there," Dash said.

"Dash? Promise you won't tell Mom that I answered the phone? She told me not to, but I heard your voice on the answering machine..." she said, her voice shaky.

"It's okay, I won't tell. You did the right thing. I'll be right home," Dash said, hanging up the phone. His heart cried for his baby, who had been literally unattended all day, and also for his young step daughter, who had been forced into this position. As he drove home, he imagined grabbing McCartney and a few of her things, and fleeing with her. He didn't know where they would go, but any place he and his daughter could live a normal, peaceful life, and not be controlled by this unfeeling, self-centered woman he had taken for his wife. How had Shelley become like this? Didn't she care about her own baby? How could she just leave a two month old baby with a young girl who couldn't even take care of herself?

He could take McCartney to his parents' house, but that would be the first place Shelley would look. He could take her to Seattle and stay with one of his friends, and file for divorce. He knew that judges usually favored the mother over the father during a custody battle, but surely a fair judge would weigh the facts and justice would be done.

By the time he turned onto their street, Dash had his escape planned. He would take Britney Emily to get some dinner and then take her to her dad's house. Then he and McCartney would be on their way, away from here. He would not let Shelley destroy both of their lives.

As he pulled up to their house, his plans diminished. Shelley's car was parked in the driveway. He entered the house and the screaming. Suzie and Shelley were yelling at each other, over the sound of McCartney's crying. Britney Emily sat staring at the TV, in a world of her own.

"Well, then, you can just do it yourself!" Suzie screamed.

"I don't NEED your help!" Shelley screamed louder.

"You will never change!"

"You can't tell me what to do!"

"No one can get anything through that thick skull of yours!"

"Mama, I can do it--"

"Don't you 'mama' me! I can't trust you!"

"Can anyone trust YOU? You're a liar!"

"You lie!"

"I do not!"

"You're going to need me, and I won't be there!"

"I don't need you! You need me!"

"You are going to be sorry!"

"YOU are going to be sorry!"

"I already AM sorry -- sorry that I ever had you!"

"GET OUT OF MY HOUSE!"

"I never want to talk to you again! Don't you call me!"

"Don't worry, I won't!"

Suzie stormed out of the house, slamming the front door.

"Did you feed McCartney?" Dash asked, over McCartney's cries.

"You know how to feed her, or don't you care about her?" Shelley said.

"I was just asking," Dash said calmly.

"Just LEAVE ME ALONE!" she shouted, slamming the bedroom door.

Dash went into the kitchen to prepare McCartney's bottle. When he returned to the living room, he picked her up and she stopped crying immediately and began drinking the formula. She finished the bottle in a couple of minutes.

"Did your mother bring you something to eat?" Dash asked Britney Emily.

"No, I'm not hungry," she said quietly. Dash's plot returned to his mind. "Why don't you get your things, and I'll take you to get a hamburger, and then you can go back to your dad's?"

"Okay," she said, unenthusiastically.

Dash looked around the room and took a mental inventory of what he would need to take care of McCartney.

He would just take the car seat, some diapers, blankets, bottles and formula. He had more than a hundred dollars in his wallet; that would get him to Seattle, where he would be able to call O.K. and then buy a few things.

He strapped McCartney in the car seat and packed the necessary items into one of her bags. He was just about to get the formula and bottles from the kitchen when Shelley came out of the bedroom.

"I better not leave you alone with these two young girls for long," Shelley said.

"What?" Dash asked, his plans upset again.

"You know, men and your urges. You have to be watched all the time."

"What are you talking about?"

"If you leave a man alone with young girls, there's no telling what he will do."

"Well, I'm not just a man, I'm a father, and a step father," Dash said defensively.

"That's the worst kind, because you think you can trust them," Shelley said. "You be careful about that, Britney Emily. Remember what we talked about before?"

"Yes, I remember," Britney Emily said quietly.

"Are you going somewhere?" Shelley asked, taking note of what Dash was doing.

"I was going to get a hamburger for Britney Emily, and I thought McCartney might want to ride along," he said.

"I'm hungry too! Let's go!" Shelley said, gathering the baby things.

In the car, Shelley scooted close to Dash while the girls sat in the back seat. She put her head on his shoulder and rubbed his arm and his leg while he was driving.

"Shell, I'm driving," he said, pushing her hand away.

"You used to like it when I did this," she purred.

"Not now, we have the girls in the back seat," Dash said.

"Britney Emily needs a few lessons," Shelley said.

"Lessons in what?" Britney Emily asked.

"Never mind," Shelley said, grinning. "Oh, Dash, you'll never guess what I did this morning."

"What was that?" Dash said, afraid to attempt to guess.

"I found us a house! Mama went with me, and we put a down payment on a house!"

"What?"

"Ours is way too small, so we found a bigger one, in a much better neighborhood. It has a yard, so we can get a dog, and it has a room where you can play your guitar. And it has four bedrooms, so Britney Emily can have one, Mama can have one when she visits, and McCartney will have her own room. And the master bedroom is big enough, I can use it as an office, too."

"Yay! I get my own room!" Britney Emily cheered.

"Shell, we didn't talk about this."

"Yes, we did. It's all we've been talking about."

"When? When have we talked about moving to a bigger house?"

"All along."

"No, we haven't."

"You never listen to me."

"Yes, I do, and we haven't talked about this."

"What, are you calling me a liar?"

"I'm just saying that we didn't talk about it."

"You're calling me a liar in front of our girls?"

"What about the house we have?"

"We can sell it, easy, and make a profit."

"We have enough expenses already."

"You're saying that I don't know how to manage money?"

"I'm not saying that, I'm just saying --"

"Did you go to college?"

"Shell--"

"You don't know anything! You're just lazy and you don't know anything!"

Six weeks later, they were moving into their new house, which, Dash discovered, was only four hundred dollars per month more than they had been paying in the small house. They were fortunate that their house sold quickly, although they didn't get much from it, because they had been buying it from the owner and hadn't built up much equity. The new house was on the outskirts of Spokane, and had a nice, big yard with lots of pine trees. The house was two levels, with four bedrooms and two bathrooms upstairs, and a huge family room, bathroom and a double garage downstairs. The kitchen opened into the dining room, which had a sliding glass door to the deck. Dash liked the neighborhood, but now they lived so far from everything. Shelley was satisfied with the schools in the area, and so now they were prepared to have Britney Emily come to live with them full time.

In August, Britney Emily moved some of her things to her new bedroom in their new home. They had a barbecue and invited MaYohimbi to see their new home.

"How do you like it?" Shelley asked proudly.

"Do not put da trust in all dese tings," he warned.

"But isn't it nice? Do you like it?" she asked.

"Da home is comfortable, but better to dwell in da corner of da housetop, dan wit a brawling woman in da wide house," MaYohimbi said. "Now, show to MaYohimbi da baby."

Shelley brought McCartney to him, and he held her close to him, as precious cargo.

"What da baby name?" he asked.

"McCartney," Shelley said.

"Ah, yes, Ma-Cartney, after you good friend, MaYohimbi."

"Something like that," Dash laughed.

MaYohimbi held her up to look in her face.

"Dis chil' is starving," he said.

"No, she isn't," Shelley said. "She just ate."

"What she eat?"

"She had her bottle."

"Bottle of what?"

"Formula, that's all she can have. She's not even four months old."

"She not have breas milk?"

"No, I have bad milk," Shelley said. "You remember that from when I had Britney Emily."

"She need someting more," he said.

"No, she's okay, just look at her."

"MaYohimbi see a hungry baby."

"She's not hungry. She's not crying."

"Ah, she learn to not cry, crying don't do no good."

"You don't know what you are talking about, MaYohimbi," Shelley said.

"MaYohimbi have fourteen brother and sister, all younger, an MaYohimbi know what a hungry chil look like."

"She isn't even hungry, can't you tell?"

"What you fixin' on da grill? Give the chil a drumstick."

"We can't just give her a piece of chicken."

"Why not? When you hungry, you want chicken."

"But she's just a baby."

"We all start off to be baby, den we grow up. But da baby do not grow if you do not feed da baby."

"We feed her. I told you, she just ate."

"MaYohimbi bring Ma-Cartney home, and MaYohimbi fatten Ma-Cartney up."

"Oh, I love you, MaYohimbi, you're so funny!" Shelley said, not taking him seriously. She took McCartney from MaYohimbi and placed her in the crib.

"So, MaYohimbi, what do you say?" Dash asked, when Shelley left the room.

"Let him not deceive himself by trusting what is worthless, for he will get no-ting in return."

"Okay..." Dash said.

"Da house is nice. But da house is not ever-ting."

"Yeah, I know that."

"You, mon, you put you trust in da Lord."

"Yeah, I do."

"Dat's da only way you can make it in da world today."

One warm evening when Dash didn't have to practice, Shelley suggested that they go out, alone together, something they hadn't done since McCartney was born.

"We can't leave the girls at home alone," Dash said.

"They'll be all right," Shelley said.

"No, I won't be able to relax. Britney Emily is only 10 and McCartney is just four months old."

"Oh, they'll be fine. We won't be out that long."

"I don't think Britney Emily is comfortable taking care of a baby."

"It's her own sister, of course she's comfortable."

"Let's ask her how she feels." Dash suggested.

"Oh, all right, we can ask Manny to come and stay with them," Shelley said.

"Does Manny know how to take care of a baby?"

"Oh, sure, he is great with children."

"Are you sure you are comfortable leaving our two girls with him?"

"They'll be fine. I'll go call him. Come on, get dressed! I want to go out dancing!"

Manny agreed to watch the girls while Dash and Shelley went out to the club. They sat with Duane Packard, the bass player from NorthStar who was recently divorced. After a couple of drinks, Shelley started to flirt with Duane. Dash was surprisingly not at all jealous, even when Shelley sat on Duane's lap, or when they slow danced together. Dash's mind was on his precious daughter, and he didn't feel like being at the club.

"Hey, man, are you all right?" Duane asked, as they returned from the dance floor.

"I'm just really tired, I guess," Dash said.

"Don't you want to dance?" Shelley asked.

"Not really. Let's get ready to go," he said. It was almost eleven o'clock.

"No! This is our night!" Shelley protested. "We haven't been out in months!"

"I really would like to get home. We told Manny we

wouldn't be out late."

"Manny won't mind," Shelley said.

"Really, let's go, after this set," Dash said.

"You're not feeling well. Why don't you go home, and Duane will bring me home later?" Shelley suggested.

"It's so far out of the way," Dash said.

"Duane doesn't mind, do you, Duane?" Shelley asked, pouring his drink into his mouth.

"Yeah, man, go ahead. You know I'll take good care of her," Duane said.

Dash was happy to leave Shelley in the arms of another man. He drove home feeling free, and Manny met him at the door.

"Hey, thanks, Man, for doing this for us," Dash said.

"Where's Shell? Passed out in the car?" Manny asked.

"No, we met a friend at the club, and she decided to stay later, but I wanted to get home."

"Yeah, I understand."

"So, thanks again," Dash said.

"Hey, Dash," Manny said tentatively.

"Yeah?"

"Can we talk?"

"Sure."

"Do you ever feel like you're... different?"

"All the time, in this family."

"No, I mean... different."

"Different? Like how?"

"Well, you have those gorgeous curls. Do you ever feel... beautiful?"

"I'm not following you."

"Do you ever wish you were a woman?"

"No, that's one thing I have never wished."

"Well, how about when you are holding your baby? Don't you wish you could be a mother?"

"No... why, do you?'

"Well... I never have felt like a man. I always liked to play house when we were kids, but I wanted to be the mom."

"Oh, I see," Dash said, although he didn't really see. He glanced at Manny's face, which he had been avoiding, and noticed that he seemed to be wearing eye shadow and cheek coloring. He thought of Manny's feminine movements, his delicate ways, and began to understand. Dash remembered how angry Manny had been when Shelley had called him 'Manly.'

"I'm a woman, trapped in a man's body," Manny said.

"Ahh," Dash said, just for something to say.

"Remember Richard? He filmed McCartney's birth?"

"Yes, the cameraman?" Dash said.

"He's my boyfriend," Manny said.

"Okay," Dash said.

"We've been together for nearly three years."

"Oh, really?" Dash tried not to show surprise.

"Yes, and..., oh, Dash, you have to promise not to mention any of this to Shelley. She would never understand."

"She doesn't know?"

"No, and I don't want her to know."

"Okay, I won't tell," Dash said.

"Thanks, my brother," Manny said.

"No problem, Man. Mum's the word."

"Well, I better get going. Hey, any time you need me to watch the girls, just let me know. Britney Emily and I had the greatest time playing with her Barbies," he winked.

"Hey, let me give you a few dollars for watching them," Dash said.

"Oh, no, it's my pleasure. Besides, I'm loaded," Manny grinned.

Dash didn't want to know what he meant by that.

24

For Thanksgiving, Dash and Shelley decided to take McCartney to meet Dari and her family for a gathering at Dash's parents' home. Shelley's mom was invited to join them. Britney Emily stayed with her dad, so Dash thought this might not be as stressful holiday as they usually had.

Zaqui was amazed at her little cousin who looked so much like her own baby pictures. Dari was thrilled to hold her niece, although she did remark about McCartney acting very hungry. Shelley instructed everyone to give McCartney only water when it wasn't feeding time. Over Shelley's protests, Dari and Dash's mom took turns holding McCartney.

"Grandparents and aunts are allowed to spoil babies," Dash's mom said.

"Well, if she cries all the time when we get home, it will be all your fault," Shelley said.

"We just don't want her crying while she's here," Dari said.

Dash saw Zaqui creep out of the room, looking a little unhappy. He followed a few steps behind her as she found her grandpa in the family room. Dash stood back and listened as they talked.

"Grandpa Dan?" she said.

"Yes, my little Rascal Lady?" he asked.

"Are you named after the Daniel in the Bible?"

"I was named after my great-grandfather, Daniel, who was named after the Daniel in the Bible," he said.

"I know a song about the Daniel in the Bible, and it says he had a purpose."

"Yes, he did," Daniel said.

"Grandpa Dan, do I have a purpose?"

"Yes, you do. Of course you do!"

"What is it?"

"Your purpose is... to make people happy."

Her face lit up like a light bulb. "Like Uncle Dash?"

"Yes, just like Uncle Dash," he answered.

Dash slipped away before they saw him, thinking about what was known to the family to be his 'purpose.' He had lost focus of his purpose, to make people happy, because he had not been happy.

"So, how's my brother-in-law?" Pastor Wright asked, coming up behind him.

"Fine, great," Dash said.

"Do you want to talk?"

"Yeah, let's sit in here," he said, indicating the front room.

"What's on your mind?" Pastor Wright asked, when they were both seated.

"Marriage, the baby, these kinds of things..."

"Do you have a pastor up in Spokane?"

"No. We haven't been going to church," Dash admitted.

"Everyone needs a good pastor, someone to pray for him, and seek God for him, and give spiritual advice."

"That's true," Dash agreed.

"You can have the best doctor in the world, but only God can spare your life. You can have the best lawyer in the world, but only God can give you real freedom."

"That's a fact."

"So, what is it? What's going on?"

"Shelley and I... we are just not getting along like we should."

"What do you mean?"

"I mean, I can't talk to her without her freaking out. And she does things without telling me, and she makes things up that aren't true."

"Is she seeing another man?"

"No, I don't think so," Dash said, "but I almost wish she would."

"I was there when you took your marriage vows. Your whole family was there. You promised to love her forever."

"But she lied about so many things, and she got us so deep in debt, I don't know if we'll ever get out."

"It sounds like she needs some help," Pastor Wright said.

"She won't listen to anyone," Dash said.

"I mean, it sounds like she has a mental problem."

"I agree with you there."

"You agree with what?" Shelley asked, bringing McCartney into the room.

"We both agree that God has all the answers," Pastor Wright said, "and that your baby is beautiful."

"I agree with that too!" Shelley said.

Shelley's mother called to say she couldn't make it to the Thanksgiving dinner. Instead, she wanted Shelley and Dash to go with her to a casino near her house after dinner. Shelley was hesitant to leave McCartney with Dari and Victoria, but they assured her that they knew how to take care of a baby. Dash would have preferred to relax at home with the family, watching football with the guys, or playing his guitar for the girls, but Shelley insisted he go with her, to spend some quality time with her mother.

Dash and Shelley picked up Suzie and took her to the smoke-filled casino.

"Are you hungry?" Suzie asked. "Because they are serving turkey dinner for just two bucks," she said.

"No, thanks, none for me," Dash said, full of his mom's turkey dinner.

"Let's go sit with Mama while she eats," Shelley said. Dash followed them to the restaurant, feeling sleepy. Shelley and her mother ordered drinks for the three of them, but Dash was too tired to drink. Shelley helped herself to his drink, and the two ladies began acting giggly and silly, her mother chain smoking the whole time. Dash's eyes were burning from the dense smoke in the place.

"I'm really feeling sleepy," Dash said. "I'm going to go out to the car and take a little nap."

"It's freezing out there," Suzie said, triggering a coughing fit.

"I just need to close my eyes for a few minutes," Dash said.

"You're going to miss all the fun," Shelley said.

"I know, I'm a fun misser," he said, leaving them at their table.

As soon as Dash crawled in the back seat and covered himself with his coat, he fell asleep. He was brought back some time later by screams and shouts of somebody outside. After a moment, he realized where he was, and he recognized the voices of Suzie and Shelley. He thought about staying hidden in the car, then he heard men's voices also. He looked out the window to see both women being held by the police. He reluctantly got out of the car and began to walk across the parking lot to them.

"You have been told before not to come back here," a huge sheriff told Suzie.

"I was just aarrccgglllyyy--" she said, wavering drunkenly.

"Leave Mama alone, you, you--" Shelley said, swaying back and forth.

"Which one of you is driving tonight?" the smaller police officer asked.

"N-n-n-neither one-uv-us," Suzie stammered.

"So, you were just expecting to pick up someone to drive you home?" the large sheriff asked sarcastically.

"Look, lady, you've been warned before about soliciting. It's not allowed here," the smaller officer said.

"Don't talk to Mama that way," Shelley yelled, slurring her words. "Do you think she would bring her daughter out and solicit with me? Are you calling my Mama a hooker?"

"Honey, I've seen stranger things," the big officer said.

"Is there a problem, officers?" Dash asked. "This is my wife."

"Well, you got here just in time. Take these women away, and don't bring them back, ever! We don't need their kind of trouble here."

"Come on, let's go home," Dash said, taking Shelley's hand. Suzie was about to fall over, so he grabbed her also, and pulled them both to the car. He helped them get into their seats and fastened their seat belts.

"It wasn't our fault," Shelley began.

"I know," Dash said.

"Those stupid cops were just picking on Mama," she said.

"I know."

"She never hurt anyone, and they just don't like her."

Suzie started snoring, and Dash was grateful that they were pulling into her driveway.

"Help Mama get into the house, and I'll wait here," Shelley said.

"Help me help her," Dash said.

"Can't you do ANYthing by yourself?" Shelley asked, getting out of the car. She struggled to unlock the front door of her mother's house. They both helped Suzie to the couch and covered her with a blanket.

"Let's just stay here for the night," Shelley said. "I don't feel like going all that way. Besides, someone has to take care of Mama."

"But what about McCartney?" Dash asked, missing her.

"Victoria and Dari can take care of her," Shelley said, heading for her old bedroom.

"But we didn't tell them we would be gone all night," Dash protested, following her.

"They're so smart, they'll figure it out," Shelley said.

"I'll just call them to let them know," Dash said.

"Mama doesn't have long distance on her phone," Shelley said, flopping on the bed.

"I'll just go back to Mom's and get McCartney and bring her here," Dash said.

"No way! You are NOT leaving me here! You are staying here. She'll be okay," Shelley said, falling asleep. Dash went to sleep in a chair.

When they arrived at Dash's parents' house the next morning, his mom was in the kitchen, unloading the dishwasher.

"What happened to you last night?" Victoria asked.

"We stayed at Shelley's mom's," Dash said.

"Were you drinking and couldn't drive?"

"No, it was just too late to come home, and Suzie doesn't have long distance so we couldn't call."

"It's a good thing McCartney didn't have any problems," his mom said.

"Where is she?" Dash asked.

"Dari has her in the family room."

"You FED her? What did you give her?" Shelley was shouting at Dari. Dash ran out to the family room. He saw McCartney in Dari's arms, looking happier than she ever had before, actually smiling instead of scowling. Dari handed her to Dash.

"She had some baby food, pears, some baby cereal, two bottles of milk, and an egg. She was really hungry. That was this morning. Ask Mom what she had last night."

Dash's mom was just coming into the family room.

"How dare you feed her! She can't eat food yet!" Shelley said loudly, upsetting McCartney.

"She did," Dash's mom said.

"She's going to get sick," Shelley said.

"She was so hungry, after we gave her the formula, we gave her some milk and some baby food. Dari fed her in the middle of the night, and she ate again this morning."

"She's going to get all clogged up," Shelley said.

"She's seven months old. She needs to be eating food," Dari said.

"You just want her to get fat!" Shelley screamed.

"Babies are suppose to be fat," Dash's mom said.

"I am not going to let my daughter get FAT," Shelley said.

"She needs to eat, Shelley," Dari said.

"That's why she has formula, four ounces for breakfast,

four ounces for lunch, and four ounces for dinner. The rest of the time she gets water," Shelley said.

"Shelley, she's not much bigger than she was when she was born," Victoria said.

"She's just tiny, and I want her to stay that way," Shelley said.

Christmas time was hectic again, going from home to home in a rush. This time, Britney Emily was upset, because McCartney's car seat and baby things took up so much room in the car, Britney Emily couldn't bring all of her gifts to open on Christmas morning. She was pouting and McCartney was crying, yet Shelley wouldn't let anyone feed her. The family was afraid to say anything at all to Shelley, for fear that she would start screaming. As soon as all the presents were opened, Shelley cleared her throat, indicating that she wanted everyone's attention.

"This is our last Christmas coming here," she announced.

"Shell! What are you talking about?" Dash asked.

"It's just too stressful, traveling from place to place, especially with a baby," Shelley explained.

Zaqui started to cry.

"We can't keep trying to please everyone, so next year, we are just going to stay home, and if you want to see us, you can come up to Spokane and stay in a motel," Shelley said. "We aren't going to do this any more."

"Then how will I get all my presents from all my grandparents?" Britney Emily asked.

25

In January, Shelley decided to home school Britney Emily. Shelley was tired of getting up early to wake her up, and she wanted Britney Emily to be home to watch McCartney during the day when she had errands to run.

"But how can she keep up with the other fourth graders?" Dash asked, appalled at the idea.

"I have ordered her all these computer programs, so she can do all her lessons on a computer."

"But what about the socialization? That was my favorite part of school. She can't get that from the computer."

"She doesn't have any friends anyway. She doesn't need to go to school. I can teach her as well as those teachers can."

"Did you ask her if she wants to be home schooled?"

"No, she doesn't know what she wants. She's just a kid. This will help the whole family."

Britney Emily began to sleep until eleven every morning, then she stayed with McCartney while Shelley went shopping and other places with Jessie. All afternoon Britney Emily watched TV. She didn't like the computer, so she never used it. Shelley didn't check her progress, or even ask her about her school work. Dash was not happy with the arrangement, but he knew better than to interfere with what Shelley was doing.

Manny had been staying with the girls on the nights Dash played with NorthStar since September, and Shelley had been coming to all the performances. Shelley loved the arrangement because Manny wouldn't accept any money for baby sitting. Manny really enjoyed the motherly role. Dash was happy that Britney Emily was not left alone to take care of McCartney at night - he still didn't like the fact that she took care of her during the day, but at least Manny was there in the evenings, training her how to take care of a baby.

One Friday evening in March, the doorbell rang. Dash answered the door, and there stood Manny, wearing full make up, a long black wig that looked like his own hair, only longer, a blue dress and high heels. He actually looked very pretty. Richard was with him, dressed in a tuxedo, holding Manny's hand.

"Manny, Richard... come in," Dash said. He knew they wouldn't be able to keep Manny's secret from Shelley any longer.

"Oh, Manny, you're here-- AAHHH!" Shelley screeched.

"Shelley, I think it's time we told you," Manny began. "We are tired of keeping everything a secret. We want to live our lives in the open."

"Manny, you're wearing a dress," Shelley informed him.

"Yes, I know. We just got married," Manny said.

"Married? You can't marry a man," she stated.

"I can if I'm a woman," Manny said. "I had my name legally changed. So, from now on, call me Esmeralda Richardson."

"Esmeralda Richardson?" Shelley asked in disbelief.

"Yes, and my husband, Richard Richardson."

"Manny, I'm not calling you Esmeralda, no way!" Shelley said.

"Then just call me Esme," he said.

"Esme? Are you crazy? What is Mama going to say?"

"What can she say? I'm 35 years old. What's she gonna

do?"

"I'm going to call her right now," Shelley threatened.

"Go ahead."

"I will."

"So call her."

"I am."

"Go ahead, break the news. Then I won't have to tell her."

"I'm not going to tell her!"

"Then don't."

"You just want me to do your dirty work!"

"Go ahead."

"No way."

"Then I'll tell her. Do you want me to call her now?"

"Shell, I need to get going, or I'm going to be late," Dash said.

"Dash! Do something?" Shelley insisted.

"What do you want me to do?" he asked, slightly amused.

"I don't know... something!"

"I can't, I need to go."

"Well, I can't go. I'm not leaving my girls here with-with-with this PERSON," she said.

"Okay, then I'll just go," Dash said.

"We'll be going too, then," Esme said, "if you don't need us."

"Need you! Need YOU?" Shelley shouted. "You just stay away from my little girls! Who knows what you might do to them?"

"Shell, if Manny, er, Esme, is now a woman, he's-I mean, she's not going to be interested in little girls."

"You just be quiet, Dash! You don't know ANYTHING!" she shouted at Dash, as he escaped out the door. Esme and Richard followed him down the sidewalk.

"And YOU!" she shouted at Esme. "You are not welcome in this house! I NEVER want to talk to you again! Stay away from us!" she shouted at them, and slammed the door.

The next day, Shelley approached Dash with an angry look in her eyes. "I found out that Manny molested McCartney," she told him.

"What? What are you talking about?"

"I don't want him around her, or around here ever again."

"What did he do? When?"

"When he was baby-sitting. He molested her."

"I just don't think he would do that."

"Well, he did!"

"He really loves McCartney, and he wouldn't even think of hurting her."

"Are you calling me a liar?"

"No, I just--"

"Well, he did it, and he's not coming back here ever again!"

"We better take her to the doctor to be sure she's all right."

"No way! I'm not putting my baby through that kind of torture! What kind of mother do you think I am, anyway? We just need to make sure Manny is never around McCartney again!"

A few weeks later, Dash was very surprised when he

came home to find Manny baby-sitting McCartney. Dash thanked him, and Manny left. Dash asked Shelley about it when she and Britney Emily came home a few hours later.

"Why did you let Manny stay alone with McCartney? I thought you said he couldn't come over any more. What if he did something to her again?"

"Oh, we talked out and he's okay," Shelley said casually. "He didn't do it."

"Shelley, you told your mom and my parents and my sister that your brother molested our daughter. Now you're saying it's okay. How do we explain to our family that he's okay, nothing happened, and he's baby-sitting for us again?"

"Oh, they'll never know. Just tell them that we worked it all out."

In August, after several big performances, a music producer from Nashville approached Walter, offering NorthStar a contract there. Walter and Janeena began considering the possibility of moving, but the rest of the band had their families and lives established in Spokane. When Dash mentioned the opportunity to Shelley, she insisted that they stay in their great new house, with their blooming business. Since Janeena was the star of the band, she could easily assemble another group of musicians in Nashville. As she and Walter prepared to move, they asked Dash to reconsider and come along as their lead guitarist. However, Dash had to decline. The band had a going away party for Janeena and Walter. They wished them well on their journey to stardom.

The rest of the band decided not to stay together without Janeena, so Dash began to look for another band. Dash had lost all interest in Shelley, but he was staying at the house for the sake of McCartney, who was just beginning to walk. Dash usually slept in the basement, where he stayed up late writing songs in his practice room. Shelley started going out with Jessie quite often.

One afternoon in late autumn, Shelley asked Dash if he would consider moving to Nashville. She had had another argument with her mother, and wanted to put as much distance between them as possible. Dash listed all the reasons Shelley had given him just last month why they couldn't move, but she excused them all, saying they had to move now, for the sake of his career.

"You are getting older," she said. "Nashville is your only chance of making it big. Let's give it five years, and if you don't make it, then we'll come back here. We need to move right away, before winter."

"But we just bought this house."

"We can sell it and buy one there."

"Our business is just starting to really take off."

"We can move the business there."

"It will take time to establish another business in a new town."

"It won't take that long."

"I don't really want to move that far away from my family."

"What about your dream? This is for your dream. We need to do this for your career. This is your last chance. Can't you see that this is God's plan for us to move to Nashville?"

In the end, Shelley convinced Dash they had to move to Nashville. She arranged to sell their house, and she flew to Nashville. In one day she found a house in a nice area for them to purchase. Dash was left to take care of the kids and pack everything into a U-Haul truck. Britney Emily was excited to be moving with them. Herbert protested, not wanting his daughter to move so far away from him. They made a schedule with him so Britney Emily could fly back to Spokane for holidays and vacations. Dash and his family were disappointed that they had to move so far so quickly, before the holidays, but everyone encouraged him and they were happy for this great career opportunity.

They drove across the country just as snow was beginning to fall in some states. Dash drove the U-Haul truck, crammed with their belongings and towing Shelley's car, while Shelley drove Dash's car with the girls and her cat.

In the rush to move, Dash didn't realize until he had some time alone while driving the truck that Shelley had cut herself off from the people she considered to be closest to her. She hadn't said goodbye to her mother or her brother/sister, or Jessie. As a matter of fact, he thought, Shelley had stopped going out with Jessie more than a month ago, and she hadn't even mentioned her at all in quite a while. Now Shelley was taking Dash farther away from his family, for the price of fame, she had said. Dash didn't feel right about the move to Nashville; however, he felt it was inevitable. The force was going forward, and he couldn't do anything to stop it.

When they moved into their new house in November, Dash was not comfortable. The weather was unnaturally warm so close to Thanksgiving. He didn't like the abundance of bugs. The city was so large, he didn't know how he would ever find his way around it. How would he find the band that would lead him to stardom? He didn't want to join a country band, but he couldn't find any rock bands who needed a guitarist in Nashville. He didn't see how his dream matched up with being in Nashville; but he still did his best to be a good father and a faithful, yet unhappy, husband.

Dash and Shelley didn't have the cooking pans and utensils they needed to make Thanksgiving dinner, so they found a restaurant that was open and celebrated their holiday there. They ordered the special of the day: turkey dinner.

"I have an announcement to make," Shelley said, tapping her spoon on her glass.

"What is it, Mom?" Britney Emily asked, grabbing another dinner roll.

"We are going to have another baby!" Shelley said with a smile.

26

During the holiday season, Dash was quiet and reserved. He loved McCartney and Britney Emily, but he was so angry with Shelley and the way she had been manipulating his life. He knew the baby couldn't be his; he and Shelley hadn't slept together in nearly a year. Now he was trapped in Nashville. He wondered if Jessie had known about Shelley's unfaithfulness. He guessed that might be the reason Jessie had disappeared from their lives so quickly. As Dash went from audition to audition for country and western bands, he felt like he could finally identify with many of their songs: his life had become a broken-heart country song. He missed his family and friends, during this Christmas season so far from home. Shelley went overboard decorating the house and filling it with presents. The Christmas tree and holiday lights around town seemed out of place, since the weather was so warm. On Christmas day, while eating leftovers which had been heated in the microwave, Dash couldn't help thinking of his mom's traditional Christmas dinner, with the whole family around the table: Zaqui's favorite kind of Christmas. Dash wondered how much Zaqui had grown. Shelley had been in such a hurry to move, they hadn't had a chance to see Dari and her family before they left.

Although Shelley was rapidly gaining weight, she was able to get Dashell Wiring established and in business shortly after the beginning of the new year. She began scheduling jobs for Dash, which took much longer than they had in Spokane, mainly for two reasons. First of all, he didn't know his way around Nashville, which was so much bigger than Spokane, so it took him a lot longer to get from place to place. Secondly, the entire pace of the whole area was so slow. Every time he spoke to clients on the phone or went to buy supplies, people just talked and moved more slowly than they did in Spokane. People were always asking him to slow down and repeat himself. Dash tried not to get impatient, but his working days were longer and their income was smaller.

Dash missed the fellowship of friends and other musicians, so he frequently went into music stores to meet people and check the job boards. He called Janeena, who already had a working band and was quite well established with the contacts she and Walter had made in Nashville. She gave Dash a couple of possibilities, but they didn't lead anywhere. Dash didn't have a place to practice playing his guitar; their third bedroom, which he had envisioned becoming his music area, had already been decorated for the baby. Shelley didn't want the girls to share their room with the baby.

Shelley decided that Dash needed a cell phone so she would be able contact him any time he was on the job. She told Dash she again had a high-risk pregnancy and was confined to the house until the baby was due in June. Dash spent his days working, driving from one side of Nashville to the other several times per day. In the evenings when he arrived home, he fixed dinner for the family, as Shelley spent more and more time sitting at the computer. She was living on Pepsi, ice cream and peanut butter cups, insisting that every other kind of food made her sick. When Dash made dinner for his family each night, he fixed a plate for Shelley. He included foods from the all the food groups, but she wouldn't touch it. She refused to go the doctor during her pregnancy, since they didn't have insurance. Shelley said they didn't have anything in their budget to pay for health care. She was so easily irritated all the time during the pregnancy, Dash couldn't wait for her to have the baby so she might start behaving somewhat normally again.

Britney Emily was losing patience with Shelley. One day she confided to Dash that she was afraid of her mother and wanted to move back to Spokane with her dad. As she was speaking quietly to Dash, Shelley interrupted their conversation.

"What are you two talking about, so secretive?" Shelley asked.

"I hate it here!" Britney Emily shouted at her mother. "I want to go home!"

"This IS your home!" Shelley screamed at her.

"I mean my real home, with my real dad!"

"No! Your real home is here, with your mother!"

"I don't have any friends here!"

"You didn't have any friends there!"

"I want to go home, where I have my own room, and can go to school!"

"Don't even talk about that! You can't leave us! You have to STAY HERE!"

"I hate it here!" Britney Emily yelled, running into her room and slamming the door.

"I wish I had left Herbert when I first found out I was pregnant," Shelley said to Dash, after Britney Emily had left the room. "Then he would never know about Britney Emily and she would never know there was another kind of life."

Shelley's confession stuck in Dash's mind. He knew at that moment that if he ever left Shelley, he would never see his kids again. She gave him no choice. He had to stay with her if he wanted to have a relationship with his children.

One evening when Dash got in his car after finishing

a job at a small business, his cell phone rang. Shelley sounded frantic.

"Where have you been?" she asked.

"I was working," he answered. "Is everything all right?"

"Why didn't you answer your phone?"

"I was working. I couldn't answer the phone. I was pulling wires."

"What if it was an emergency?"

"Was it?"

"It coulda been."

"But was it?"

"No, but I coulda been in labor."

"The baby isn't due for another six weeks."

"That doesn't mean anything."

"So, why are you calling?"

"Oh, never mind. It's not important." She hung up. Dash wasn't sure why she had called.

When Dash came in the house, Shelley was sitting at the computer, and she was very angry.

"Get me some more Pepsi," she demanded, without moving her eyes from the computer screen.

"You already had, what, eight cans today? You shouldn't be drinking so much pop."

"You're not my boss! You can't tell me what to do! I need another Pepsi!"

"How can that be good for you? And for the baby? Have you eaten any real food today? The baby needs nutritious food."

"Don't tell me what to do! Just get me some Pepsi, and get it NOW!"

Dash went to the store, bought another case of Pepsi, and brought it home. Once she opened the can, she was in a much better mood.

"So, what do you want to name the baby?"

"I thought we already decided on Heather for a girl or Tyler for a boy."

"Tyler, okay, Tyler Daniel, after your dad."

"Are you going to change it at the last minute, like you did with McCartney?"

"No way!" she said.

"Because I don't want Harrison or Ringo for a son."

"I wouldn't do that! We decided on Tyler together, so it's going to be Tyler."

"Or Heather, for a girl."

"Heather, for a girl," she agreed.

On a Sunday morning in June, Shelley woke up with a scream.

"I'm going into labor!" she shrieked.

"Get up, let's go," Dash said, as calmly as he could.

"You know I can't get out of bed by myself! I'm too fat!"

"Here, I'll help you. Take my hand."

"Owww! It hurts! Call the ambulance!"

"Just get up, come on, I'll take you to the hospital." He pulled her up and out of the bed. He went down the hall to the girls' room and opened the door.

"Brit-Em, I'm taking Mom to the hospital to have the baby. I'll come and get you as soon as the baby is born so you and McCartney can meet your new brother or sister."

The girls were still in bed. Britney Emily nodded. By now she had plenty of experience taking care of McCartney.

She had been McCartney's primary caregiver since they had moved to Nashville.

The baby came quickly after they arrived at in the birthing room. They didn't have time for any drama or for anyone else to be with them for the birth. Shortly after noon, Shelley gave birth to a healthy baby boy.

Dash was so thrilled to hold his baby boy in his arms.

"Tyler, my son," he said. "Tyler Daniel."

Shelley fell asleep, exhausted. The nurse took Tyler Daniel and told Dash to go home. Dash wanted to stay, but she told him he should get some rest and come back later.When he brought Britney Emily and McCartney to the hospital later that day to meet their brother, he was not surprised to learn that Shelley had officially named their son Lennon.

Lennon did not look like anyone in the family: instead of curly brown hair like Dash and McCartney, or straight blond hair like Shelley and Britney Emily, he had coarse red hair. His face was oblong, not wide like the rest of the family members' faces. He didn't smile the first four months of his life. He looked angry and cried often, and he wouldn't respond to his mother at all.

Dash loved little Lennon so much. He identified with his unspoken pain. He wanted to comfort him, to make him feel better. He made sure Lennon felt wanted. Lennon bonded with Dash, but he didn't bond with his mother. She didn't have much time for him. She spent between fourteen and eighteen hours each day sitting at the computer, 'working.'

27

After nearly a year of searching for an opportunity to play with a band in Nashville and leaving his number in every music store in the city, Dash finally got a call on his cell phone from an interested party.

"May I speak to Dash?" a male voice asked.

"This is Dash speaking."

"Hi, Dash. My name is Corby Waste and I got your number from Jimmie Thomas down at the music store. He said you play guitar."

"Yes, sir."

"Do you play country?"

"Yes, sir."

"Do you play rock?"

"Yes, I can play just about anything."

"Do you play by ear, or do you read music?"

"I can do both."

"Have you heard of Patrick Neptune?"

"Yeah, sure! He's the fastest rising star in Nashville right now."

"That's what we believe. He's in need of a good guitar player, right away. Can you come on down and let us hear what you can do, say, this evening at 5:00?"

"Sure!" Dash got the address from Mr. Waste and called his five o'clock appointment and rescheduled. He didn't call Shelley; she wasn't expecting him to be home until about nine anyway.

Dash drove to an unfamiliar part of town and found the offices of Neptune Enterprises. He arrived a few minutes early and entered the elegant building. A pretty young woman was standing in the lobby.

"You must be Dash," she said, smiling.

"Yes, I have an appointment at five with Mr. Corby Waste."

"I'm Melissa. I work for Neptune Enterprises. Come on in, meet the gang."

"I was wondering which guitar I should bring with me, my acoustic or electric?"

"Oh, they have plenty of guitars inside for you to use."

Dash followed Melissa to a large room where two men were waiting.

"This is Dash," said Melissa, "and this is Mr. Neptune and his manager, Mr. Waste."

"Nice to meet you, both of you," Dash said.

"Dash," Patrick Neptune said, extending a hand. He was tall and blond with brilliant blue eyes that smiled. Dash shook his hand and then Corby's.

"Do you know any of Patrick's stuff?" Corby asked.

"I have heard a few of his songs on the radio, but I haven't ever tried to play them."

"Here, can you play this?" Patrick asked, handing Dash some sheet music. "Feel free to improvise on this part right here."

"Sure, I can do this," Dash said, looking over the music. It looked like a basic chord progression, not too difficult to follow.

"Can you play a twelve-string?" Corby asked.

"Yeah, I have one at home," Dash said.

"Great! Why don't you play this song on that guitar?" Corby asked, indicating one of the guitars in a row of about twenty.

Dash glanced at the song one more time, heard it in his head and memorized it. He picked up the guitar and started to play. He played it well. During the second verse, Patrick started to sing. When they finished that song, Corby handed Dash another song and then another. At about seven-thirty, Corby stopped the duo and took Patrick aside for a few minutes.

"We would like for you to play with us," Corby announced. "Patrick is going on his first world tour, beginning in Europe. We are leaving next Friday. We've tried out a dozen or more guitarists, and you are by far the best. You've got what it takes. What do you think? Do you want to go with us, as lead guitarist?"

Dash's heart leaped in his chest. Then he thought about Shelley. She had to support this venture. This was their reason for moving to Nashville in the first place. This was what he had worked toward ever since he was a child.

"I'll let my wife know, and I'll be ready to go," Dash said, trying to contain his excitement.

"We'll also be recording some of the shows so we can make a live concert video and a CD," Corby said. "I'll call you and we'll get a contract set up for you to sign. Oh, about the pay. We'll be going to 60 cities in 90 days. All your expenses will be paid. Plus you'll get $1000 for each show. If you get sick or can't do a show, you don't get paid."

"That sounds great," Dash said.

"Now, if you'll just fill out some papers so we have your personal information on file, Melissa will hook you up with everything you need."

"Shell, our dream is finally coming true," he said as soon as he came in the door.

"What do you mean?" she asked, turning from the computer to look at him.

"I auditioned for Patrick Neptune! They thought I was great, and they want me to go with them on a world tour, starting next Friday!"

"I didn't know you had an audition scheduled today," she replied, irritated.

"They just called me today, and I went over and auditioned."

"You can't go," she said.

"What do you mean? This is what we've been waiting for."

"If you start going on tours, your kids will never see you. They'll never know you. You won't know them."

"Shell, this has been our plan all along."

"Maybe this was YOUR plan all along."

"When we got married, you said you were supporting my music and my career as a musician."

"It was different then. Now you have a family."

"They will be paying me a huge amount, and we can use it to pay off our bills, or where ever we need it. We'll have lots of extra money, and this could lead to a permanent position with a world-famous band."

"You can't go," she repeated.

"Shell, this is why we moved to Nashville in the first place, so I could make it big. This is big."

"No! You can't leave me alone in this God-forsaken place to take care of your kids. You can't do that to me."

"You can take the kids and live anywhere. You don't have to stay here. I'm going to be making a lot of money, and when I come home, I'll come to where ever you are."

"No, you can't do this to me."

"I'm not doing anything to you. This is for us."

"You can't go!"

"Shell, this is what I've always wanted to do, my whole life."

"What about what I want? Don't you care what I want?"

"I thought you wanted this. I thought you were supporting me. I told you all about this before we even got married."

"Well, now we are married, and you have responsibilities, to me and to your children."

"Shelley, I'm going to go on tour with them."

"You are just going to abandon us?"

"No, I'll be back after the tour."

"Forget it, you're not going."

"Yes, I am going. This is why we came to Nashville. This is about the best offer I could ever have."

Despite Shelley's protests, Dash was determined to go. He began collecting items he would need to take with him on the world tour. He decided to take all three of his guitars, and he bought plenty of spare strings and picks. He couldn't believe this was finally happening! He had been dreaming about this all of his life, for as long as he could remember.

He finished the wiring jobs he had in progress, and didn't make appointments for any new clients. He and Shelley wouldn't need the income from Dashell Wiring any more. He was so excited, he couldn't eat.

Dash called his mom and told her the good news. She was so excited for him. She promised to call Shelley weekly to check on her and the kids. He called Dari and she prayed with him over the phone. He tried to call O.K., but couldn't get him, so he left a message.

Dash got his passport and all the shots he would need. He got his luggage together and selected a few outfits he would be wearing over the next few months. Neptune Enterprises would be providing his stage outfits.

He talked with Shelley a few more times and she reluctantly agreed that this would be good for both of them. He promised that he would stay in touch and if either of them or one of the kids had any type of problem, he would come back to Nashville. His cell phone had a worldwide calling plan, so she would be able to reach him almost anywhere he went.

By the next Tuesday, Dash was finishing up his final job before the tour. He hadn't yet heard from Corby Waste about signing the contract. He tried to call him using his cell phone, but the phone didn't work. When he got home, he went to the computer to ask Shelley about it.

"I have been trying to call you all day!" she shouted at him as soon as she saw him.

"My cell phone isn't working," he said.

"Oh, that's right! It must have been turned off."

"Turned off? Why would it be turned off?"

"Because you didn't pay the bill."

"What are you talking about? You told me you were paying all the bills online."

"No, this one YOU were supposed to pay."

"Why didn't you tell me you weren't paying it?"

"I don't have to tell you every single thing."

"So, now my cell phone is turned off, and I've been expecting a call from Patrick Neptune's manager."

"Oh, he called here yesterday and I already talked to him."

"What did he say?"

"He wanted you to come down and sign some papers

and stuff, but I told him you changed your mind and you weren't interested."

"You WHAT?"

"I told him you weren't interested in going on the tour."

"Shelley! You know I want to go! Why did you tell him I wasn't interested?"

"I told him you are looking for something closer to home. You can't leave us alone like that. We talked about it and we decided that this wasn't the best career move for you."

"We didn't decide that!"

"Yes, we did! Don't you care about your own wife? Don't you care about your own flesh and blood? Do you want your kids to grow up and not know who you are?"

"This is only for a few months, and then I'll be back home."

"I would never let you do that to your own kids! They have a right to see you, even if you don't want to see them."

"This is my career! This might be the only chance I'll ever get!"

"You'll get another chance, a much better chance. That will be best for the whole family."

"Shell..." he began, then he realized that nothing he said would make a difference to her.

He dialed Corby Waste's number from their home phone.

"Neptune Enterprises, Melissa speaking."

"Hi Melissa, this is Dash. I met you last week. How are you doing?"

"Oh, hi, Dash. I've been really busy getting everything ready to go so we can all leave on Friday. I'm so sorry you're not coming with us on the tour."

"Can I please speak to Mr. Waste?"

"He left for London this morning. You know, you were so much better than the guy they chose, but since you can't go with us, they had to take the second best. He was a really far second, too. You were really great. I was wishing you could come, but Corby told us that you had changed your mind. I'm really sorry."

"Okay, thanks. Well, maybe I'll see you around.

"We'll all be back in a few months," she said.

28

After living in Nashville for nearly two years, Dash and Shelley were deeper in debt than ever. Dash wasn't any closer to being in a band than when they first arrived. Shelley scheduled Dash to work for Dashell Wiring from eight in the morning until nine or ten at night, seven days a week. She made a practice of scheduling his jobs and estimates so he would have to drive from one side of town to the other several times each day. He didn't have any time for himself. Every day he deposited all the checks he received for the jobs he did, and he gave Shelley the cash he earned. She was aware of every dollar he had, and she made sure he gave it all to her. She gave him ten dollars each day for gas and lunch. He usually skipped lunch. When he arrived home, Shelley was always sitting at the computer, the kitchen had no food in it, and the kids were hungry. Every night, Dash went to the grocery store to buy something for dinner, then he came home and cooked it. Their normal dinner time was near midnight. Shelley didn't eat dinner. She stayed on the new computer she had just purchased until three or four in the morning, much to the irritation of Dash, who had a hard time sleeping while she was pounding on the keyboard in their room.

Shelley also traded her little car for a new van, insisting that she needed it with the three kids. Dash wondered about that, since she didn't go anywhere; but Shelley said she had figured it all into their budget. One night when Dash came home, he found the kids in front of a large screen TV in the living room.

"Where did this come from?" Dash asked Britney Emily.

"Some guys delivered it."

"Where is our other TV?"

"Mom told them to put it in Lennon's room so he can watch cartoons."

"He's just a baby. He doesn't need a TV in his room."

"I wish we had a TV in our room," Britney Emily said, "like I do at home at my real dad's house."

Dash went to the bedroom to ask Shelley about her latest purchase.

"Shell, why did you buy that huge TV?"

"We need it."

"We don't need it."

"The kids need something to do all day while I'm working."

"So you bought a giant TV to baby sit them?"

"Are you saying that I'm not a good mother?"

"No, I'm just wondering. How much did it cost?"

"That's none of your business! I got a great deal over the Internet!"

"Shell, we need to talk about these kinds of things before you go out and just buy them."

"If you don't like it, why don't you just divorce me? And don't forget, you'll be paying lots of child support!"

Dash didn't bother to respond.

About a month later, Dash was surprised to see Shelley in the front room when he came home.

"Come and see what I got!" she said, grinning.

"What did you get?" he asked apprehensively.

"Out in the back yard," she said, pulling him to the back door.

"She got us some puppies!" Britney Emily said.

"Puppies! Shell, we haven't talked about getting a dog."

"They were on special! I got a real bargain."

"Bargain dogs?"

"Yeah, they were real cheap."

She opened the door and Dash saw two puppies chained to a stake.

"What kind are they?" he asked, going down the steps to pet them.

"They are twin pit bulls."

"Pit bulls! Shell, we shouldn't have pit bulls around the kids."

"Oh, they'll be all right. They'll grow up together."

"Out of all the kinds of dogs, why did you get pit bulls?"

"They are worth a lot of money. I got them for just three hundred bucks each, and they're worth almost a thousand bucks!"

"What are their names?" he asked.

"That one is Rigby, and that one is MacKenzie," Shelley said.

"So, we can call them Eleanor and Father?" Dash asked.

"No! I told you, Rigby and MacKenzie!" Shelley insisted. She yelled to Dash that she had an errand to run and would be back in a few hours.

Dash took the kids into the house and the phone rang.

"I need to talk to Shelley," Suzie demanded.

"She isn't here right now," Dash said politely.

"Where is she?" Suzie barked.

"I don't know, she just took off. She said she had an errand to run," Dash said.

"I just want to let her know that her Uncle Rocky is out

of prison, and he might be coming to get her."

"Uncle Rocky?"

"Didn't she tell you about him?" Dash could hear Suzie smoking.

"No, she hasn't mentioned an Uncle Rocky."

"Well, it's ancient history. She should have told you all about him by now."

"Who is he?"

"Her dad's brother, the one she sent to prison."

"The one she what?"

"She said he raped her, so he went to prison. He said he would get her for falsely accusing him. After he had been in for a couple of years, Shelley told me he didn't really do it, but she was mad at him for telling Herbert that she cheated on him. Her Uncle Rocky saw Shelley at a motel with another man."

"Oh, really?"

"Yep. He's been in for almost fifteen years, and he just got out. He always swore that he would get her as soon as he got out."

"I'll be sure to tell her," Dash said.

When Shelley came home, Dash told her about the phone call.

"Shell, your mom called right after you left."

"Did you talk to her?"

"Yeah, and she told me about your Uncle Rocky."

"My what?" she screamed. "I don't have an Uncle Rocky! You stay out of my business! Don't you have enough to do without trying to make up some garbage about someone who doesn't even exist?"

"Your mom was just trying to warn you--"

"Don't bring Mama into it! I don't need her help! Do you think I don't see what's going on? I know exactly what you are trying to do, and it' s not working! You are not going to get away with it!" Shelley slammed the bedroom door.

One evening a few weeks later, Dash bought a latte when he stopped for gas after his last job of the day. As he was driving home, he felt enshrouded in dread. He loved his kids more than anything and wanted to be with them, but he couldn't stand living with Shelley for another day. He saw a semi truck coming towards him in the opposite lane, and he imagined it veering over into his lane and killing him. The idea of death was a welcome alternative to the life sentence he was currently serving. He didn't want to go to his own house and face Shelley again. He went home anyway.

When he came in the house, Shelley noticed the cup in his hand. "Did you buy an Expresso?" she asked accusingly.

"Do you mean Espresso?" he corrected, not caring how angry she might get. She was angry all the time now, no matter what Dash said or did.

"You know what I mean."

"No, I bought a latte."

"I thought you didn't like coffee."

"I don't."

"Then why did you buy that?"

"I just wanted to try it."

"Those are so expensive."

"I know, I just wanted to try one."

"Have you ever bought one before?"

"No, have you?"

"No, I don't drink coffee, it's not good for you."

"It's not coffee, it's a latte."

"Are you going to start buying them every day? Because that is going to be pretty expensive."

"No, I might buy one a year. Or less."

"You shouldn't waste your money on them."

"I'm not planning to buy them any more. Ever."

"Good. You shouldn't."

The next night when Dash came home from work, he found a brand new Espresso maker, still in the box, on the table.

"What's this?" he asked.

"It's an Expresso maker," Shelley said.

"I can see that. Why is it here?"

"I bought it for you."

"Why?"

"To save money."

"How can this save money?"

"It was on sale for only two hundred bucks, so now you can make Expresso at home and you don't have to buy them any more."

"I wasn't planning to buy them any more."

"Well, now you don't have to."

"Thanks."

Dash knew Shelley's spur-of-the-moment purchases where partly the cause of their financial struggles. He tried to approach the subject, but Shelley refused to discuss it.

"Just leave me alone! You have no idea how hard this is!" she yelled.

"Shell, I'm just wondering how we are paying for all these things."

"You do your job and I'll do mine!"

"But you have been saying we were tight on money."

"You just have to work harder! You are so lazy! And you don't know anything!" she shouted. "Now, just LEAVE ME ALONE! I have WORK to do!"

During the summer, Shelley took three trips home to visit her mother, who was dying of cancer. Britney Emily spent the summer with her dad, so Dash was left to take care of McCartney and Lennon, who had just turned four and two. This was the best summer he had had in a long time. He was able to make his own schedule, and he took the kids to a nearby day care while he worked eight hours a day, five days a week. He hadn't had a break from work in so long, he almost forgot what to do when he wasn't working.

He took the kids to the park the first day Shelley was gone, and he immediately realized that they didn't know how to play. They wouldn't even try to run across the grass. Lennon held his head to the side and just kind of shuffled his feet, while McCartney just walked. He took them to the swings, and they were afraid to get in them. He put them both on his lap and demonstrated how to swing. He convinced them that this was a fun activity. Neither of them would go on the merry-go-round, but they did finally go down the small slide after much coaxing and sliding by Dash. Had Dash not been having so much fun playing with his kids, he might have felt sad that they had been deprived of this for so long. He made up his mind that he would spend more time with them, especially after Shelley came home.

Lennon hadn't started talking yet. McCartney, glad to finally have an audience, was talking nonstop. She told her daddy all about things they had seen on TV, their only exposure to the world. She asked for all kinds of things she had seen on commercials, and Dash promised they would find them in the stores to see if she still liked them when she saw them in real life. Lennon, whom Shelley had described as uncooperative and incorrigible, was actually very obedient and eager to please his daddy.

"Daddy," McCartney said.

"What is it, Carty?" Dash answered.

"Do you really love us?"

"Of course I do. I love you more than anyone in the world."

"Then why don't you work harder?"

"What do you mean?"

"Mommy said that if you really loved us, you would work harder so we could have more money to buy good food that we like."

"Sweetheart, I love you and I work very hard. Mommy has money for food."

"She said she doesn't have enough because you are too lazy and you don't work hard enough."

"I work as hard as I can. But from now on, I'm going to be spending more time with you and Lennon."

"You are?"

"Yes, I am."

"Promise?"

"I promise."

Dash envisioned what life would be like without Shelley, with just his children. He loved them so much. The summer was so peaceful and wonderful. He wondered if he had any chance of getting custody of them if he asked Shelley for a divorce. He was cleaning up the kitchen after baking brownies with McCartney and Lennon when the phone rang.

"Dash?" It sounded like Shelley's mom.

"Yes, this is Dash."

"Put Shelley on the line," she demanded.

"Who is this?" he asked.

"Don't you recognize your own mother-in-law's voice?" she yelled. She sounded as if she might be drunk.

"How are you doing?" he asked.

"I'm fine, what do think? Since when do you care about me? Now, put Shelley on!"

"Shelley isn't here," he said.

"Of course she's there," she said, coughing. "Where else would she be?"

"She's out visiting you."

"What are you talking about? I haven't seen her since you moved away."

"Oh, well, she said --"

"Tell her to call me as soon as she can. The police have been all over here, asking about Jessie."

"Jessie? What about Jessie?"

"She's missing, you dim wit! Don't you know anything?"

"I hadn't heard that she was missing."

"Don't you ever read the paper?"

"Actually --"

"She's been missing for almost a month. Did she come down and visit you?"

"Not that I know of. I haven't seen her since before we moved."

"Well, join the club! You two are the hardest people to contact in the world!" Suzie hung up without saying good-bye.

Dash didn't care where Shelley was, and he almost wished that she were the one who was missing. He was concerned about Jessie, but he couldn't do anything for her. All he could do right now was to take care of his kids and spend precious time with them. Shelley's mother obviously wasn't dying of cancer. Shelley was spending her summer somewhere else, most likely with someone else. Dash hoped she would meet a man she liked better than Dash and would leave him and the kids for her new man.

When Shelley returned a few days later, Dash watched her carefully to see if she would betray her whereabouts all summer. She quickly returned to her routine of 'working' at the computer for hours on end, completely ignoring the family and not mentioning anything about her three vacations. Dash decided to not ask her about them.

Although Shelley still scheduled Dash to work late hours, he finished early as often as possible, so he could spend a lot of time with his kids. One evening when he came home early, he was playing with McCartney and Lennon in the above ground swimming pool in the back yard. Rigby and MacKenzie, starved for attention, were running around the yard in a frenzy. Shelley came outside and was surprised to see Dash there.

"What are you doing here?" she demanded.

"I live here," he answered.

"Why aren't you working?"

"I got finished a little early and came to play with the kids."

"You should be at work!" she screamed.

"I'm all finished for today," he said. "Come on, do you want to play in the pool with us?"

"Unlike SOME people, I HAVE to work," she said. "You shouldn't be playing with them now."

"Are you saying I shouldn't be playing with my kids?"

"They ARE NOT your kids!" she shouted, loud enough for all the neighbors inside their houses to hear. McCartney and Lennon both began to cry.

"Yes, you are my kids," he said quietly, comforting them.

"McCartney may be, but Lennon definitely is NOT!" she yelled.

"You are BOTH my kids," he said. They looked up at him, reassured.

"Why don't you get a DNA test and find out?" she challenged.

"I don't need to find out anything. These are my kids." He was the only father they knew, and he felt as if they were his kids more than they were Shelley's.

"You just try and divorce me, then we'll see whose kids they are," she warned.

"We're just playing, okay? Don't you have to get back to work?"

"Don't YOU tell me what to do! You don't own me!" She slammed the door.

Dash continued playing in the pool with McCartney and Lennon until sunset.

At the end of summer when Britney Emily returned from Spokane, she was determined to go back to Spokane to live with her dad. Shelley refused to entertain the idea, although she did agree, after a long, heated discussion over the phone with Herbert that Britney Emily could go to school this year. The placement tests showed that Britney Emily was nearly three years behind her ninth grade class; however, the school officials agreed to let her enter the eighth grade. Shelley was outraged and enrolled Britney Emily in a private school across town. Dash would need to drive her to school every morning.

Dash was not pleased with the fact that the two younger children were virtually on their own all day. He made an effort to stop by the house to check on them between jobs whenever possible. McCartney was quite satisfied to watch TV on the big screen all day, patiently waiting to eat until Dash came home. Lennon, on the other hand, liked to explore the house and look for food, so Shelley put a lock on his door and kept him locked in his room.

"How can he go to the bathroom?" Dash asked her, since he was in the process of toilet training him.

"Until he learns to behave, he will just have to wear his diapers while he is in his room," she snorted.

The next week, Dash was extremely upset to see that Shelley had fastened Lennon's diaper with duct tape.

"Shell, why is this diaper taped to Lennon's skin?"

"He keeps taking it off," she explained, her eyes fixed on the computer. "You just try going in that room with all those diapers all over the floor."

Dash looked in Lennon's room. The floor was covered with every toy and every piece of clothing Lennon owned. Several old diapers were scattered around the room. Dash got a plastic bag, collected the diapers, and put them in the trash. He felt sick to think that his son had been playing among them. Dash called Lennon to help him, and together, with McCartney volunteering also, they put all of the toys in the toy boxes and the clothes in the dresser. Lennon still didn't say a word, but he did smile at Dash and hug him whenever the opportunity arose.

At Christmas time that year, Dash felt very homesick. This is my favorite kind of Christmas, with all the family here together at Grandma and Grandpa's house, Zaqui's little voice said in his head. He missed his family so much.

Zaqui was almost ten now. He couldn't imagine how much she had grown. If Dari had sent any recent pictures, he hadn't seen them.

As Dash put Britney Emily on the plane to go visit her dad for Christmas, Dash wished he were going home to Washington State also. Shelley had purchased a pile of presents which were sitting under the pre-decorated artificial Christmas tree she had bought. Business had slowed a little; people weren't thinking of wiring their houses and business at this time of the year. Dash had more time to spend with McCartney and Lennon. He bought a turkey and prepared Christmas dinner for the family. Shelley left the computer long enough to watch the kids open their gifts, then she said she had to get back to work. Dash enjoyed Christmas day with McCartney and Lennon, and they ate their feast without Shelley, who was too busy to join them. Dash said a silent prayer, believing that God was working on the situation, and that all things would work out for the best, because of God's love and Dash's faithfulness to his family.

29

The next summer, one afternoon between jobs, Dash was at the gas station when his cell phone rang.

"Dash!"

"Dari!"

"Where are you?"

"I'm in Nashville. Where are you?"

"I'm at home. I mean, are you on your way to the airport?"

"No... should I be?'

"Aren't you going to pick up Zaqui? Or is Shelley going to pick her up?"

"What are you talking about?"

"Zaqui is waiting for you at the airport."

"She's here?"

"Didn't Shelley tell you?"

"Tell me what?"

"That Zaqui was coming to visit you for a week."

"Really? No, she didn't say anything about it."

"She didn't? We've been planning this since the beginning of summer. She said you knew all about it."

"Man! She didn't say anything to me about it."

"Well, Zaqui just called me, and she is at the airport waiting for someone to pick her up. I just talked to Shelley yesterday, and she said you would be there to meet her."

"I'm on my way. I'm only a few minutes from the airport."

He got the flight number and sped to the airport. He saw ten-year-old Zaqui waiting near the ticket counter. She had grown so much in five years! Her face lit up when she saw him and she ran to give him a hug. He lifted her up and swung her around.

"Uncle Dash!"

"Kwee-Kwee!"

"Where's Britney Emily and McCartney and Lennon?"

"Britney Emily is at her dad's for the summer and McCartney and Lennon are at home with Aunt Shelley."

"I'm so glad you came to get me. I thought you forgot about me."

"How could I forget about my favorite niece?"

"Uncle Dash, I'm your only niece."

"You're still my favorite," he said.

"Uncle Dash, my hair is just like yours now! Look!"

"I think mine is longer when I pull it down," he said. "Let's compare." They each stretched a curl down nearly to their waists.

"Uncle Dash, they are just the same! See?"

"You're right!"

"We have the good hair, don't we, Uncle Dash?"

"Yes, we do, my little Z-Bug. Good and curly."

"Uncle Dash, what are we going to do while I'm here visiting you?" Zaqui asked.

"Well, I don't have it all planned, but on my day off, we can go to the zoo."

"Do you have to work while I'm here?"

"Yes, most of the days I have to work."

"But Aunt Shelley told Mommy that you had time to do stuff with me."

"I do have to work, but I'll make time to be with you."

"Thanks, Uncle Dash."

"I'll tell you what. I have just one more job to do today. Do you want to go with me and help me?"

"Can I?" Her eyes grew wide.

Zaqui proved to be a good helper, and they finished the next job quickly. Dash took her home. McCartney and Lennon were so excited to see another child in the house. They didn't know who she was. About an hour after they got home, Shelley came out of the bedroom.

"What's going on? What's all this noise?" she snapped.

"Hi, Aunt Shelley," Zaqui said.

"Hi, Sweetie!" Shelley said, her voice immediately different. Dash recognized that familiar voice from long ago... yes, that was the sweet voice Shelley had used before they were married.

"Shelley, did you forget to mention that I needed to pick her up at the airport today?"

"No, I told you."

"When?"

"The other day."

"You didn't mention anything about it to me."

"You never listen to me."

"You didn't tell me. Dari called me and I was near the airport, so Zaqui didn't have to wait too long."

"That's why I scheduled you to work over in that part of town," she explained.

"You didn't even tell me she was coming."

"Yes, I did."

"I don't recall you mentioning it."

"You have to work all day tomorrow, you know. You

can't be playing with Zaqui."

"I know."

"And McCartney starts school on Monday, you know."

"I know. Is this really the best time for Zaqui to be here?"

"Sure, we have been talking about it all summer. Zaqui can play with McCartney and Lennon."

"I just think it's a little strange that you didn't mention it to me."

"I did too! You weren't listening!" Shelley stomped back into the bedroom.

The next evening Dash finished working early so he could spend some time with Zaqui, McCartney and Lennon. When he came in the house, McCartney and Lennon were sitting on the couch watching TV.

"Carty, where's Zaqui?' he asked.

"She's outside, in the back," McCartney said, keeping her eyes on the screen.

"What's she doing out there by herself?" Dash asked, going to the back door.

"I don't know. She didn't come in when we did," McCartney said.

Dash opened the door and saw his niece huddled in the pool, shivering. Rigby and MacKenzie were running loose in the yard. He called them and put them on their chain.

"Z-Bug, what are you doing in the pool?" he asked.

"Uncle Dash, please don't get mad at me," she begged, nearly in tears.

"Mad? I can't get mad at my favorite niece."

"I couldn't get out," she cried.

"Why not?" he said, reaching to help her.

"I was scared of the dogs. When Aunt Shelley came out and told us to go in the house, the dogs were running around and they kept barking at me. McCartney and Lennon just ran by them. I tried to get out of the pool, but the dogs wouldn't let me."

"Come on, they're chained up now," Dash said, pulling her out of the pool. He wrapped a towel around her. Although the evening was warm and muggy, the water in the pool was cold.

"Thanks, Uncle Dash. Look, I'm pruning," she said, holding out her hands so Dash could see her wrinkled finger tips.

"How long were you in the pool?" Dash asked.

"Since the afternoon," Zaqui said.

"Was Aunt Shelley out here with you while you were swimming with McCartney and Lennon?"

"No, she just let us come out here and told me to watch them in the pool, then she came out later and told us to come in."

Dash was very upset with Shelley when they went inside. He left Zaqui to change into her clothes while he went to confront Shelley quietly in the bedroom.

"Shell, did you know Zaqui has been in the pool since this afternoon?"

"Oh, really? I told her to come in a long time ago," Shelley answered, uninterested.

"She's afraid of the dogs. Why didn't you chain them up?"

"I told her not to be afraid."

"Shell, those are pit bulls, and they were barking at her. She was scared of them."

"She didn't have to be scared. I told her not to be."

"That's not the point! She was scared and you didn't help her!"

"What's your problem? Why are you always accusing me?"

"Shelley!"

"What's the matter with you? Why are you freaking out over nothing? You always do that."

"And you left the kids out in the pool unsupervised!"

"I was watching them from the window."

"Yeah, sure you were."

"Are you saying that I'm a liar?"

"I'm saying that you were not being responsible for the kids. We agreed that they can't go in the back yard with the pool and the dogs without one of us with them."

"Zaqui was there. She's big enough to watch them in the pool."

"Shell, we don't even know if she can swim!"

"But she can stand up in the pool. It's not over her head."

"Shell, I can't believe you."

"You ARE calling me a liar!" she screamed.

"You don't have to yell."

"You just get away from me and stop accusing me! If you don't like the way I handle things, why don't you just divorce me? You don't know anything!"

The next day was Monday, McCartney's first day of school. Zaqui helped Dash pick out an outfit for her to wear, and she combed McCartney's hair. McCartney looked so cute. Dash thought about how, at Zaqui's age,

Britney Emily had become an unwilling baby-sitter of her tiny baby sister.

"Uncle Dash, what am I going to do all day today when you go to work?" she asked, as he was leaving to drive McCartney to school.

"You can play with Lennon until I come home. I'll be home early."

"Okay, Uncle Dash. When is your day off?"

"Tomorrow," he decided.

That evening when he returned, the three kids were watching TV in the living room.

"Daddy!" McCartney said, leaping to give him a hug.

"Uncle Dash!" Zaqui said, getting up to hug him. Lennon didn't say anything, but he also hugged his dad.

"How are you doing today?" Dash asked.

"I hope you're not mad that I let Lennon out of his room," Zaqui said apologetically. "He was pounding on the door. You said I could play with him. I changed his diaper and got him dressed and helped him clean his room."

"Good girl, Kwee."

"I think Lennon is hungry," Zaqui continued, "because we couldn't find anything to eat after we had our cereal this morning and all the milk was gone."

"Didn't Aunt Shelley make some lunch for you?"

"I haven't seen her all day."

"Who wants to go to Burger King?" he asked. Three hands shot up and little voices shouted happily, "Me! Me! Me! Me!"

Dash called his two clients scheduled for the next day and rescheduled the jobs for the next week. He had so much fun with the kids at the restaurant. They were all laughing - even Lennon - and playing with each other, behaving as if they had a normal life. When they returned, Shelley was asleep in her chair at the computer. Dash didn't bother to wake her when he went to bed. At about three in the morning, he heard her pounding on the computer keyboard, as was her usual fashion.

Dash woke up early and fixed pancakes for the kids. Again, Zaqui helped him get McCartney dressed. She and Lennon rode with Dash to take McCartney to school. When Dash sent Lennon to go to the bathroom by himself, Zaqui had a few questions for Dash.

"Why doesn't Lennon talk?"

"He's just not ready yet, I guess."

"He's really smart. He can understand what I say to him, but he never answers. When McCartney is with him, she answers all the questions for him."

"Yeah, I noticed that."

"Uncle Dash, why is McCartney so skinny?'

"She just doesn't eat much."

"Why is she afraid of getting fat when she is so little?"

"She's not afraid of getting fat."

"She told me she doesn't want to eat very much because she doesn't want to get fat. Last night she didn't even eat her French fries! Lennon ate all of them."

"Lennon is hungry all the time," Dash said.

"McCartney's head looks too big for her body, like one of my dolls I have at home."

Dash considered this and realized it was painfully true. Zaqui continued.

"Her legs at the top are skinnier than my arms right here," she said, pointing to her wrists. "I can see all her bones."

Dash felt his heart ache. He was so accustomed to

how McCartney looked, he hadn't noticed that she was unnaturally thin for a five-year-old.

"Let's get ready to go to the zoo!" he said, as Lennon came out of the bathroom.

The three of them enjoyed their day at the Nashville Zoo. Zaqui rode on an elephant and they saw all the animals. Lennon looked as if he might say something. The uncommon smile on his face showed how happy he was. Dash noticed how cute Lennon was when he smiled. He didn't have that serious, worried look, like he usually did, as if he had the world on his shoulders. He looked at his daddy with trust and love.

Dash bought a pizza to take home, and they arrived just before the bus brought McCartney home from school. She handed him a note from her teacher as she went to play with her cousin.

Mr. and Mrs. Farrah, it said, Does McCartney have an eating disorder? She refused to eat any lunch yesterday or today. It was signed by Mrs. Bates.

As they ate the pizza, Dash observed McCartney. She took one bite and played with her food. Lennon and Zaqui each finished one piece and then a second piece before McCartney took another bite. She pushed away from the table. Lennon grabbed her pizza and devoured it.

"Carty, you didn't really eat," Dash said.

"I'm not hungry," she answered.

"Lennon always eats the rest of her food," Zaqui said.

Dash realized that McCartney had a problem that could be very serious, but he had no idea what to do about it.

"Carty, come back and eat some pizza," he said.

"I don't really like pizza," she said.

"Come on, it's really good."

"I don't want to get fat," she explained.

"Nobody can get fat from eating one piece of pizza."

"Are you sure?" she asked doubtfully.

"Yes, I'm sure."

"Promise?"

"Look at me. I ate three pieces, and I'm not fat, am I?"

She examined him carefully and then returned to the table and ate two pieces of pizza.

"Carty, you have to eat something at every meal. Your teacher is worried about you. You need to eat at school. I promise you won't get fat."

"Okay, Daddy," she agreed.

Dash felt bad about leaving Zaqui alone with Lennon the next couple of days while he went to work, but she seemed to enjoy taking care of him. When he came home early on Friday to take her to the airport, Zaqui was buzzing with excitement.

"Uncle Dash! Uncle Dash! Lennon talked!" she said, jumping up and down.

"He did?" Dash asked, astonished.

"Yes! He said, 'Don't go,' when I told him I have to leave today!"

"He said that?" Dash asked. He wondered what his son's voice sounded like.

"And then he told me when he had to go to the bathroom! He said, 'Lennon go potty.' It was really hard to get the duct tape off his diaper, but I pulled it and he didn't even cry when it stretched his skin, and then he went to the bathroom all by himself!"

"That's great, Zaqui! Lennon, you can talk! You've just been listening all this time, haven't you?"

Lennon nodded seriously.

"Let's all go to take Zaqui to the airport," Dash said.

"No!" Lennon shouted. Dash was stunned to hear him speak. With tears in his eyes, he picked up his son.

"You don't want Zaqui to go?" Dash asked.

Lennon shook his head.

"You CAN talk, Len!" he said.

Lennon nodded.

"Whenever you get ready, you just say what's on your mind."

The three of them went to the airport and said good-bye, each one trying not to cry. Lennon hugged Zaqui as if he would never let her go.

"Thank you, Uncle Dash. You're the best uncle! I had fun in Tennessee, but I miss my Mommy and Daddy too."

"I know."

"When can you come and visit us?"

"I don't know. As soon as we can."

"Bring McCartney and Lennon too!"

"I will."

"Tell McCartney and Aunt Shelley 'bye' for me."

"Okay. We love you, Kwee."

"I love all of you, too!"

They gave each other one last group hug and Zaqui got on the plane. Dash and Lennon watched until the plane was out of sight.

30

One morning the next spring, Dash left just after seven o'clock to go to work. He was finishing a job near eleven-thirty when his cell phone rang. The caller ID indicated that the call was coming from his house. He didn't answer it. It rang again. As he decided to answer it, Dash was dreading what Shelley had to tell him today.

"Hello?" he said.

"Daddy?" McCartney cried.

"Carty? What's the matter? Why aren't you in school?"

"Daddy, Mommy won't wake up," she sobbed.

"What do you mean?"

"She won't wake up. She's asleep and she won't wake up. I dialed 9-1-1 and told them that my mommy won't wake up."

"I'm on my way home, Carty."

Dash packed his tools and supplies as quickly as he could and drove across Nashville to his house. It took him nearly 45 minutes to get home.

When he arrived, two police cars and an ambulance were in front of his house. Dash parked across the street and ran to find out what had happened. He saw a policeman guiding a somber McCartney into his patrol car. Dash didn't see Lennon anywhere.

"What's going on, officer?" Dash asked.

"Do you live here?" the officer replied.

"Yes, sir, I'm her dad, Dash Farrah" he said.

"Daddy!" McCartney said, running to him. Dash picked up his daughter.

"We responded to a 9-1-1 call. Apparently your wife tried to commit suicide," the officer told him.

"She what?"

"If you don't mind, I have a few questions." Two more officers joined them.

"Does your wife have a history of narcotics abuse?"

"No, sir, she doesn't take any drugs."

"Where were you this morning?"

"I was working across town."

"Can you prove your whereabouts?"

"Well, I just got a check from this guy, and he was there in his house while I was working. I got there about seven-thirty this morning, and I just left when my daughter called me on my cell phone." Dash handed him the check and all three officers examined it before handing it back to Dash.

"As far as we can tell, your wife ingested a bottle of pills and a bottle of booze," the officer said. "Do you know where she got the pills?"

"No, sir."

"Did you provide her with the pills or the alcohol?"

"No, sir, I didn't even know she had them. Where is she? Is she all right?"

"We'll answer your questions in a minute," he said. The three officers stepped several feet away from Dash and spoke as if he couldn't hear them.

"Do you believe his story?"

"He seems legit."

"Can you believe a long-haired hippie like that?"

"He does have it in a pony tail."

"He looked surprised, like he didn't know anything about it."

"The best killers do."

"I don't think he had anything to do with it."

"We'll just keep an eye on him."

They walked over to Dash.

"What kind of work do you do?" the big officer asked him.

"Wiring, for cable and Internet, homes and small businesses." He started to reach for his wallet to give them one of his business cards and they all drew their guns.

"Hold it, boy!" the big officer said.

Dash put both hands up in front of him.

"I just want to show you my business card, it's in my wallet," he explained. They withdrew their guns while he took out a card.

"Let me see that," one of the officers said, grabbing the card. "How much do you charge?"

"It depends on the size of the building and what exactly you want done," Dash said.

"Well, my house is--"

"Oh, can it, Hoffer," the thin officer said.

"Keep the card, and call me, if you want. I can come and do a free estimate," Dash said.

"About your wife," the other officer said, "they are taking her to the hospital. She was unconscious when the EMT arrived and has continued to be unresponsive." The ambulance left without Dash having the opportunity to see Shelley.

"Why isn't this child in school?" Hoffer asked.

"Can't you see, she's too small to go to school," the big officer said.

"You take it easy," Hoffer told Dash.

"You can go and see your wife at the hospital," the thin officer said. "But you better call first. She might not be able to have visitors for awhile."

After everyone had left, Dash took McCartney in the house. He found Lennon locked in his room, lying on a pile of toys on the floor, watching TV. He was oblivious to the emergency that had just taken place. Dash called his mom and told her what just happened. She said Goliath had just called her, so Dash called Goliath.

"Hey, dude, how's it going?" Dash asked him.

"I'm great. What's up with you, Mr. Out-of-Touch?" Goliath asked.

"Well, we just had a little excitement. Shelley was just taken to the hospital."

"What happened?"

"I'm not sure. I was at work, and apparently she tried to commit suicide, pills and alcohol."

"Dude, I'm on my way."

"What?"

"I'm catching the next flight down."

"What for?"

"My wife and kids went to a family reunion in Alaska, so I have a week free. I'm there."

"You don't need to do that."

"I need to do it, believe me."

Goliath arrived at midnight. He rented a car and found his way to the house. Dash still hadn't heard any news about Shelley. Dash brought Goliath up to date on his marital situation.

"Dude, now I understand."

"What?"

273

"We all wondered why you had fallen off the face of the earth. It's not like you to be out of touch with everyone for so long."

"I know. It's just that--"

"You've said enough. No need to explain. So, what does she do on the computer all day? And all night?"

"I don't know, I don't even use it."

"Well, let's take a look."

"I don't know anything about it. That's her thing."

"It's my thing too." Goliath turned on the computer and started opening windows and documents.

"Look at this," he said. "Your business records haven't been opened in more than six months."

"What? Then what's she doing all the time?"

"Ah, here it is. She's been chatting. Her screen name is 'stormingbottom'? Why would she be stormingbottom?"

"I don't know," Dash laughed, "but you should see it when she gets mad."

"Do you want to read her conversations?" Goliath asked.

"No, I don't care about that," Dash said.

"It looks like she sent some guy a lot of money," Goliath said.

"She did?"

"Yeah, and this other guy too, like, a couple thousand. He's asking her for more."

"Really?"

"Yeah... and this guy, well, she seems to have a relationship going on with him."

"I'm not surprised."

"Whoa, dude! Look at this!" Goliath opened a file that was a porno movie. Dash couldn't believe what he was seeing. Then Goliath found thousands of pornographic pictures that had been downloaded. They opened a few, but soon got bored and turned off the computer.

The next morning, Dash called the hospital again and learned that Shelley had been transferred to the psychiatric unit. Her case worker told Dash that she had tried to commit suicide, and they needed to check her mental stability. They were holding her for observation. She wasn't allowed to have visitors or talk to anybody for three to seven days. Dash called the clients he had scheduled for the next few days to postpone his jobs. He and Goliath spent the day cleaning the house and fixing dinner. They took the kids to a movie and had a wonderful, relaxing evening. McCartney and Lennon didn't ask about their mother at all, nor did they seem to miss her.

The next morning, Dash and Goliath were making plans for the day when a taxi delivered Shelley to the house.

"Shell, what are you doing home?"

"I live here, remember? Oh, so, is this what you do? I'm in the hospital dying, and you invite your friends to have a party in my house?"

"Shell, aren't you suppose to be in the hospital for another day or two?"

"What for? I'm fine. I don't belong in a loony bin. You're the one who is crazy."

"Shell, I didn't try to commit suicide."

"What are you talking about? I didn't try to commit suicide! You tried to kill me! You know you can't divorce me, so you tried to kill me!"

"What are you talking about? I wasn't even home! I didn't know anything about what you were doing!"

"Oh, yeah, of course you have to say that in front of your friend. I'll show him what kind of person you are! Just come and look at all the pictures he downloaded from the

Internet!" she yelled at Goliath.

As soon as she turned on the computer, she knew they had used it while she was gone. She stormed into the living room where Dash and Goliath were sitting.

"I wasn't even dead yet, and you were getting all involved with pornography!" she shouted.

"Shell, I didn't --"

"You just STAY AWAY from my computer! Don't you dare touch it again, or I will have you arrested, I swear!" she stomped across the room and Goliath began to laugh.

"Look at that," he said, laughing so hard he was barely able to talk.

"Hey, man, don't laugh at her." Dash warned. "She's really mad."

"I know why she is stormingbottom!"

"Shhh! She'll hear you," Dash whispered. "Stop!"

"Did you see that? It describes her perfectly!" Goliath was laughing so hard, he fell on the floor.

"Come on, man, let's go outside," Dash urged.

Dash and Goliath retreated to the back yard.

"The next time she says 'why don't you get a divorce,' I'm going to do it," he told Goliath. "I'm going to tell her yes, I will."

"Be careful, man, she's dangerous."

"I know that. I live with her."

Dash looked around the yard for Rigby and MacKenzie, but he didn't see them anywhere.

"What's wrong, man?" Goliath asked.

"I was just thinking, I haven't seen our dogs in a couple of days. I wonder where they are?"

"What kind are they?"

"Twin pit bulls."

"Twins? Can dogs be twins?"

"That's what Shelley calls them."

"Do they look alike?"

"No, not at all."

"Why did you get pit bulls?"

"Shelley got them, a real bargain."

"She bought bargain dogs?"

"My question exactly."

Dash opened the door to go inside, and Shelley was standing right there.

"Shell, where are Rigby and MacKenzie?"

"Look in the garage."

"It's too hot to keep dogs in the garage," Dash said, hurrying to let them out. Goliath followed him. When Dash opened the door to the garage, a giant beast was looking in his face. Dash quickly closed the door.

"Did you see that?" he asked Goliath.

"What was that? A horse?" Goliath asked.

"Shell, what is that giant animal doing in our garage?"

"That's Yellow Submarine," she said.

"Yellow Submarine?"

"Yeah, he's a Great Dane. He's really friendly. I traded Rigby and MacKenzie for him, and I only had to pay three hundred bucks. He's a lot better with kids." Shelley took a can of Pepsi and went back to the computer in the bedroom.

"Dash, in case you didn't know..." Goliath said.

"Know what?"

"She's crazy."

31

After Goliath had gone home, Dash's life returned to its normal, unpredictable state. Dash finally found a country rock band, The Burnt Bridge Boys, who was looking for a lead guitarist. He began to practice with them three times a week. When Shelley over-scheduled him to work, he rescheduled his appointments so he could spend time with McCartney and Lennon and practice with the band. The three guys in the band, Mike Daily, Marty Groth and Derron Pryor, were laid back, mellow musicians who really admired Dash's skill and talent. Dash became close to Derron, one of the most friendly people Dash had ever met.

One evening Dash was getting McCartney organized for school the next day. Dash asked Shelley for the keys to the van and she exploded.

"What do you need them for?" she snapped at him.

"I need to get McCartney's backpack."

"It's not in there!" she yelled.

"She said she left it there."

"She doesn't know what she's talking about!"

"Can I look?"

"You stay out of my van! You have no right to invade my personal property!"

"I don't want to invade anything. I just want to look for McCartney's backpack."

"You keep away from MY things!"

"So where's her backpack?"

"How should I know?"

"I'm just asking, if it's not in the van, where is it?"

"You just stay away from my van!"

"Shell, it's our van, not just yours."

"Then why don't you just divorce me? Will THAT make you happy?"

"Yes, as a matter of fact, it will."

Shelley was taken aback. She looked away from the computer at Dash.

"You're joking, right?" she asked.

"I'm serious."

"You're kidding."

"No, seriously. I'm not kidding."

"You're just kidding."

"No, I'm serious. I want a divorce."

"No way. You can't do that to me."

"I'm tired of your games. I want a divorce."

"You're going to be sorry! You are going to PAY! If you leave us, you will NEVER see your kids, ever again!"

Dash called his mother for advice. He nearly broke down when he confessed to her what was really happening in his marriage. Victoria suggested that Dash should look in the phone book for a divorce lawyer. Since lawyers in Nashville weren't listed by specialty, Dash selected one who didn't have a fancy advertisement: Beckworth Dolittle Bargemarjer. Dash called him and set up an appointment to file for divorce.

O.K. called Dash the next day. He had talked to Goliath and was calling Dash to lend a sympathetic ear.

"Man, I just can't take any more of this insanity," Dash explained.

"Goliath told me how crazy she really is," O.K. said.

"No doubt about it."

"He told me she tried to kill herself, and then she blamed it on you?"

"That's what she's claiming."

"So have you talked to a lawyer?" O.K. asked.

"Yeah. You'll never guess what his name is."

"I hope it's Perry Mason or Matlock."

"No, not quite. It's Beckworth Dolittle Bargemarjer," Dash told him.

"So do you just call him Becky Doo?" O.K. asked.

Dash laughed. O.K. always knew how to break the tension and make any situation into a comedy scene. Dash wondered how he would ever be able to speak to his lawyer now, because he would always think of him as Becky Doo.

Shelley's mother arrived at their house a few days later. She planned to stay with them until they went to court. Besides constantly reminding Dash that he was a failure, she filled their house with her continual smoking. McCartney developed a cough, and could get no relief from the smoke.

Dash continued to live at home after he filed for the divorce. Beckworth Dolittle Bargemarjer recommended that he stay so Shelley wouldn't accuse him of abandoning his children. Becky Doo was very reassuring, telling Dash that he had nothing to worry about, and that because they had evidence that Shelley was a neglectful parent, Dash would have no problem getting custody of the children. He told Dash to document everything that happened. For the first time in years, Dash felt a bit of hope.

Dash's mom came to visit him in May, to give her support to Dash. Shelley did her best to let Victoria know she was not welcome in their house. Victoria stayed in a motel because she didn't want to get into an argument and she couldn't stand the smoke. She visited with the kids daily, although Shelley wouldn't let her come in the house when Dash wasn't there.

On Saturday afternoon, the day before Dash's mom was going home, they took McCartney and Lennon to the park to play. Dash and his mom wanted a couple of hours alone with the kids, without the constant screaming from Shelley and her mother. Dash and Victoria had to fight with Shelley for the opportunity to take the kids with them, but Shelley finally agreed, insisting that they bring them home within two hours. Dash, his mother, McCartney and Lennon got into Victoria's rental car and went to the playground at McCartney's school, just a few blocks away. The kids, feeling the tension in their house, but not understanding it, had been quiet and subdued for the past few weeks. Today, they had so much fun playing with their daddy and their grandma. They ran and jumped and went on the swings and slide.

They stayed at the playground for more than an hour, then they stopped to get ice cream on the way back to the house. They were all laughing and singing in the car when they arrived at Dash's house. They were surprised to see a sheriff's car in the driveway. Two officers approached the rental car and motioned for them to get out of the car.

"Are you Dash Farrah?"

"Yes, sir, I am."

"And are you Victoria Farrah?"

"Yes, officer. What is this all about?"

McCartney started crying, then Lennon did too.

"We have a warrant for your arrest, both of you."

"What for?" Dash asked.

"Kidnapping."

"These are my kids!"

"Sure they are. Don't touch them. Keep your hands in plain sight."

"She is crazy!" Victoria said.

"Daddy! What's happening?" McCartney cried.

"These are my kids," Dash explained. "We took them to the park and now we're bringing them home. I live here with them, and this is my mother, visiting us from Washington state."

"You fit the description and this is the stolen car you were reported to be driving." The officer put handcuffs on Dash and his mother.

"It's not stolen! It's a rental!" Dash said.

"Excuse me, officer, but we just took my grandchildren to the park," Victoria explained.

"There they are! They kidnapped MY babies!" Shelley screamed as she came out of the house.

"We didn't kidnap them," Victoria said. "We just took them to the park to play."

"We went to the park and you weren't there! You were trying to take them away from me!"

"We went to the playground, just around the corner."

"You liar! You kidnapped my babies! McCartney! Lennon! Get in the house and away from these kidnappers! NOW!"

McCartney and Lennon began to cry. Shelley's mom came out and drunkenly started yelling incoherently. Shelley shoved Lennon so hard he fell down on the lawn, increasing the volume of his cries.

"Get up and get it the house!" she yelled.

"I want my daddy!" he cried.

"Get in the house! He's not your daddy! He's a criminal!"

"Do you really think it's necessary to cuff the lady?" one

officer asked the other.

"What is your involvement in all this?" the second officer asked Victoria. "You were driving the getaway car?"

"No, I'm their grandmother and I came from Washington state to visit my son and my grandchildren," she said.

"I'm their grandmother!" Suzie shouted from the porch.

"We are both their grandmothers," Victoria explained.

The officers examined Victoria's driver's license. They decided she wasn't a threat, so they took off her handcuffs.

"What about my son? He lives here. Those are his children. How could he kidnap them?"

"Look, lady, we had a report of a kidnapping, we've located the perpetrator, and we have to take him to jail."

"There was no kidnapping. His wife is crazy. We just took them to the playground to play, and then we brought them home."

"You can follow us in your car, and then post bail for your son." the officer said, leading Dash to the patrol car.

Dash couldn't believe he was being arrested, accused of kidnapping his own children! He got into the back seat of the police car, his heart breaking as his kids screamed and cried from the front yard. His mother followed them to the police station. Dash was very cooperative. After having his fingerprints taken, he was put in a holding cell overnight. The next day, he was released to the custody of his mother, after she posted bail and solemnly swore that he wouldn't flee the state.

When Dash's mother took him home, Shelley and her mother behaved as if nothing unusual had happened. Shelley was on the computer and didn't acknowledge that they were in the house. Her mother continued her drinking and smoking in the kitchen. McCartney and Lennon greeted their daddy and asked their grandmother if she would take them to the park again.

"Mom, I wish you could stay longer," Dash said at the airport, needing someone on his side.

"Either Dad or I will come back when you go to court," she promised.

"It would help if you could both be here."

"I know. We'll see."

32

The divorce proceedings were scheduled for mid-August. Dash's dad arrived the day before they went to court. Beckworth Dolittle Bargemarjer was confident that the judge would be favorable to Dash, until he saw who was to be the judge for his case. Judge Mardell was known as a man-hater who always sided with the mother, regardless of the circumstances or evidence. During the proceedings, she wouldn't let Dash say anything, and she didn't want to hear from his lawyer either. She had made up her mind about the outcome of the case before they even arrived in the courtroom. Shelley's mother sat behind her in court, and Dash's dad sat behind him.

Although Shelley was put on the stand and couldn't answer a single question honestly, she was considered to be the injured party who deserved everything. Shelley stated that they had earned more than $130,000 last year, and the judge asked her if that were gross or net. Shelley didn't know the difference. Dash whispered to his lawyer that they had earned closer to $30,000 but he didn't have any paperwork to prove it. Shelley had all the records for the business. She hadn't completed a tax return in three years, so they really had no record of how much they had made.

At the end of the proceedings, which were like a nightmare where Dash was unable to talk, Becky Doo explained what had been decided. Dash could have the kids every Wednesday and every other weekend. He would get the house and everything in it, along with the $2000 monthly mortgage payment. Dash would get the business and pay Shelley $2500 per month for spousal support, since now she would be unemployed. She would get the computer, but he could have everything else connected with he business. She would get the van, and he would make the $675 monthly payment for the next seven years, until it was paid off. For each child, he would be required to pay $750 per month child support. In addition, he would be required to pay all of the outstanding bills, including their taxes for the past three years, when that amount was calculated. The only financial burden given to Shelley was her student loan that she had brought into the marriage.

"I don't have that kind of money," Dash told Beckworth Dolittle Bargemarjer.

"According to the financial records Shelley gave the judge, you make well over $10,000 per month."

"Where did she get records like that? We didn't make anywhere near that much."

"That's what she said you have been making."

"No way. I don't even make a thousand dollars a week."

"Well, after two years, we can appeal. And, by the way, here is my bill."

Dash nearly fainted when he saw he owed Beckworth Dolittle Bargemarjer more than $7,000.

"One last thing," Becky Doo said. "Shelley has filed a harassment suit against you. For the next two years, watch your step. She can have you arrested any time, for any reason, if she says you are disturbing her domestic tranquility. If she does that, you will stay in jail for one year."

"Well, he lived up to his name," Daniel told Dash, as Beckworth Dolittle Bargemarjer walked away.

"What do mean?" Dash asked.

"He did do little," his dad answered.

"Yeah. Maybe he should change his name to Worth-less Do-little Charge-alot," Dash remarked.

33

Shelley bought a house just around the corner from the house that was now Dash's. She and the kids moved one week after the court decision. Although the judge had awarded all the furniture and appliances to Dash, he let Shelley take the beds for the kids, the two smaller televisions, and some of the living room furniture. Her house had all the large appliances and some furniture left by the previous owners. Shelley took her personal belongings and some of the children's clothes.

About two weeks after the court date, Dash decided to go home after work, before he went to band practice. When he opened the front door, he saw that his house had been burglarized. Everything in the house, with the exception of his clothes had been taken. The TV, couch, bed, refrigerator, washer, dryer, dishwasher, stove, microwave, and even the carpeting had been removed from the house. Judge Mardell hadn't mentioned Yellow Submarine in the settlement. He was gone too. The house had been stripped. Before calling the police, he called Shelley.

"Shell, I was robbed today," he said. "Someone came and took everything out of the house."

"It's all mine! I just came and got what's mine!"

"Shell, you took everything!"

"That was all my stuff!" she shouted. Dash heard a man's voice in the background.

"Who are you talking to?" he asked.

"That's my friend, Ed. He's very special to me. He cares about me. He's my soul mate."

"Shell, I don't care about Special Ed. You already have a stove. And what are you going to do with two refrigerators?"

"None of your business! Now you just leave me alone, or I'll call the police! You know you are not allowed to disturb my domestic tranquility!" She slammed down the receiver.

Dash tried to become accustomed to the routine of seeing McCartney and Lennon on Wednesdays and every other weekend, but it was so painful. Dash bought foam mats and blankets for sleeping, since he didn't have any furniture, but he had to take the kids out to eat for every meal because he didn't have a stove or refrigerator. He couldn't afford to purchase appliances. Lennon stopped speaking, and McCartney was growing resentful toward her daddy.

"Daddy, why did you steal our house?" she asked him.

"I didn't steal your house. I live here, and you can come and visit me any time."

"You stole our house. Mommy told me."

"That is not true. The judge gave me this house, and then Mommy bought your house where you live with her. You were in the courtroom. You heard what the judge said."

"You are a liar."

"No, this is the truth."

"I don't believe you," she said, and went to sit on the floor in the corner. Lennon gave Dash a hug, silently indicating that he did believe his daddy was telling the truth.

One evening, Dash was on his way home from band practice when he saw red flashing lights in his rearview mirror. He pulled over to the side of the road, his heart pounding. Shelley was probably having him arrested.

Dash was given a ticket because one of his tail lights wasn't working. He was so relieved that it was only a traffic ticket. He drove slowly the rest of the way home, thanking God that it hadn't been anything worse.

When he arrived home, two sheriff cars were parked in the driveway. He parked in front of the house and went to see what they wanted.

"Dash Farrah?" one of the officers asked, looking in a little book.

"Yes, sir."

"We have a complaint against you. Where were you approximately thirty minutes ago?"

"I was clear across town, just leaving from band practice."

"Do you have any witnesses?"

"Yeah, the other band members were all there."

"Band members, huh?" He wrote something in his book.

"What is going on?"

"I'm afraid we are going to have to arrest you. Your ex-wife saw you peeping in her windows, and that is against the law. On top of peeping, you have frightened her, disturbing her domestic tranquility. We have a court order to arrest you."

"I wasn't there," Dash said. "I was clear across town."

"Unless you have a more reliable witness than some band members, I'm afraid we're going to have to take you in."

"Wait! I do have another witness," Dash remembered. "Another one of Nashville's finest."

"What are you talking about, boy?"

Dash pulled out the ticket he had just received.

"See the time on that ticket?" Dash said, pointing to the time. "And the street where I was stopped?"

The officers examined the ticket carefully, then one of them called someone on the police radio.

"Well, boy, you got lucky this time. But one day, your luck is going to run out, and we are going to be there to catch you," he warned.

"Yes, sir," Dash said. He knew the officer was telling the truth.

Without Shelley to solicit clients and schedule jobs for Dashell Wiring, business slowed to a crawl. Dash's income was barely $1500. per month. He wasn't able to make the required payments. Within three months, he knew he had to sell the house. He met with a real estate agent, who put the house on the market, then he temporarily moved in with Derron. He didn't want to put Derron in jeopardy by bringing McCartney and Lennon to his home, so he rented a motel room where they stayed when Dash had them on the weekends.

Dash soon had no money. His parents sent him some, but it wasn't enough to pay any of his bills. Shelley was very angry that he wasn't paying her all she was owed, and Dash was afraid she would have him arrested during one of her episodes.

The real estate agent brought good news: a family was interested in his house, and was willing to pay his asking price. Dash made preparations to make the deal, but on the last day they changed their minds. Dash found out that Shelley had seen the family looking at the house and had told them that the roof leaked whenever it rained, and that it had a lot of hidden damage. Although none of it was true, the family didn't buy the house, and Dash missed another house payment. He knew he was going to lose the house.

34

Dash had only one option: he had to move back home with his parents. In Nashville, he was in constant danger of being arrested. He was broke and going deeper into debt daily. He really liked the members of the band, especially Derron, but the day came when Dash had to tell them goodbye.

"Dash, I hope you don't take this the wrong way," Derron said, "but I'm going to miss you when you're gone."

"I'm going to miss you too," Dash said. "You have been a great friend to me."

Dash put the few items he owned in his car, and began to drive back to Washington State. He didn't tell Shelley that he was leaving, for fear that she would make up a reason to have him arrested on his way out of town. After spending Wednesday evening with McCartney and Lennon, with McCartney extremely hostile and Lennon clinging to Dash, begging him not to make him go back to his mommy, Dash began to drive. He didn't stop until he was out of Tennessee.

His parents were happy to have him home and out of the awful situation with his ex-wife. They were also grieved that he couldn't see his children. Dash set up a wiring business and had a few jobs, but with his enormous debts, his finances disappeared quickly. Every time he saw a child, he ached to see his own children. When he called Shelley's house to talk to them, she either didn't answer the phone or she told him the kids weren't at home.

One night he had a dream that he was standing at the foot of Mt. St. Helens, looking up at it. He heard Dari's voice but didn't see her.

"Ready to dash, Dash?" she asked.

"On the dot, Dot," he replied.

Dash began to climb the volcano. He knew what the ash was like because he had been in Yakima when Mt. St. Helens had erupted in 1980. After the ash had fallen over the Yakima valley for more than a week, the landscape looked as if it were covered in snow; but the ash was not cold. It was soft and heavy, like fine sand.

Dash took a few steps onto the mountain. His feet sank deep into the ash, at least ten inches or so. He looked up and could see the summit, or rather, the top edge of the crater, not so far above him. He had flown over the mountain several times since the eruption, so he knew what it looked like on the other side of that rim: the crater was at least a mile deep, with a lava dome building inside it. In the dream, he tried to climb the ash mountain, but for every step up he took, he sunk down deeper. After only a few steps, he nearly waist-deep in the ash. He looked up to the summit again, and saw McCartney and Lennon at the top. He could see their mouths moving, calling to him, but he couldn't hear what they were saying. They were waving and calling. Patrick Neptune stood by Lennon, holding his hand and waving Dash to come up. Beside them were Dash's guitars, and his car, all the important things in his life. Dash used all his strength to pull one leg out of the ash, and then the other, to attempt to crawl a little closer to his goal. The kids were waving more frantically. Suddenly Shelley was standing on the rim. She pushed Dash's car over the edge, into the crater. She turned and laughed at Dash. She pushed Patrick Neptune and he toppled over the edge, into the crater. Then Shelley picked up Dash's guitars and threw them into the crater. Dash was moving so slowly, his feet sinking in the ash. He finally managed to move within a few feet of the summit – he could almost reach Lennon's outstretched hand - when Shelley yanked the boy away from his father, and shoved Lennon and then McCartney into the crater.

"You'll never amount to anything, never a mountain to anything! It's all mine! You are going to pay for all these things!" she shouted.

Dash awakened with a start, covered with sweat, his legs aching from the attempted climb of the volcano. The phone was ringing.

"Dash, guess what! I climbed Mt. St. Helens yesterday," Dari told him.

"Really? Did you make it all the way to the rim?" he asked.

"Yeah, the south rim. It was really tough, especially the top part where it is covered with ash. For every step up I took, I slid down a couple of feet. It was so hard to make any progress, so I really prayed and asked the Lord to help me. Suddenly, I found myself at the top of the south rim, along with the rest of my group. I'm not sure how I made it that last hundred yards, but I know other people were praying for me and then suddenly I was there, at the top."

"Wow, I just now had a dream that I was climbing Mt. St. Helens," Dash said. "I know what you mean about stepping up and sliding back, because I did the same thing."

"Seriously?"

"Seriously."

"You need lots of prayer, huh, Bro?"

"I need an incredible amount of prayer."

"Let's pray right now," Dari said. "Dear Lord, You know Dash's needs and You know his heart. We know You haven't brought him all this way just to leave him. We know You care about him, and that You are in control of everything. Touch him right now, and let us see the miracles that we know You are able to do. In Jesus' name we pray, Amen."

"Amen."

"Dari, I've lost everything. I've lost my kids. I'm too far away to see them. I don't have the money I am suppose to be sending them. I lost my house. I'm filing for bankruptcy. I missed my chance to play in a really big band. I've lost everything."

"Dash, you still have Jesus. If you don't have anything else, and you have Jesus, you have enough. He's all you need. You don't need all those other things."

"Yeah," he agreed, but he didn't feel any better.

After declaring bankruptcy and living with his parents for nearly two years, falling further and further behind on his support payments, Dash was somewhat despondent. He longed to see McCartney and Lennon, but he couldn't. Although he was going on with life, working part time and had joined another band, his life felt so empty.

One afternoon, Daniel brought a certified letter to Dash. The return address was the Nashville courthouse.

"It doesn't look like good news," Daniel said.

Dash opened the letter and quickly read it. He handed it to his dad, his mind not wanting to comprehend what it meant.

"Oh, no," said Daniel. "I don't believe this. You have got to sue her for slander. Shelley is accusing you of molesting Lennon! You're going to have to go back to Nashville to court."

35

Victoria helped Daniel find another lawyer in Nashville. His new lawyer, Rutherford Clancy, obtained a copy of the new charges. After contacting the court, he learned that Dash was required to undergo a psychiatric evaluation by a psychiatrist in Nashville selected by Shelley before the court date.

Dash explained everything to Rutherford Clancy over the phone: Shelley's history of false molestation accusations, her neglect of her children, her computer addiction, her extramarital affairs, her suicide attempt, and the fact that she had stolen everything out of the house after it had been awarded to him. Dash mentioned the debt she had accrued while they were married, and the income she hadn't reported to the IRS. Rutherford Clancy assured Dash that he didn't have to worry about anything. Dash asked him how Shelley could press charges against him for something that she said happened more than two years ago, and Mr. Clancy said that if they were phony charges, they would be able to clear up the matter quickly and nothing would go on Dash's record. When Dash told him about the divorce settlement and how much he was required to pay Shelley each month, Mr. Clancy was quite upset.

"Who was your divorce lawyer?" he asked. "Maybe I can get your records from him. That would help a lot."

"He has a strange name," Dash said, trying to recall. "Oh, yeah, Mr. Bargemarjer."

"Not Beckworth Dolittle Bargemarjer, I hope?" He stretched out the name with his southern drawl, 'Bahhhgemaahhja.'

"Yes! That's his name," Dash said.

"Oh, well, we won't be able to get any records from him."

"Why not?"

"He's doing some time and his office is locked up and under investigation."

"Great," Dash said.

"It's okay. We probably won't need any of that information anyway."

Rutherford Clancy had an investigator gather information about Shelley's life since Dash had moved from Nashville and called him a few days later to share what he had learned.

"You're not going to believe this," he told Dash.

"What?"

"Seven different men have lived with your ex-wife in the past two years. After you moved from Nashville, apparently she didn't know you were gone, and three times she filed harassment complaints against you, resulting in three warrants for your arrest. In addition, she claims to have been robbed at gunpoint in her own house by an unknown intruder, and another time, she claimed an unknown intruder raped her in her house. Your children missed so many days of school last year that they were each held back one grade. Social services has tried to investigate reports of your little girl-- McCartney -- being physically abused as well as nearly starved, but they have not been able to contact your ex-wife. She doesn't have a chance in court."

"McCartney was physically abused?" Dash asked, his heart hurting for his little girl.

"That's the subject of investigation by social services."

"What about those warrants for my arrest? When I get there, will I be arrested?"

"No, they were all dropped when the authorities

discovered you had moved out of the area months before they allegedly happened."

Dash and his mother flew to Nashville so he could undergo the psychiatric evaluation with Dr. Von Hollen, the psychiatrist Shelley had chosen. As soon as the evaluation was finished, they flew back to Washington state the same day, not giving Shelley an opportunity to know Dash was in town.

Two weeks later, Rutherford Clancy called Dash with the results of the evaluation.

"You're good to go, Dash. The report says you are a normal, healthy man with no deviant tendencies. Nothing to worry about. I'll FAX you a copy of the full report."

"Can we have them do an evaluation on Shelley?"

"I tried, but she refused. The judge said she is not required to be evaluated, unless she volunteers."

"Do you know who the judge will be? That last one didn't really give me a fair chance at all."

"Yes, this time we will present your case before Judge Wackenhut, another female judge, but she's known to be fair."

O.K. called Dash that night to see how he was doing. Dash brought him up to date on what was happening.

"So, the report from the psychiatrist said you are normal, huh?"

"Yeah, Dr. Von Hollen was really cool."

"Van Halen? You were evaluated by Van Halen?"

"No, not Van Halen, Dr. Von Hollen. He said that nothing in any of my responses was abnormal or unusual. I'm a perfectly well adjusted man."

"He said that?"

"That's what the report says. Do you want me to FAX you a copy?"

"Nah, I believe you. Do you want me to go with you when you go to court?"

"My dad's going with me."

"I could go too. You need all the support you can get."

"Thanks, but it would probably make Shelley even madder if I have a friend there with me."

"So, are you getting the same judge this time? Wasn't her name Mardell?"

"Not the same judge, no. This one is also a woman, but her name is Judge Wackenhut."

"Whack-a-what?"

"Wackenhut."

"Dude! You don't have a chance!"

"What do you mean?"

"With a name like Whack-a-nut, you are dead in the water."

"No, it's Wacken-hut. Hut! Hut! As in Jabba-the-Hut. Not nut."

"Oh, okay. That's better. Maybe you do have a chance."

Dash and his dad flew to Nashville to go to court. Dash tried his best not to show how nervous he was when he walked into the courtroom with Rutherford Clancy. Dash nearly cried at the sight of his children. McCartney hadn't grown at all and was as thin as ever. Lennon was taller and thinner than he had been. Both were sullen and looked at him with anger. A man was sitting beside Shelley's mom. Shelley had gained a lot of weight since Dash had seen her. Her teeth had deteriorated to dirty little nubs. She had the same female lawyer as she had had during the divorce.

Neither of them looked at Dash.

Judge Wackenhut entered the courtroom and instructed everyone to be seated.

"I have read the petition. Child molestation is a serious crime and you can expect to serve a long sentence if you are found guilty," she said sternly, looking directly at Dash. She turned to Shelley and smiled. "Mrs. Farrah, please tell us in your own words what happened."

"My baby, Lennon, told me that his Daddy touched him in his private area inappropriately."

"When did this happen?" Judge Wackenhut asked with concern.

"One night when he was spending the weekend with Dash, before Dash ran away from Nashville."

"Where did this happen?"

"He took my babies to MOTEL."

"A motel?" the judge repeated, as if nothing good could happen in a motel.

"Yes, and Lennon said he touched his privates."

"Does Mr. Farrah have a history of inappropriate sexual behavior?"

"Yes, Your Honor," Shelley lied.

"Would you please tell us all about it?" the judge asked.

"Yes, first of all, on the computer we had at home, the one I used for business, he downloaded thousands of pornographic pictures, the same day he tried to kill me and I was in the hospital recovering."

"That's not true!" Dash said.

"Mr. Farrah, I will not tolerate outbursts in my courtroom," Judge Wackenhut said sternly. "You will have your chance to speak." She turned to Shelley. "Now, go on, my dear."

Dash whispered to Rutherford Clancy that Shelley was the one who downloaded the pictures, and that he never tried to kill her, but she had tried to kill herself. Rutherford Clancy nodded knowingly.

"I can prove the pictures were downloaded that day," Shelley said confidently. "Also, he has had many young girlfriends, even when we were married. He's in a rock band."

"A ROCK band!" Judge Wackenhut exclaimed, disgusted.

"Yes, so he is always involved with underage girls."

"I see," said the judge, shaking her head.

"And also, he had to go to a psychiatrist because of his unusual sexual behavior. You have a copy of Dr. Von Hollen's report. It tells all about his sexual deviation and unnatural tendencies." Shelley held up her copy of the report.

"It does not say that!" Dash said, unable to contain himself.

"Mr. Farrah, one more outburst from you, and I will hold you in contempt of court."

"I'm sorry, Your Honor, but--"

"Silence! You will have your chance to speak! Please continue, Mrs. Farrah."

"Another time both of my babies witnessed Dash wrestling nude with another man," Shelley continued.

"How awful!" the judge said.

"I don't know where she got that idea," Dash whispered to Rutherford Clancy. "That never happened."

"Another thing," Shelley continued. "On the Internet, his band has a web site. On Dash's personal web page, and this is a print out of his bio, see, he is admitting that he is bisexual!"

"Let me see that," the judge said, examining it closely. "Yes, this is a bio, so that means he is bisexual."

"A 'bio' is a biography," Dash whispered to Rutherford Clancy.

"Don't worry about it," he said, patting Dash's hand.

"Dash ran away after he molested Lennon," Shelley continued, "and his parents gave him a big house, so he lives there for free, without paying any rent. I have been working at three full-time jobs and going to school, just to keep food on our table to feed my babies."

Rutherford Clancy looked at Dash, puzzled. "I live with my parents, in the basement," Dash whispered.

"He molested his son," Shelley said, "then he ran away, and he owes us almost two hundred thousand dollars. He has tons of money. He's the sole heir to the Farah jeans fortune."

The judge shook her head sympathetically. "These rich young men, running around the country, taking advantage of women and then leaving their own children penniless," she commented.

"We're not related to the Farah jeans people," Dash whispered to Rutherford Clancy. "It's not even spelled the same."

"It's okay, we'll take care of it. You don't have anything to worry about," Rutherford Clancy assured him, again patting his hand. Dash recalled Beckworth Dolittle Bargemarjer had told him the very same thing.

Dash's heart nearly broke when they asked Lennon to take the witness stand. He was eight years old now, and clearly confused. He acted as if he wanted to look at Dash, but had been warned against it.

"Lennon, can you please tell me what happened?" the judge asked sweetly.

"When?" Lennon asked.

"Tell me what happened with your daddy."

"Which Daddy? Daddy Ed or Daddy Terry or Daddy ----"

"No, the one who is in the courtroom today."

"Daddy Dennis, right back there?" Lennon pointed to the man sitting near Shelley's mother.

"No, the man sitting over at that table, Dash Farrah."

"Dash is not my daddy," Lennon said.

"Tell me what Dash did," Judge Wackenhut said.

"Dash touched me on my privates," he said, as if he were reciting a speech. Lennon kept his eyes on his mother. He would not look at Dash.

"In this courtroom, you need to call him 'Dad' or 'Daddy,'" the judge instructed. Lennon looked at his mother for confirmation, and she nodded.

"Dad touched me on my privates."

"When did this happen?"

"When he took me and McCartney to a motel."

"And how did he touch you?"

"He put his hand right down here."

"Did he move it around or anything?"

"No, he just put his hand right here."

"On top of your pants?" the judge asked.

"No, inside my pajamas. On top of my underwear."

"I was checking to see if he had wet his pants," Dash whispered to Rutherford Clancy. "I was toilet training him. You can't feel when those fleece pajamas are wet. You have to feel the underwear."

"Don't worry, we'll take care of it," Rutherford Clancy whispered back.

"How long did he keep it there?" the judge asked.

"About three seconds," Lennon answered.

"She told him to say that," Dash told Rutherford Clancy. "How would an eight year old know how long three seconds was, more than two years ago?"

"Is there anything else you would like to tell the court about your daddy?" Judge Wackenhut asked Lennon.

"Yes, I saw Daddy wrestling with a man and they were both naked."

"Where did this happen?"

"In the bedroom. They were on the bed together."

"Anything else?" Judge Wackenhut asked.

"Dash let our dog die," Lennon said.

"Oh, I'm so sorry, sweetheart," the judge said. "That is downright cruel."

"I didn't know the dog died," Dash whispered to his lawyer.

"That's sad," Rutherford Clancy replied quietly.

"Would you like to tell us anything else, Lennon?" the judge asked.

"No, that's all," Lennon said, jumping down and returning to his seat.

"Mr. Farrah, can you please tell the court in your own words what happened?" The judge did not look at him, but began writing something. She didn't seem to be paying any attention to Dash.

"I took my kids to a motel for the weekend because I was living with--"

"Mr. Farrah, we don't care about your living arrangements. Just tell the court what happened," the judge said, irritated. She began writing again.

"I was checking to see if Lennon had wet his pajamas, because he was just being toilet trained--"

"Mr. Farrah, do you expect us to believe that a six-year-old boy was just being toilet trained? It is not going to help your case if you don't tell the truth."

"He wasn't wet, so I removed my hand."

"I think we have all the information we need. You may step down."

"Aren't you going to say anything?" Dash asked Rutherford Clancy.

"She'll give me a chance to speak later," he replied.

"We will recess and reconvene after lunch, at one-thirty." Dash saw Lennon jump when Judge Wackenhut pounded the gavel on the desk.

"What kind of a circus is this? What is going on here? That woman hasn't said one thing that was the truth," Daniel told Rutherford Clancy.

"We'll get a chance to present our side of the story," Rutherford Clancy replied.

"Is this your first trial? I think you missed your chance," Daniel said.

"We do things different in Tennessee than you do in Washington," Rutherford Clancy said.

Dash wanted to talk to his children, to hold them, but they refused to even look in his direction. He watched them leave the courtroom with Shelley and her mother.

"I have reached my decision," Judge Wackenhut said when court reconvened. "First, the matter of support. During the divorce, the amounts of support were unusually high. I don't see any supporting documents warranting payments of that size. Mr. Farrah, you are still responsible for the amounts already accrued, but beginning this month, you will no longer pay spousal support, nor Mrs. Farrah's van payments. Child support shall be reduced to five hundred dollars per child."

"Yes!" Rutherford Clancy said.

"Mr. Clancy, please keep your reactions to yourself, or I will hold you in contempt of court."

"I apologize, Your Honor."

"Now, may I continue?"

"Please, Your Honor."

"The matter of child molestation is very serious, as I previously stated. I believe that this has happened as charged, so I will only allow Mr. Farrah to visit his children with supervision, for one hour at a time.

"Before the visits begin, Mr. Farrah must be examined by three psychiatrists, each of whom must be pre-approved by Mrs. Farrah. After being examined and if you pass their qualifications, the supervised visits may begin. I must add that Mr. Farrah's parents are not qualified to supervise these visits because Mr. Farrah's mother is a known kidnapper."

Out of the corner of his eye, Dash saw his dad poke Rutherford Clancy in the back.

"Ow!" Rutherford Clancy yelled.

"Mr. Clancy, do you wish to say something?" Judge Wackenhut asked.

"No, Your Honor," he said meekly.

The judge continued. "Mr. Farrah will be responsible for all costs related to the visits, including airline tickets, motel costs for the children and their supervisor, and any incidental costs.

"Mr. Farrah, you have painted a very negative picture of yourself in the eyes of your children. They are terrified of you. They are afraid that you will try to kidnap or hurt or kill them. They know you tried to kill their mother. Both children feel that you stole their house from them.

The psychiatric report states that you are not to be trusted around children and that you have many sexual deviations. You were unfaithful during your marriage with underage girls. You haven't changed. You currently are in a rock band, which entails all kinds of illegal drug use and kinky sex, and you have admitted to the whole world on the Internet that you are bisexual."

"None of this is true!" Dash whispered frantically to Rutherford Clancy.

"Mr. Farrah will be allowed one phone call per week to call his children."

"Dash never calls us and I hate him!" McCartney yelled.

"Mrs. Farrah, please keep your children quiet."

"Yes, Your Honor," Shelley said.

"This case is closed."

The courtroom cleared. Dash watched sadly as his children walked away from him. They did not acknowledge him.

"What's the matter with you?" Daniel asked Rutherford Clancy.

"What do you mean?"

"None of those things are true!" Daniel said.

"I don't follow you," Rutherford Clancy said, puzzled.

"My wife is not a 'known kidnapper'!" Daniel said angrily. "And 'bio' is short for biography, not bisexual! And even if someone is confessing to be bisexual, the Supreme Court has ruled that sexual preference can't be a factor in court! You should have this case thrown out of court! And didn't you read the psychiatric report? It didn't say any of those things! It said the exact opposite! Why didn't you object?"

"We'll get them on the appeal," Rutherford Clancy said.

"Look at the bright side. Your monthly payments have been reduced to a thousand dollars."

"I'll never get to see my children."

"Sure you will, you just have a few rules to follow."

"Where am I going to find three psychiatrists that are approved by Shelley? She set it up so it's impossible for me to see my own children."

"Like I said, once you pay my bill, we can file an appeal. I took some good notes and we can win, if we get the right judge," Rutherford Clancy said confidently.

"I'm out of money," Dash said. "I can't afford to file an appeal."

Rutherford Clancy looked at Dash. "I thought you were the sole heir to the Farah fortune. Aren't you loaded?"

"Wrong Farahs. We're not related," Daniel said.

"But you've got lots of money," Rutherford Clancy said.

"No. I'm broke," Dash said. "I filed for bankruptcy a while back, and I owe my parents more than twenty thousand dollars for court costs and lawyer fees and trips to Nashville."

"And we're retired," Dash's dad added. "We don't have any more to lend him."

"Well, give me a call when you get some more money, and we'll see what we can do about the appeal," Rutherford Clancy said, shaking Dash's hand and leaving the courtroom.

36

Dash was in a daze. He felt as if he had lived through a movie scene in a courtroom, where someone else had written the script and he was doomed from the beginning. The judge had believed all the lies and wouldn't even listen to the truth. Since returning from Nashville two weeks ago, Dash had been numb. If he allowed himself to feel, he would only feel pain. He lived inside a cloud of nothingness. His dream was gone. His children were gone. His hope was gone.

Once again, the thought occurred to Dash that if he were killed in a car accident, he would be in a better position than he was right now. He didn't see the point in living. His parents were terrific and extremely supportive. Dari had been sending encouraging notes in the mail, which he didn't bother to open any more. He had nothing and he felt nothing.

"When all you have is Jesus, that's enough," he heard Dari's voice say.

Dash was driving by a church and read the billboard. "Hope offered here," it said. He turned into the empty parking lot of the church and let himself begin to feel again. He hurt. He let the tears flow for a long time. He got out of his car and walked to the door of the church. He figured it would be locked, since it was Tuesday, but to his surprise, the door opened. The atmosphere was quiet inside, as if he had stepped into another world.

He walked into the sanctuary and was enveloped by a feeling he couldn't describe. He knelt and asked God to forgive him for his anger and bitterness. He felt unworthy in the presence of God. God was perfect, and Dash was not. He didn't deserve anything from God; yet after he prayed, he felt forgiven. He felt a little bit lighter. He knew he needed to forgive Shelley. Dash couldn't do it by himself, so he asked God to help him. He had to let go of the weight of anger and hate. He gave it all to God.

"Good afternoon," a man's voice said, startling him. "I'm Pastor Houston."

"I'm Dash Farrah, and I..." he trailed off, unsure what to say or why he was there.

"Give your burdens to the Lord, son, and leave them there," Pastor Houston said kindly. "You are very troubled, aren't you?"

"Yes, but I feel a little better now." What he meant to say was that he could feel now.

"Would you like to talk?"

"No, it won't do any good," Dash said.

"Then tell it to the Lord. He knows the truth. He's the only One who can help anyway."

"Yeah, you're right," Dash agreed.

"Well, you just take your time here," Pastor Houston said. "Stay as long as you like. I'll be in my office if you need me. I have a pile of paperwork to sort."

"Okay, thanks," Dash said.

"And feel free to come visit us on Sunday morning, eight o'clock or eleven," Pastor Houston said as he left Dash alone with God.

The next Sunday, Dash decided to go to church. He wasn't interested in being one of the church musicians or even being known by the other people there. He just went because it felt right, deep inside, for him to be there.

He felt God wanted him to be there. Dash made church attendance part of his regular schedule, and slowly, his hurt began to heal. He began to feel hope that somehow, God would make things right. Dash finally felt that he had forgiven Shelley, even though she didn't deserve to be forgiven, the same way God had forgiven Dash when he didn't deserve to be forgiven.

One Sunday morning when his parents had gone to Reno, Dash was getting dressed for church. The doorbell rang. Dash fastened the buttons on his shirt as he opened the door. A woman was standing on the porch with McCartney and Lennon.

"Dash Farrah?" she said, comparing him to a picture.

"Yes," he said tentatively. His heart began pounding. Both of his kids were staring at him with big eyes.

"My name is Laura Young, and I work for the Nashville department of children's services. We were called to the home of your ex-wife. Apparently she has had a major mental breakdown. She has been taken for observation to the state mental hospital for women. She will be there for a couple of years, at least. Your children were sent to us, and we did an investigation. We discovered that the charges against you were all false, and that you were unjustly accused. Has your lawyer been in touch with you?"

"He's not my lawyer any more," Dash said, not believing that this could be happening.

"I was under the impression that you were going to file an appeal. Well, no need, the case has been overturned. You have been awarded full custody of your children."

"Full custody?" he asked incredulously.

"That's right," Ms. Young said, smiling. "My job was to deliver your children to you, and now I have a flight to catch. Have a good day."

Dash watched her drive away in a rental car as he opened the door for his children to come in the house. They stood a distance away from him, holding each other.

"Daddy, do you still hate us?" McCartney asked.

"Sweetheart, I love both of you so much. I have always loved you," Dash said, blinking back the tears.

McCartney stared at Dash. Lennon broke free from his sister and lunged to hug his daddy.

"Come on," Dash said. "Let's go to church and say a prayer for Mommy."